Diagnosis Murder: The Silent Partner

"Producer Lee Goldberg wrote the very best *Diagnosis Murder* episodes, so it's no surprise that this book delivers everything you'd expect from the show. This is a clever, high-octane mystery that moves like a bullet train. Dr. Mark Sloan, the deceptively eccentric deductive genius, is destined to join the pantheon of great literary sleuths. . . . You'll finish this book breathless. Don't blink or you'll miss a clue. A brilliant debut for a brilliant detective. Long live Dr. Mark Sloan!"

—Janet Evanovich

"An exciting and completely satisfying read for all *Diagnosis Murder* fans. We were hooked . . . Lee Goldberg's skill in bringing our favorite characters to the printed page left us begging for more."

—Aimée and David Thurlo, authors of the Ella Clah, Sister Agatha, and Lee Nez Mysteries

DIAGNOSIS MURDER

THE DEATH MERCHANT

Lee Goldberg

BASED ON THE TELEVISION SERIES CREATED BY
Joyce Burditt

SIGNET
Published by New American Library, a division of
Penguin Group (USA) Inc.,
375 Hudson Street,
New York, New York 10014, U.S.A.
Penguin Books Ltd, 80 Strand,
London WC2R 0RL, England
Penguin Books Australia Ltd, 250 Camberwell Road,
Camberwell, Victoria 3124, Australia
Penguin Books Canada Ltd,
10 Alcorn Avenue,
Toronto, Ontario, Canada M4V 3B2
Penguin Books (N.Z.) Ltd, Cnr Rosedale and Airborne Roads,
Albany, Auckland 1310, New Zealand

Penguin Books Ltd, Registered Offices:
80 Strand, London WC2R 0RL, England

First published by Signet, an imprint of New American Library,
A division of Penguin Group (USA) Inc.

First Printing, February 2004
10 9 8 7 6 5 4 3 2 1

Printed in the United States of America

PUBLISHER'S NOTE
This is a work of fiction. Names, characters, places, and incidents either are the product of the author's imagination or are used fictitiously, and any resemblance to actual persons, living or dead, business establishments, events, or locales is entirely coincidental.

To Valerie and Madison

ACKNOWLEDGMENTS

Once again, I am deeply indebted to Dr. Doug P. Lyle, who inexplicably continues to answer all my bizarre medical questions with humor, patience, and ingenuity. I also owe thanks to Bill Dinino, Jason Stoffmacher, Gerald Elkins, Jacquelyn Blain, Aimée and David Thurlo, and Rich and Marie Colabella for their wise counsel.

Finally, I could not have written this book without the continued enthusiasm and support of William Rabkin, Tod Goldberg, Gina Maccoby, and Dan Slater.

PROLOGUE

Roger Standiford stood alone in the pitch darkness of the desert night, holding two suitcases bulging with $4.5 million in cash, just as he'd been told to do five hours earlier. That's when he got the call on his private line at the T-Rex casino and an electronically distorted voice told him they had his eighteen-year-old daughter and the price he'd have to pay to get her back.

They also told him not to call the police. Not to alert his security staff. Not to do anything but get the money together from the cashier's cages at his three casinos and await instructions. He had six hours, not a minute more, to deliver the ransom or his daughter would be killed. And in case he didn't believe they were serious, they'd left one of Connie's pinkie fingers on the cutting board in his kitchen.

Roger rushed home in his Lincoln Town Car, trying in vain to reach Connie on the cell phone as he crawled through the Las Vegas traffic, cursing at the herds of slow-moving tourists who clogged the streets, the medians, and the sidewalks. Until that day, he'd never minded the crowds and the gridlock; it had been a reassuring sign of his own continuing prosperity. Now they were cattle blocking the road.

Roger Standiford lived in a sprawling, Mediterranean-style estate on three acres of reclaimed desert on the outskirts of Las Vegas, an area he was transforming into an enclave for the city's wealthiest residents. Bulldozers, excavators, and huge earthmovers were clearing and grading the barren landscape all around his property for the lakes, golf courses, and residential palaces to come. His showplace was the first to be completed, but fifty more were already on the way.

When he arrived at the house, the gate was wide open when it should have been closed. Ordinarily, his wife, Emily, would have been at home, but she was traveling in Spain, looking for artwork to adorn the walls of the high-roller suites at his Alhambra casino, which meant Connie came home from school each day to an empty house. But Connie was an adult now; they weren't worried about her.

The fact was, they'd stopped worrying about anything after Roger made his first $10 million.

He followed the circular driveway around a huge fountain, its decorative geyser of water a sign of Roger's mastery over the dry desert that surrounded him. Connie's BMW, a surprise present on her sixteenth birthday, was parked in front of the house.

Roger peeked in her car, feeling every rapid pulse of his heart, then turned to the house. The front door was ajar. He eased the door open slowly and stepped inside. As in his casinos, it was thirty degrees cooler inside, chilling the sweat on his skin and making him shiver. Or perhaps it was the sight of Connie's car keys and book bag carelessly dropped on the entry-hall floor that gave him goose bumps.

Her things were at the foot of one of the two winding staircases that joined at the top like a giant marble wishbone.

Connie never dropped her stuff on the floor like that. *Never.*

Roger called out her name, and heard his desperation echo unanswered through eight thousand square feet of emptiness. He hesitantly stepped into the kitchen, saw the splatter of dried blood on the granite countertop, and knew with horrifying certainty that the call he'd received wasn't a sick joke. He staggered back, his daughter's terror and agony almost palpable in the cold air.

The only thing that kept him from crumbling, that pulled him from the edge of emotional collapse, was a sudden, energizing flush of pure rage.

He'd get his daughter back. And then he'd get them. He'd bury the kidnappers in the foundation of his next casino for the pleasure of walking over their bodies every single day.

The phone rang.

He knew who it was before he answered it.

"You've wasted forty minutes, Roger," the voice said. "Tick, tock."

Click.

Roger considered going upstairs and getting the .38 from his nightstand. But it was 102 degrees outside, and he'd left the T-Rex in a polo shirt and tan slacks. If they were actually watching him and he emerged in this heat wearing a jacket, he'd look ridiculous and they'd know he was concealing a weapon.

So he reluctantly left the gun behind, ran to his car, and drove back to the T-Rex as fast as he could, which was not very fast at all. Another thirty minutes evaporated.

The T-Rex towered above the lush rain forests of prehistoric earth, where enormous volcanoes spewed lava and monstrous, animatronic dinosaurs roamed, roaring at tourists, swatting helicopters out of the sky, and crushing cars in a fiery display twice an hour every weeknight.

Roger parked in front, ordered the doorman to keep the Lincoln where it was, and dashed into the lobby, which looked like it had been carved out of solid rock. Lights cleverly disguised as stalactites dangled from the ceiling. Mist rose from the steaming pools of Dinosaur Grotto, where a brontosaurus chewed on leaves and idly watched the tourists playing the $5 slots.

As Roger walked across the casino floor, past the gaming tables and rows of slot machines, he scanned the faces in the crowd, wondering if one of them belonged to a kidnapper.

But no one met his gaze, no one looked away too quickly, no one stared. They were too busy losing money and gawking at the ferocious pterodactyl that soared over the casino, hunting for prey.

Roger went straight to the gift shop, grabbed two T-Rex souvenir suitcases from the window display, and, without stopping to explain himself to the stunned salesgirl, marched to the cashier's cage.

He punched his code into the keypad, the door buzzed open, and he hurried inside. The cashiers whirled around, surprised to see the resort magnate in their midst. He dropped the bags on a table and ordered the cashiers to quickly fill them with $1.5 million in cash. Then Roger called ahead to his other casinos, demanding that they each prepare $1.5 million and have it ready for him within the hour. He hung up before anyone could ask questions.

Moments later, Nate Grumbo, Roger's head of security, strode into the cage. The ex-Fed with the flat-topped head, square jaw, no neck, and permanent squint had obviously been alerted by his people at all three casinos about Roger's outrageous demand.

"Is there a problem, Mr. Standiford?" Nate asked, his voice a low grumble rising from deep within his wide linebacker's body.

"Nothing that concerns you." Roger looked at his diamond-studded Rolex, then back at the cashiers counting the money. It was taking too long.

Nate glanced at the cash, the bags, then back at Roger. It didn't take a genius to figure out the broad strokes of what was happening. "Are you sure this is how you want to play it?"

Roger nodded. "I don't have a choice."

He pictured the terror on his daughter's face when they held her hand down on the cutting board, and he wanted to scream but he swallowed it back.

Nate must have seen the muscles tensing in his employer's neck, the momentary flash of fear in his eyes.

"I'm going with you," Nate said.

"No," Roger said firmly. "I need you to leave this room now, go back to your office, and wait for my call. I don't want anyone doing anything except their usual routine, is that clear?"

Nate nodded and walked out.

Of course, what Roger asked for was impossible, and he knew it. The kidnappers had to know he couldn't keep this quiet. There was no way Roger Standiford could walk into the cashier's cage, stuff a million and a half bucks into a couple of bags, and walk out again without every employee in the building hearing about it. By nightfall, half of the citizens of Las Vegas would know.

Maybe that was the point. Maybe that was how the kidnappers were tracking his compliance. Maybe they were on his payroll. It would certainly explain how they knew his wife was away, the time his daughter got home from school, all his private phone numbers, and the security code to his front gate.

It was something he'd think hard about later, when his daughter was home safe, when he wasn't counting minutes while his cashiers were counting cash.

The cashiers had his bags packed in forty-five minutes, and then he was on his way to Gilligan's Island, his first casino. He'd built it a decade ago, shrewdly capitalizing on the world's incomprehensible affection for the inane sitcom. Since then, thousands of people had posed for pictures in front of the shipwrecked SS *Minnow* and the bronze statues of the seven stranded castaways. It was what passed for a historical landmark in Las Vegas. He honked the sightseers out of his way and scrambled out of the car.

The money was waiting for him in neat stacks in the cashier's hut. He was out of the casino again in ten minutes, "The Ballad of Gilligan's Island" ringing in his ears.

Twenty minutes later, he was driving away with the last third of the ransom money from the vaults of the Alhambra, his lavish re-creation of the Moorish palace in Spain, when his cell phone trilled.

It was them. They told him where to drive. Then they called back a few minutes later and gave him new directions. And then they did it again. And again. Each time never giving him a chance to respond and to make demands of his own.

Night fell as they made him drive in circles around the city for an hour and then, finally, miles and miles out into the desert.

And now he stood in the vast emptiness, swallowed by the impenetrable darkness, "The Ballad of Gilligan's Island" playing in his head on an endless loop, just like it did in his casino.

He was in hell.

His cell phone rang. He flipped it open.

"Drop the bags, walk away, and drive back to your house," the voice said. "You will be told where to find your daughter."

They broke the connection before he could speak, before he could ask what guarantee he had they would call once they had the ransom.

He looked around, trying to see into the darkness. Were they out there somewhere, watching him now? How close were they? Was Connie with them?

"I want my daughter back now!" he yelled.

But the darkness absorbed his cry and gave nothing back. After a long moment, he turned and walked away. He got into the car, tossed the phone onto the seat beside him, and drove back toward the city.

It was the longest hour of his life. The phone was like a physical presence on the seat. He could almost feel the kidnapper sitting there beside him, sneering with pleasure at Roger's impotence and fear.

Roger steered the car up to the house, parked behind Connie's BMW, and got out. The outdoor flood lamps had come on, bathing the property in light, turning his house into a glowing castle that could be seen for miles at night. His cell phone rang. He dived back into the car, laid his stomach across the seat, and picked up the phone.

"Where is she?" he shouted.

"Next door."

And that was it. Roger stared at the phone. *Next door?* What the hell did that mean? He crawled back out of the car, stood up, and looked through the wrought iron fence that surrounded his property. There was nothing next door, just tractors and bulldozers and miles of graded desert.

Something caught his attention on the pad beside his fence, at the outermost edge of light cast by his flood lamps. A metal pipe stuck a foot or so out of the ground, right at the spot where he'd watched crews digging a gigantic hole over the last few days. Something sparkled around the pipe, attracting him like a tourist to the blinking lights outside of one of his casinos.

Roger quickly scaled the fence and dropped down on the other side. He ran over to the pipe, recognizing with a pang of fear what was catching the light before he got there.

It was his daughter's necklace.

He realized everything in one horrible instant.

She had been just a few yards away from the house the whole time.

She was buried alive.

Frantic, Roger dropped to his knees beside the pipe and yelled down into it.

"Connie? Can you hear me? *Connie?*"

He heard his voice bouncing off a hollow space below, but Connie didn't reply.

"Hold on, honey, we're going to get you out."

It took another hour just to get a construction crew out there to set up lights and operate the excavator. The gigantic scoop clawed at the earth, revealing a metal storage container buried a few feet below ground.

Roger jumped down onto the container and opened it up. The first thing he saw illuminated in the narrow space were five plastic jugs of Sparkletts water. The next thing he saw was Connie, curled up in a corner, her hastily bandaged hand clutched to her chest, her eyes wide open.

He dropped into the container and went to his daughter, taking her in his arms, stroking her hair. But she was cold and unyielding and beyond his comfort, her eyes staring forever into the abyss of death.

Chapter One

Although Dr. Mark Sloan often recommended that his patients relax and take a vacation, he studiously avoided following his own advice. He found the practice of medicine, as chief of internal medicine at Community General Hospital, and the intellectual challenge of solving homicides, as an unofficial consultant to the LAPD, far more relaxing and energizing than sunning himself on a beach somewhere.

Besides, he lived at the beach. What would be the point of going to another beach to do nothing when he could do nothing at home?

Not that he would *ever* do nothing at home, not when there was so much interesting work he could being do instead.

That was classic workaholic thinking, according to his friend Dr. Amanda Bentley, a confirmed workaholic herself who juggled two jobs as the hospital's pathologist and as an adjunct county medical examiner.

She was among Mark's friends who tried to convince him that he didn't have to lie around somewhere, that he could enjoy an active vacation, exploring foreign countries and meeting people from different cultures.

While Mark conceded his friends had a point, he knew he'd soon be bored and anxious, stressed out and miserable, exhibiting all the symptoms of a man who desperately needed a vacation.

The same symptoms that his son, Steve, an LAPD homicide detective, had been showing for weeks. Mark urged his son to take a much needed, and long overdue, vacation. Steve reluctantly agreed on one condition—Mark had to come with him.

Steve lived with his father, so Mark knew the last thing his son really wanted to do was go on a vacation with him. Mark saw the condition for what it was: a transparent ploy to avoid taking time off from work.

So Mark called his bluff.

Which was why the chaise lounge closest to the activities hut at the Kiahuna Poipu Shores resort on the garden island of Kauai had become an impromptu beachside medical clinic, where Dr. Mark Sloan happily treated the minor injuries of his fellow guests.

Mark looked like just another tourist in his wide-brimmed Panama hat, colorful aloha shirt, baggy white shorts, and flip-flops—except for the stethoscope around his neck. He sat on the edge of the chaise lounge facing Buddy, a chalk-skinned and sunburned teenager from New Jersey who'd scraped his legs on sharp coral while snorkeling in the shallow bay.

Buddy winced as Mark finished gently dabbing disinfectant cream on his wounds.

"If you keep those scrapes clean and dry, they should heal just fine," said Mark, sorting through the grocery bags beside him for the right Band-Aid. He'd stocked up on some basic medical supplies at a tiny market in Old Koloa Town. "But you're going to have to stay out of the water for a few days."

"You're joking, right?" Buddy asked.

"The water will sting and you risk infecting the wounds," Mark said as he carefully applied the Band-Aid. "Besides, you're already pretty badly sunburned—your skin could use a rest. I don't want you going outside again unless you're wearing a shirt."

"But I'm only here for two more days," Buddy whined as he stood up. "What am I supposed to do?"

"I'm sure there's plenty that you haven't done," Mark peeled off his surgical gloves and dropped them in the trash can, on which he'd thoughtfully taped a bright yellow-and-black DANGER: BIOHAZARD placard.

"Not all the pleasures of Kauai are in the water." Mark exchanged the damp towel on Buddy's chaise lounge for a fresh one from the stack he kept near his supplies. "You can enjoy the spectacular views from Waimea Canyon, which Mark Twain called 'the Grand Canyon of the Pacific.' Or you can take a boat ride up Wailua River. Or you can go horseback riding to Kalihiwai Falls. Or do some shopping at the—"

The kid interrupted Mark midlist, thanked him for his help, then shuffled away sadly, idly scratching his red shoulders. Mark shrugged and tossed Buddy's towel in the hamper in front of the activities hut.

"How would you know what there is to do?" asked Moki Kaohi, the young Hawaiian man behind the counter. He wore the hotel's uniform floral shirt and shorts and spent his days making sure guests had all the fun he wished he was having. "You've been sitting here for three days handing out Band-Aids and ice packs."

"I've heard about it from my son," Mark replied. "He's been all over the island, water-skiing, surfing, hiking, and snorkeling."

"Have you considered going with him?" Moki asked.

"I wish I could," Mark said, "but my patients have been keeping me pretty busy."

"Your *patients?*"

"It's been one thing after another with them," Mark sighed wearily, motioning with a wave of his hand at the vacationers splashing in the massive pool and frolicking in the crashing surf. "Sunstroke, coral scrapes, stubbed toes, twisted ankles, even a lady who stepped on a sea urchin. Frankly, I'm a little understaffed."

Moki looked at him in astonishment for a moment, then said, "I'm afraid I'm going to have to ask you to leave, Dr. Sloan."

Mark was shocked. "You're throwing me out of the hotel?"

"No, of course not. We're pleased to have you as our guest," Moki stepped out of the hut with a big smile on his face. "I just need you to move. This is where we do the barbeque buffet and salad bar every Saturday."

Moki tilted his head toward a half-dozen kitchen staffers standing off to one side, looking at Mark impatiently as they waited with their barbeques, chafing dishes, tables, and iceboxes.

Mark hadn't noticed them before, and now that he did, he was terribly embarrassed.

"Oh, I'm so sorry, Moki. I didn't mean to hold up the barbeque," Mark scrambled to his feet and quickly started gathering up his supplies. "Where would you like me to set up my triage?"

"Actually, I think we can manage without one for an hour or two," Moki picked up Mark's grocery bags. "Why don't you let me take your things back to your room, while you enjoy a nice *long* walk?"

Mark looked over the scene around him. People bodysurfing and boogie boarding in the mild waves. Children building sand castles on the pristine beach. Couples strolling hand in hand in the frothy surf. Kids charging down the water slides, squealing with delight. Bartenders mixing tropical drinks at the swim-up bar in one of the pool's rocky grottos. Afternoon nappers sprawled lazily in hammocks strung between the palms. Sunbathers lying side by side on row after row of chaise lounges, each reading one of the same ten best-selling paperbacks.

"Things do seem to be under control for the moment," Mark said, handing over his stethoscope. "I suppose I could take a short break."

"Take your time," Moki said. "Please."

Mark sighed, slipped on his sunglasses, and reluctantly strolled down to the clean white sand. As soon as the doctor was out of sight, Moki tossed Mark's things in the hut, tore the DANGER: BIOHAZARD warning off the trash can and quickly carried the receptacle away, holding it from his body at arm's length.

As Mark walked on the beach, soaking his feet in the warm surf, it occurred to him that he hadn't seen much of Steve since they arrived. His son was off early every morning, eagerly looking forward to some adventure or another. Not the behavior Mark expected from someone who, only a few days ago, was so reluctant to go on vacation.

Mark was beginning to wonder who'd actually played whom. Still, he couldn't get too upset. Steve was enjoying the relaxation he needed, and that was all that mattered. Mark would find ways to occupy himself.

It wasn't that Mark was blind to the enchantments of Kauai. He appreciated the smooth sand with its almost sugarlike consistency and the astonishingly clear azure sea. He marveled at the tropical plants, the jagged mountain peaks, and the quaint plantation architecture. He breathed in the moist, clean air and admired the bright blue skies.

He did all that during the drive from Lihue airport and his first hour at the resort.

It was great, wonderful, terrific.

Now what?

He didn't feel like bodysurfing and getting tossed by the waves. He didn't see the interest in snorkeling, paddling around to look at fish he could see in the aquarium at his dentist's office. He didn't want to drive around sightseeing; he spent way too much time in his car at home. And just thinking about horseback riding made his back ache.

Mark supposed he could keep on treating the minor medical needs of the hotel guests for the next week, but that wouldn't keep him sharp. His mind was craving a challenge beyond applying Band-Aids, doing crosswords, or finishing a John Grisham novel.

Maybe he'd call Jesse Travis, the ER resident and his young apprentice of sorts, and have him FedEx the stack of medical journals in his office that he'd been meaning to get to for so long.

The beach curved along a small bay with sprawling resorts on either end and lavish private homes in between. The houses were tucked back behind low fences and ringed by palm trees and bougainvillea.

Most of the homes were raised on stilts a few feet above the ground to avoid flooding and to allow rising surf to pass under them. But the height would offer them little protection if another hurricane, like the one that ravaged the island in 1992, pounded the shore. Amid the row of homes, the cement ruins of a three-story condo complex still stood wrapped in vines, as if to warn the home owners they were on borrowed time.

Mark noticed that there were fewer sunbathers on this stretch of sand, and they seemed to be mostly locals. Few tourists appeared willing to venture beyond the range of a waitress with a drink menu. The sunbathers shared the beach with three monk seals who lazed undisturbed on the dry sand, as blasé as seasoned movie stars to the dozens of cameras and camcorders trained on them at any given moment.

One of the seals rolled over and huffed as Mark passed at a respectful distance. Mark huffed back, but the seal was unimpressed.

Mark turned to look at the sea, enjoying an ocean view unobstructed by clouds, fog, or a brown layer of smog. He could see a swimmer beyond the waves, cutting a smooth, confident course along the shore. The man was moving at a precise, even clip when he suddenly faltered, let out a cry of pain and surprise, splashed about, and then swam toward shore, clearly in distress.

Something was very wrong, but Mark had no idea what it could be.

Mark waded into the surf to meet the man, who he could

see was in his forties, deeply tanned, and well-muscled, with flecks of gray in his close-clipped hair.

The man staggered out of the water, dragging one leg behind him, clutching himself and wincing in pain.

Mark rushed to his side and helped him to the beach. "I'm a doctor. What happened?"

"Swam into a school of jellyfish," the man hissed between clenched teeth. "It felt like swimming into a beehive."

Mark could imagine how easy it would be to swim in amid the transparent creatures and not realize it until they were stinging you with their poison tentacles.

"How did you hurt your leg?" Mark asked, leading the man back toward the Kiahuna Poipu Shores resort.

"Playing football in college," the man said. "One tackle and I was finished as a quarterback."

"Have you ever had an extreme or allergic reaction to bee stings, mosquito bites, anything like that?"

"No," the man gasped.

"You're a quite a swimmer."

"I live on the beach," he said, wincing. "I do a mile every day, rain or shine."

"Ever encountered jellyfish before?"

"Once. And when I came out of the water, a big old Hawaiian peed on me." The man gave Mark a worried look. "You're not going to pee on me, are you?"

"Don't worry, modern medicine has progressed beyond that." Mark smiled and led him to a chaise lounge. "Wait right here."

Mark rushed to the barbeque buffet, where he was surprised to find Steve among the long line of guests who were helping themselves to lunch. His son was barefoot, wearing shorts and a tank top that showed off his strong shoulders and dark tan. Anyone looking at Steve standing there would have pegged him as a surfer, certainly not as a cop.

"Hey, Dad," Steve said. "Where's your little clinic?"

"Over there," Mark motioned to the man sitting on the

chaise lounge, grimacing in pain. "The guy got stung by some jellyfish."

"Ouch," Steve said.

Mark squeezed in front of the line at the salad bar. "Excuse me, medical emergency."

He reached into the salad bar, lifted away the pot of Italian dressing from the crushed ice, and carted it back to the chaise lounge. The mystified guests all watched him go, except for Steve, who concentrated instead on piling bay shrimp on his salad.

As soon as Mark reached the chaise lounge, he set the pot down and began ladling dressing all over the swimmer's body, coating him in oil and vinegar.

"You call this modern medicine?" the man shrieked, reacting both to the surprise and the chill of the cold salad dressing on his skin.

"Practical medicine, actually. It won't help the pain, but the vinegar in the dressing will stop the jellyfish's undischarged nematocysts from firing and giving you more stings."

He made sure the man was covered from head to toe in Italian dressing, then dropped the ladle back in the empty pot. "Stay here."

Mark turned, oblivious to everyone in line staring at him, and hurried over to the barbeque, where the cooks were grilling steaks, hamburgers, and hot dogs. He motioned to a jar of steak tenderizer.

"Would you mind if I borrowed that?" Mark asked, holding out his hand insistently. "It's a medical emergency."

The cook handed him the jar and watched as Mark raced back to the chaise lounge and began seasoning the oily man.

The man was now wincing more in embarrassment than pain. "Are you sure you're a doctor?"

"I can vouch for him," Steve said, clearly amused, sauntering over with his salad. "He's actually chief of internal medicine at a major Los Angeles hospital."

"Really?" The man turned back to Mark. "Now that I've

been marinated and seasoned, I hope you're not intending to cook me for lunch."

"The jellyfish poison is a protein," Mark explained. "I'm sprinkling you with meat tenderizer because the active ingredient is an enzyme that breaks down protein, thus neutralizing the poison and lessening the pain."

"That's a relief, because barbequing me would have been way too ironic," he said. "I own a restaurant."

The man held out his hand, which was dripping oil and vinegar. "Danny Royal."

Mark shook his hand. "I'm Mark Sloan, and this is my son, Steve. We're staying here at the hotel for two weeks."

Danny offered his hand, but Steve declined with a polite smile. "No thanks, I've already got plenty of dressing on my salad."

Moki came over, obviously upset. "Do you want to explain what's going on, Dr. Sloan?"

"This gentleman was stung by jellyfish," Mark said. "I'm treating him."

"With our buffet?" Moki asked incredulously.

"I hadn't thought to ask," Mark said, then turned to Danny. "Would you like something to eat? The food here is really quite good."

"You already know how good their salad dressing is," Steve said with a smile.

"Actually, I'm feeling much better already," Danny said, rising slowly. "I think I'll go home and wash up."

"Afterward you'll want to treat the welts with some antiseptic spray or ointment."

"I'll do that," Danny said. "Thank you so much for your help. I hope you'll come to my restaurant tonight and let me treat you to dinner."

"That's not necessary," Mark said.

"I insist," Danny replied. "It's the Royal Hawaiian. Come any time."

And with that Danny shuffled off, trailing oil and vinegar behind him. Moki looked from the oily footprints to the oily chaise lounge, and then back at Mark, who smiled sheepishly.

"Is the buffet still open?" Mark asked, patting his stomach. "I'm starving!"

Chapter Two

Wyatt arrived in Kauai two days earlier, almost three weeks after his initial recon. It took him that long to formulate his plan, figure out the best way to make it happen, and then examine it from every angle. He envisioned everything that could go wrong, then devised fixes and escapes. Only when he was satisfied that every detail was worked out, every possibility considered, did he book his flight back to the island.

He could have done all his thinking on Kauai without going to the trouble and expense of returning to the mainland and coming back again. But the longer he stayed in one place, the greater the chance that someone would notice him or remember something about him if asked. When he returned, he was careful to alter his appearance. It was a matter of habit now.

Wyatt had a lanky, athletic build and unremarkable features that effectively lent themselves to simple deceptions like colored contacts, colored hair, and unshaven cheeks. Even so, the way he walked, the way he dressed, the accent he used, and even the words he chose when he spoke were different this time.

Every choice he made on his last trip he changed on this one. He used another airline, another rental car company, and didn't shop at the same store or eat at the same restaurant twice.

Wyatt booked a room in the biggest, most crowded hotel

he could find, where he'd be just another tourist among hundreds.

On his first day back, Wyatt scouted locations again and briefly shadowed his target to be sure no variables had been introduced in his absence that might impact the plan. As far as he could tell, nothing significant had changed.

On his second day back, Wyatt bought supplies for his task, paying cash whenever possible. He only used his false credit card and driver's license when paying cash would attract attention or they were required to secure a rental.

Wyatt intended to stay another few days after the job was done on the off-chance that airline or boat departures were ever scrutinized, though he doubted that would happen. Still, he liked to be thorough.

He double- and triple-checked all his equipment, took a long jog and a scalding shower, and got dressed in a Tommy Bahama aloha shirt and white pants. It was louder than he liked to dress, but here he'd blend right in.

That was his forte. Blending. Moving unseen. Slipping in and out of a crowd with the smooth, deadly precision of a stiletto blade.

After some careful consideration, Wyatt decided to bend one of his rules. He'd go back somewhere he'd been before.

He'd have dinner at the Royal Hawaiian.

Mark and Steve arrived at Danny Royal's restaurant shortly after nightfall and were immediately impressed by the relaxed luxury of the place.

The restaurant was an open-air plantation house set deep amid a lush, tropical garden with meandering koi ponds teeming with golden carp and burbling waterfalls cascading over lava rocks.

The wide terrace was lit by the glow of flickering torches, the sea breeze pushed through the dining room by the gentle churn of ceiling fans. The deep reddish-brown luster of koa-wood paneling behind the bar gave the restaurant a rich, distinctly Hawaiian elegance.

Kamalei, the attractive young Hawaiian hostess, led them out to a table on the terrace. She began to hand them menus when Danny Royal appeared, exuding refinement and polished cordiality.

"My friends won't be needing menus tonight, Kamalei," Danny said to the hostess, who took the menus but remained at the table. He turned to his guests. "I'm so pleased to see you both."

"How are you feeling?" Mark asked.

"A little itchy, but otherwise just fine," Danny said. "I'm sure I'd be feeling a lot worse if it wasn't for your quick attention. I've taken the liberty of preparing a tasting menu of some of our specialties for you. I hope you don't mind."

"Not at all," Mark said. "We place ourselves entirely in your hands."

"Excellent," Danny said. "I'll be back to join you for dessert. If there's anything at all you need in the meantime, Kamalei will be at your service."

She bowed slightly at the mention of her name. Danny excused himself, and almost immediately a waiter appeared at the table with appetizers.

"What have we here?" Mark asked the hostess.

"Lemongrass-seared island opah with udon noodles and Thai basil–lime butter sauce," Kamalei explained. "Kalua pig, luau leaf, and butterfish in a crispy lumpia wrapper with lomi salmon relish. And a warm macadamia nut, goat-cheese salad with mixed Maui greens in a passion fruit vinaigrette."

She gave Mark a mischievous grin. "I understand you're especially fond of vinaigrette."

Steve looked across the table at his father. "You've only been here a few days and already you're famous."

"Infamous is more like it," Mark said.

The appetizers were followed by course after course of cleverly prepared delicacies unlike anything they'd ever tasted before.

They feasted on quail stuffed with Lahaina corn, roasted

black olives, rosemary, soft polenta, and truffle shavings; kiawe wood-fired Molokai pork tenderloin with caramelized Maui onions; and seared swordfish in a roasted macadamia nut–lobster butter sauce.

They hardly spoke to one another during the entire meal, savoring the food, the warm night air, and the sound of the surf crashing against the shore.

For dessert, they were tempted with fresh fruit, Hawaiian vintage chocolate, and a dizzying assortment of cakes, pies, and pastries. Steve tried them all, but Mark reached his limit after two bites of coconut cream pie covered with chocolate shavings and crushed macadamia nuts.

Danny Royal joined them at the table, settling into one of the plush rattan chairs as Kamalei served them all steaming hot mugs of freshly ground Kona coffee. She left the coffeepot at the table.

"The coffee is made especially for me from Kona beans harvested on the leeward slope of Mauna Loa," Danny said. "Hawaii is the only place in the United States where coffee is grown, so I insist on having the freshest cup possible, using only the finest local beans."

Mark sipped the coffee and practically purred with delight. "An exquisite end to an exquisite meal. I don't think I've ever had anything quite like it."

"What would you call the cuisine?" Steve asked. "Pacific Rim? Hawaiian?"

"I like to think of it as a fusion of Hawaiian, Asian, European, and classic American cuisine," Danny said. "Though sometimes I think it might be a bit too eclectic for the tourists. You'd be surprised how often people ask the waiter if we can make them something simple."

"Then they are cheating themselves out of a rare treat," Mark said. "Not only is the food wonderful, but the restaurant itself is beautiful. The décor, the ambiance—it's so elegant and comfortable."

"I'm flattered, Dr. Sloan. I can't take the credit for the food—I just hired the right chef," Danny said. "But I designed the restaurant myself. I imagined it for years before I finally got the opportunity to build it."

"What were you doing before?" Mark asked.

"I was in the restaurant business, though hardly in this league," Danny said. "I operated a Croque Monsieur sandwich shop franchise in New Jersey and eventually expanded it into a couple more outlets. Still, I wasn't really happy. Financially, I was secure, but I kept dreaming of white sandy beaches, swaying palms, and running a restaurant without a drive-through window. A few years ago, the chain offered to buy me out and I jumped at it. It gave me the financial freedom to create the Royal Hawaiian."

"It's a meal we won't forget," Mark said.

"You'll have to let me return the favor next time you're in Los Angeles," Steve said, "though I'm afraid our menu is limited, our décor isn't quite as opulent, and we encourage our guests to eat with a bib."

"You own a restaurant?" Danny asked.

"It's a rib joint called BBQ Bob's," Steve said. "I never intended go in the restaurant business, but Bob was retiring. I couldn't stand the idea of not being able to eat there anymore. So I convinced a doctor who works with Dad to buy the place with me. It's been great, and since both of us have flexible schedules in our day jobs, we've been able to evenly share the responsibilities of running the place."

"Are you a doctor, too?"

"No," Steve said. "I'm a homicide detective with the LAPD."

"Really?" Danny said, a slight hesitation in his voice.

Danny's fleeting discomfort didn't surprise Steve; he was expecting it. Whenever he revealed in casual conversation that he was a cop, it made people nervous. Especially single women, to his constant frustration. The fact he still lived at home with his dad wasn't helping his romantic prospects, either.

He didn't know what it was about being a cop that made people uncomfortable around him. He didn't know whether it was because he dealt with death all day, or if everybody, no matter how honest and law-abiding, had a guilty conscience.

"How did you end up in that profession?" Danny asked, refreshing their cups of coffee.

"It's sort of the family business," Steve said, sipping his coffee and enjoying the rich, complex flavor of the Kona beans.

Danny looked at Mark. "Are you a detective, too?"

"Not officially," Mark said with a smile, "but I can't seem to stop myself from poking my nose into things anyway. My father was a homicide detective, so it must be in the genes."

That wasn't entirely the truth. Steve was competent, hardworking, and, by any professional measure, good at his job. But he knew his skills, like his grandfather's, were learned, rather than innate. Neither of them had Mark Sloan's amazing gift for solving perplexing crimes.

Mark's mind was always working, assimilating thousands of bits of seemingly unrelated information, and then, in a moment of stunning clarity, drawing it all together into a clear picture. It made Mark an information junkie, asking questions about everything, constantly poking and prodding his way through a case, aggravating just about everyone involved, including Steve.

"What is it that fascinates you about murder?" Danny asked Mark.

"It's not murder that fascinates me," Mark said. "It's the puzzle. Once I start thinking about a mystery, my mind won't let it go, tormenting me until I solve it."

"So he figures it's okay to torment me," Steve said, "and anybody else who comes in contact with him."

Danny laughed good-naturedly. "Something tells me you're quite good at what you do, Dr. Sloan."

"Not really." Mark shrugged modestly. "If the killers didn't make so many mistakes, they wouldn't be caught."

Over the next few hours, and another pot or two of Kona

coffee, they discussed what it was like living on Kauai, the volatility of a tourist-dependant economy, and the high price of just about everything on the island.

By then, despite being fortified by caffeine, the long day and the huge meal took their toll on Mark and Steve, who thanked their host for a wonderful evening.

On their way out, Mark stopped at a table by the front door, where there was a selection of souvenir photocards of individual Royal Hawaiian entrees with the recipes on the back. He took one of each.

"Do you really think you can make those dishes at home?" Steve asked.

"I don't see why not," Mark replied.

"The same reason I couldn't perform an appendectomy even if you gave me a picture and directions," Steve said. "There's more to it than you think."

Mark shrugged. "It will be fun trying, anyway."

As they left the restaurant, neither of them noticed the lean, angular-faced man at the bar, just another tanned tourist in a Tommy Bahama shirt and slacks, nursing a tropical drink. But Wyatt was keenly aware of them.

They didn't sense his presence in the shadows as they walked back to their hotel, or feel his gaze as they crossed the vast, open-air lobby to the elevators.

No one was ever aware of Wyatt until it was far too late.

CHAPTER THREE

Mark slept in until nearly ten the next morning, showered, shaved, and went down to hotel's open-air café, taking an outside table overlooking the tropical garden. Parrots, macaws, and cockatoos chirped and chattered in brass cages amid the coconut palms, brilliant heliconias, and radiant anthuria.

Waking to the birdsongs, the sweet floral fragrances, the rhythmic breaking of the waves, and the gleaming blue skies invigorated Mark.

Despite his big meal the previous night, he indulged himself with a generous helping of French toast and slices of papaya, kiwi, and pineapple, topped off with a tall glass of fresh-squeezed orange juice. He was halfway through breakfast when Steve joined him, ordering three eggs, pancakes, and a large order of thick-sliced, apple-smoked bacon.

"I'm oversleeping and overeating," Mark said, snatching a slice of Steve's bacon. "I don't know what's come over me."

"Better watch out," Steve replied, "or someone might think you're on vacation."

Perhaps I finally am, Mark thought. Something about the extravagant dinner the night before, and the glorious morning that greeted him, had a profound effect. He felt unusually relaxed and mellow; the anxious need to find new and different things to occupy his mind had ebbed. And much to his surprise, he kind of liked it.

"What's on your agenda for today?" Mark asked.

Steve gazed out at the water. "Looks like a good day for some snorkeling. Want to join me?"

"No, thanks," Mark said. "Maybe I'll take a walk, have a swim in the pool, then stop in at the Royal Hawaiian for some lunch."

"Going back so soon?" Steve raised an eyebrow. "You really fell in love with the place."

"It's hard not to," Mark said. "And Danny Royal is an exceptional host."

"He puts on a show, all right," Steve said sourly.

"I know why you're upset," Mark said. "It's the way his face fell when you told him you're a cop. Most people have the same reaction. I wouldn't hold that against him."

"I don't," Steve said. "It's being lied to that bugs me."

"What did he lie about?"

"He said he ran a Croque Monsieur franchise in New Jersey," Steve said. "They don't have outlets in the Eastern United States."

"How do you know that?"

"Jesse got us a subscription to *Restaurant Business Week*, the industry trade paper," Steve said.

"And you read it?" Mark asked incredulously.

"Once," Steve said. "It was in the bathroom, and I forgot to bring the sports page. Anyway, they had a big feature on Croque Monsieur's future expansion plans. New Jersey was among the new markets they were considering."

"So Danny wasn't entirely candid about his past," Mark said. "I'm sure he had his reasons. It doesn't make him a bad person. He certainly treated us well."

"It'll be interesting to see how long that hospitality lasts."

"Come with me and find out," Mark said. "I took a peek at their lunch menu and it looks incredible."

"I bet the prices are incredible, too," Steve said. "Incredibly steep."

"So what? We're on vacation," Mark replied. "Let's live a little. My treat."

Steve looked at his dad in surprise. "You really are loosening up. Does this mean you're leaving your stethoscope in your room?"

"I saw three new James Patterson paperbacks in the gift shop," Mark said. "I might pick up one and read in a hammock for an hour or two before lunch."

"You'll have the mystery solved in ten minutes."

"Then I guess I'll have to buy all three."

Steve was wrong.

It took Mark only five minutes to figure out everything that was going to happen in the book, and another five to skim the rest of the pages to confirm that he was right. He didn't bother with the other two books, setting them aside and taking in the view instead.

The beach was a little less crowded that morning, since many tourists departed on Sundays and new arrivals wouldn't be coming in until later that afternoon.

Still, there was a lot of activity on the sand. There were the teenagers boogie boarding in the waves, their parents documenting every wipeout in snapshots and home movies. Toddlers raced around, inflatable floaters on their arms, playing chase with the surf. A few older tourists in sunglasses stood knee-high in the water, only half committed to getting wet, letting the waves break in front of them and spill out against their waists. Barefoot honeymooners strolled hand in hand along the beach, or necked discreetly in one of the half dozen prized beachside cabanas, which some hotel guests staked out at dawn just to be sure to snare one. And a pair of monk seals scrambled out of the water onto the beach, honking and snorting excitedly, startling the adults and thrilling the small children in the surf.

The seals dragged their heavy bodies up the sand to bask in the sun and digest after gorging themselves for breakfast. In that regard the seals had a lot in common with the people around them. The casual encounter with wildlife, so close to a busy, sprawling resort, was jarring. It was like seeing an elk stroll through a crowded shopping mall. The seals took it more calmly than the tourists did.

Mark turned his gaze back to the ocean and saw Steve swimming near the rocky point, facedown in the water, his yellow snorkel bobbing as he followed the fish. He hoped his son was being careful. That was the area where most of the snorkelers and swimmers he'd treated over the last few days had scraped themselves.

Beyond Steve he could see the sure stroke and steady progress of Danny Royal, swimming parallel to the shoreline. Mark was surprised to see him braving the water so soon after his nasty encounter with the jellyfish. Danny obviously wasn't going to be dissuaded from doing what he wanted by some bad luck and a little discomfort. Perhaps it was that kind of tenacity that made him so successful.

There was something behind Danny, but Mark wasn't sure exactly what it was. Mark sat up slowly in his hammock, his heart racing, and squinted at the object in the water. He could almost believe it was a snorkeler, kicking up his feet, until the woman on the beach began screaming and his initial, gut-wrenching instinct was confirmed.

"Shark!" she yelled hysterically. *"Shark!"*

The instant after her cry, time seemed to freeze. Even the air seemed to still, as everyone's attention focused on the dorsal fin cutting through the water and diving below Danny, who was suddenly yanked under in a sickening crimson swirl of water.

The horrific sight sparked instant pandemonium on the beach and sheer panic in the water, with parents charging into the surf to rescue their kids as terrified swimmers charged out of the sea to save themselves.

Danny bobbed up once in a froth of bloody water, an arm flailing in the air, and then he was pulled down again, his screams drowned beneath the surface.

Mark rushed onto the beach and into the bedlam, trying

to spot Steve, and caught a quick glimpse of his son swimming toward a little boy in an inner tube. The child was wailing in terror, floating just a few yards from where Danny was attacked and the water still churned, bloodred.

Panicked swimmers, surfers, and boogie boarders scrambled ashore, pushing, tripping, and falling over each other in their mad rush to safety.

As one man fled, he foolishly turned away from the waves, which slammed into his back and repeatedly smashed him against the jagged rocks. Mark ran into the water, grabbed the unconscious man under the shoulders, and dragged him ashore.

Beyond the waves, Steve neared the wailing boy, who sat atop his bobbing inner tube, staring in wide-eyed horror at the spot where Danny Royal had been pulled under.

Steve reached out for the inner tube and the boy screamed, mistaking him for the shark, and lost his balance, toppling into the water and splashing around in terror. If the shark was still near, the boy was practically inviting an attack. Steve grabbed him firmly around the arm.

"Relax, you're going to be all right," Steve said, "I'm taking you back to the beach, but you have to calm down, do you understand?"

The boy sniffled and nodded, his lower lip quivering. "What about the shark?"

"He's long gone," Steve said. "We're safe."

But the truth was, Steve had no idea if they were safe or not. And as they swam back to shore, he couldn't help imagining the shark trailing after them, closing in on their kicking legs.

Back on the beach, Mark tended to the man who'd been thrown against the rocks. He gave him mouth-to-mouth until the man coughed up seawater and started breathing again, then Mark shifted his attention to his injuries. The man was bleeding from abrasions all over his body, but the worst was a deep gash on his left leg, probably caused by the jagged edge of a rock.

Mark grabbed a beach towel, pressed it against the man's gushing leg wound, and started looking for something to use as a tourniquet.

That's when Steve emerged from the water with the child he'd rescued. The child ran into the safety of his mother's arms, the woman gleaming with gratitude at Steve, who nodded in return and then crouched at his father's side.

"What can I do to help?" Steve asked.

"Hold this," Mark said, motioning to the towel. "I think he's knicked an artery."

While Steve took over applying pressure to the wound, Mark found a woman's bikini top discarded on a beach-blanket. He wound the bikini top around itself into a rope, then went back to the man and tied off the leg.

Mark did a quick scan around him as he secured the makeshift tourniquet. The water was empty now, but the beach was filled with people, many of them injured in the melee.

"Wrap him up with some of the beach towels," Mark said, studying the shivering man, who was looking very pale. "He's going into shock. Keep him warm until the paramedics arrive. I'm going to see if anyone else needs medical attention."

Mark moved among the others, assessing the injuries, mentally prioritizing them as he went along. No one else appeared seriously hurt, though there were a number of broken bones.

His supplies were up in his room, so he made do with whatever was handy. He made splints out of plastic shovels and boogie boards, securing them to the broken arms and legs with T-shirts, ski ropes, and belts from bathing robes.

By the time he'd finished with the last splint, the paramedics and police arrived. The beach quickly cleared as the injured were transported to the hospital and the frightened guests returned to the safety of the hotel.

But Mark Sloan, wet, sandy, and bloodstained, lingered behind on the beach.

The water was calm. Waves broke gently against the shore. The pair of monk seals napped peacefully in the sun. The only evidence that anything had happened were the beach towels, hats, and other belongings forgotten and abandoned along the crescent of empty white sand.

Mark stared out at the sea. Steve stepped up beside him.

"You did all you could, Dad." Steve said.

Mark nodded.

Two Coast Guard boats were speeding toward the tiny bay, but Mark knew it was too late for any rescues. All they'd find now, if they were lucky, were Danny Royal's remains.

Chapter Four

News of the shark attack spread quickly. Within an hour, it was all over the local news. Within two hours, CNN picked it up and it was all over the world. Reporters flocked to the hotel, interviewing guests as they rushed to check out.

Mark and Steve avoided the crush of reporters by spending the night in their rooms.

Steve ordered a pizza from room service, turned on the TV, and caught up on a couple action movies he'd missed in the theaters. It was better than being left alone with his thoughts. That day he'd seen a man killed by a shark. The day before Steve left for Hawaii, he stood over the corpse of a grocery clerk shot by a shoplifter stealing a six-pack of beer. He could ponder all the violence he saw or think about how James Bond was going to save the world with a laser-firing toothpick. Steve chose 007.

Mark relaxed on his lanai, the moon casting its bright glow on the water, which lapped gently against the shore.

He tried to reconcile the beauty and serenity of the moonlit water with the startling danger and violence that lurked below its surface.

He couldn't, of course.

In the same way he couldn't reconcile the joy of delivering a baby with the sadness of declaring someone else dead in the course of a typical day at Community General.

So he gave up trying and went to bed, accepting what

happened to Danny Royal as another tragedy, another fact of life, that was out of his control.

By morning, the sand had been cleaned of the belongings left behind by the beachgoers and a line of SHARK WARNING signs had been staked every twenty yards.

The reporters were gone and, apparently, so were most of the guests. The vast, teak-lined lobby of the Kiahuna Poipu Shores, open to the tropical garden, the waterfalls, and the beach below, felt empty and hollow as Mark and Steve came down for breakfast.

Mark and Steve had the dining room virtually to themselves as they sipped their fruit smoothies, ate their hot muffins with guava butter, and browsed through their complimentary copies of the *Honolulu Star-Bulletin.*

The lead story on the front page was, not surprisingly, the shark attack.

SHARK TERRORIZES POIPU;
LOCAL MAN FEARED DEAD

LIHUE, Kauai—A shark attacked a swimmer in the waters off Poipu Sunday afternoon, terrifying scores of witnesses and prompting the immediate closure of a mile-long stretch of beach.

"It was absolutely horrifying," said Wilma Manfred, 47, who was visiting the Garden Island from Spokane, Washington. "Everyone ran screaming out of the water. It was sheer panic."

She was one of approximately a hundred people, most of them tourists, who witnessed the attack, which occurred shortly after 11:00 A.M. about twenty-five yards offshore from the Kiahuna Poipu Shores resort on Kauai's south shore.

Witnesses reported seeing a dorsal fin measuring twelve to fourteen inches slicing through the water behind the swimmer. The victim struggled with the shark for only a few moments before disappearing.

Based on witness statements, authorities believe the victim was Danny Royal, owner of the Royal Hawaiian, a popular Poipu restaurant. Royal was reported missing by Kamalei Moala, 26, a hostess at his restaurant, when he didn't show up for work.

Moala said Royal swam in front of his Poipu residence each day before lunch, but that "he shouldn't have been in the water at all" on Sunday.

Royal was apparently stung by jellyfish during his swim on Saturday, but went back in the water Sunday despite the painful encounter.

"The jellyfish were an omen," said Moala, "and he ignored it."

The shark attack sparked a panic on the beach that resulted in several minor injuries. Seven people were transported to Queens Medical Center in Lihue for treatment. Six were released, while one unidentified man remains hospitalized in good condition, recovering from several broken ribs and deep lacerations suffered when he was battered against the rocks by the roiling surf. He is expected to be released today.

Authorities and witnesses credited an unidentified doctor from Los Angeles, who promptly treated many of the injured beachgoers before paramedics arrived, with saving the man's life.

Coast Guard rescue teams searched the waters off Poipu for Royal, while authorities combed the shoreline on foot. The search was called off at nightfall and was scheduled to resume Monday morning, though officials conceded they have little hope that Royal survived the attack.

The incident has closed a mile-long stretch of Poipu Beach until Tuesday at the earliest. It was the second shark attack on Kauai in less than two months and the fifth this year in Hawaii.

* * *

Mark was surprised there wasn't more background on Danny Royal in the article, or even a picture of him to accompany the piece. There was a sidebar on the mass exodus of shaken tourists leaving south shore resorts and crowding the Lihue airport, and the lament of resort owners on the immediate, dire impact the shark attack would have on the local economy.

There were several related stories recapping past shark attacks in Hawaii, most of which occurred in nearshore waters after heavy rains. The sharks were drawn to the murky waters filled with runoff from island streams. Sharks were also known to congregate around harbor entrances and channels, between sandbars, and in areas with steep drop-offs. Experts speculated on whether the shark that attacked Royal was a tiger, a Galapagos, or a great white.

The coverage continued in the feature section of the paper, with a long article exploring Native Hawaiian folklore about sharks, which seemed to be viewed either as sacred gods and guardian spirits or as terrifying symbols of unspeakable evil.

One legend Mark found intriguing told the story of Kamaikaahui, a man with a shark's mouth on his back, hidden under his clothes. Kamaikaahui would ambush unwary travelers near the ocean, devour them, and blame their deaths on sharks.

Mark set the paper aside and saw Steve still immersed in the news section.

"Looks like we're going to have the entire island to ourselves," Steve said.

"Would you rather go home?" Mark asked.

"Hell no, I've been looking forward to this vacation for too long."

It took a second before Steve realized what he'd just done. He'd unwittingly confessed that all his moaning and whining about going on vacation was just a trick to get his dad to take some time off.

Maybe his dad hadn't noticed. But Steve knew he was kidding himself. Mark Sloan noticed everything.

Steve peered hesitantly over the edge of his newspaper to see his father grinning at him.

"Uh-oh," Steve said.

"No harm done," Mark waved off Steve's worries. "I figured I was being conned, but I went along with it, anyway."

Steve lowered his newspaper. "Are you sorry you did?"

Mark shook his head. "Until the shark attack, I was really beginning to enjoy myself."

"I was having a great time from the moment we arrived," Steve said. "And I don't see why that should change."

"Because you hardly knew Danny Royal?"

"Because I'm a homicide detective. I see violence and death every day," Steve said, setting his paper aside on the empty chair next to him. "What happened to Danny Royal was terrible, but the truth is, I've seen a lot worse. At least this was a freak accident, a nasty brush with nature. You know how many innocent bystanders I see killed in senseless drive-by shootings every week?"

Mark nodded gravely. "I know what you have to deal with and the stress you carry because of it. That's exactly why you need this vacation so much. You don't have to feel guilty about staying or enjoying yourself."

"Neither do you," Steve said. "How much pain and bloodshed do you see each day at the hospital? How much more when you visit a crime scene? You need this break as much as I do."

Mark looked past the swaying palms to the mist-covered mountains in the distance, impossibly green and dramatically jagged. It was beautiful here, and going home now wouldn't change what had happened.

"You're right, we should stay," Mark said. "But maybe we should consider switching to a different hotel."

"Fine with me," Steve said.

"I'll look into it after breakfast," Mark said. "What are you going to be up to?"

"I think I'll rent a bike and explore the island a bit," Steve said. "I'd welcome some company."

Mark smiled. "I appreciate the offer, but I'll just slow you down. You havc a good time."

The waiter delivered the bill. Mark was about to sign for it when Moki appeared at the table and snatched the bill from him.

"Breakfast is courtesy of the hotel, Dr. Sloan," Moki said. "Along with your entire stay at the Kiahuna Poipu Shores."

Mark shared a look of surprise with Steve.

"It's just our small way of saying *mahalo* for what you did on the beach yesterday," Moki continued. "We were very lucky to have you with us."

"Thank you, Moki, but it really isn't necessary," Mark said, thinking about his plans to switch hotels. "I was just doing what I do."

"We insist, Dr. Sloan," Moki said. "*Mahalo nui loa.*"

Moki left, the bill in hand.

Steve watched him go. "You can't really change hotels now."

"No, I suppose not," Mark sighed.

"Look at the bright side," Steve said, rising from the table. "We're off the hook for everything but the airfare."

"But the beach is closed here," Mark said. "You can't go in the water."

"Do you really think I'm gonna swim *anywhere* on this island now?" Steve asked. "I might not even take a bath."

Mark took a long stroll on the empty beach. If it wasn't for the circumstances, he would have enjoyed having the entire beach to himself.

He was almost to the other side of the bay, and the resort tower that dominated the point, when a light rain shower hit, despite the heat and the vibrant blue sky. Rather than seek shelter at the other resort, Mark decided to wait out the rain under the cover of the palms that lined the shore.

It rained frequently on Kauai, which was why the island

was so incredibly lush and green. The showers, at least on the south shore, rarely lasted more than a few minutes and were often a refreshing respite from the heat. He'd seen beachgoers simply put their books and magazines under a towel and wait it out, happily soaking themselves in the cool rain.

Mark heard the raindrops drumming against something and turned to see an inner tube up in the ice plants, probably washed up by the tide. It was the inner tube that belonged to the boy Steve rescued.

And it was splattered with blood.

At least that's how it would look to the untrained eye. But Mark knew it wasn't blood because it wouldn't have retained its red color, nor would it have clung so tenaciously to the inner tube.

Mark crept closer to the inner tube to investigate. It was swarming with ants, drawn to the crimson splatters.

He took a leaf, dabbed it in the sticky substance, and sniffed. The smell was sweet.

Mark glanced back out at the sea and thought about the legend of Kamaikaahui. Perhaps it was true.

Steve was in the lobby when Mark returned, carrying what looked like a bloody leaf in a baggie.

"What are you doing back so soon?" Mark asked his son, who was soaking wet.

"The damn rain cloud followed me the entire ride," Steve said. "So I ducked into a café and had some coffee. They had the radio on. Did you hear the news?"

Mark shook his head.

"They found Danny Royal's body floating in the harbor," Steve said grimly. "There wasn't much left."

Mark took a deep breath and let it out slowly, thinking. That's when Steve noticed the baggie and what was in it.

"What's that?" Steve asked.

"Something I found on the beach," Mark said. "Do you have any friends on the Kauai Police force?"

Steve studied his dad for a moment, recognizing the expression on his face, knowing exactly what he was in for. He had a funny feeling his vacation was over.

"No," Steve said flatly.

"Then let's go make some."

Chapter Five

"Ho, he jus' come in. We no done da autopsy yet," Sgt. Ben Kealoha said, staring at the two *haoles* standing on the other side of the reception desk in the Lihue Police station. "We go'n, but it's no like we need to."

Kealoha was a heavyset, deeply tanned Hawaiian in his midthirties, wearing a loose-fitting, untucked aloha shirt that nearly hid the badge and gun that were clipped to the belt of his faded jeans. In his cheeks he had the permanent laugh lines of a man who found more amusement than sorrow in life.

Mark wasn't sure what Kealoha had just said, but it sounded like they weren't in any hurry to do the autopsy.

"I'm not sure I understand," Mark said.

"Da bruddah was grind by a shark," Kealoha replied. "Nothun' left 'cept his nog, brah."

Mark glanced wearily at Steve, who smiled and flashed his badge at the cop.

"I'm Steve Sloan, LAPD Homicide, and this is my father, Dr. Mark Sloan," he said. "So if you don't mind, *bruddah*, how about letting us have a look at the body?"

Kealoha examined the badge, smiled back at Steve, and motioned them around the counter. "Why didn't you say so to begin with? Always glad to oblige my colleagues in law enforcement. I'm Sgt. Ben Kealoha, but you can call me Benny."

He led them through the tiny squad room, with its three metal desks, cinder block walls, and window air conditioners, toward a door at the end of long, narrow corridor.

"So what's with the pidgin-English routine?" Steve asked.

"The tourists love it," Kealoha said. "They want us Hawaiians to be Hawaiian, brah. What's your interest in Danny Royal?"

"Nothing official," Steve said.

"We met him for the first time on Saturday. He invited us for dinner at his restaurant," Mark said. "We were on the beach Sunday when he was attacked."

"Do you know him well enough to identify his body?" Kealoha asked.

"I suppose so," Mark said.

"K'den, that will save us some trouble," Kealoha said, holding the door open and motioning them into the morgue. "I really don't want to ask a civilian to make the ID, considering the condition he's in, if you know what I mean."

They walked past Kealoha into the cold room. The floor was cement, gradually sloped toward several area drains for easy cleaning with a hose. One wall was lined with a half dozen refrigerated morgue drawers for holding bodies. There were two autopsy tables in the center of the room. On one of the tables lay the remains of Danny Royal, covered to the neck with a white sheet, not that it made much difference. What the sheet hid the imagination could readily fill in. The sheet was flat on the table below his knees.

Standing beside the table, looking as white as the sheet, was a woman in her late twenties scribbling furiously on her clipboard, taking deep breathes and letting the air out slowly. She had curly brown hair and wore a tank top, a pair of knee-length shorts, and leather sandals. There was a tape measure around her neck, the kind a seamstress might use.

"Dis da shark lady," Kealoha said.

"Veronica Klein." She offered her trembling hand to Mark and Steve. "I'm a senior field agent with the Shark

Task Force of the Hawaii State Department of Land and Natural Resources."

"You must need both sides of a business card for all that," Steve said with a smile, then introduced himself and his father to her.

Mark glanced at Danny's frozen face. His eyes were open, his mouth wide, a death mask of utter terror.

"That's Danny Royal," Mark said. "Where's the medical examiner?"

"On his way in from Princeville," Kealoha said. "But we got everything we need to know from the shark lady."

"Which is?" Steve asked.

"Da bruddah was grind by a shark," Kealoha said with a grin.

"There's a bit more to it than that," Veronica said, almost reluctantly turning toward the body. "I'm going to lift the sheet now. I want you to be prepared."

She seemed to be saying it more for herself than for the others. When she didn't hear any objections, she took a deep breath and slowly drew the sheet back to expose the corpse.

Danny's legs were missing below the knees, and both his arms were gone. His torso was also ravaged, large chunks of flesh ripped from his sides.

"As you can see, the wounds are all broad and curvilinear," she said, swallowing hard.

"*Curvilinear.*" Kealoha looked at Steve. "Funny, that was just what I was about to say."

"It means a rough semicircle," she said, a touch of irritation slipping into her voice. "Very rough. The flesh was torn by the shaking of the shark after it bit down."

Mark glanced at Steve and gave him a subtle nod. Steve gave an almost imperceptible nod back.

"How do you know the bite was from a shark?" Steve asked Veronica.

"You mean aside from the fact a hundred people saw the shark grab the guy and pull him under?" Kealoha said.

"I know the wound is from an animal rather than an implement because a knife would make a clean cut; a hatchet or meat cleaver would show multiple chops, as well as nicks and cuts into the bone." Veronica pointed to the edge of one of the wounds. "You can tell it wasn't a bear or a wolf, for example, because those animals have a muzzle, which would create a narrow, longer bite."

"Plus bears and wolves don't attack people in the ocean thirty yards offshore," Kealoha said. "At least not in Hawaii. Does it happen often in California?"

Veronica ignored Kealoha and pointed to the edge of the wound. She was enjoying Steve's attention and the opportunity to show off what she knew. "If you look at the curvature of these bites, the outline of the teeth can actually be seen in the flesh."

Mark found a box of rubber gloves, slipped on a pair, then took a scalpel from a nearby tray. No one seemed to notice as he carefully examined the wounds with the tip of his scalpel.

"Can you tell us anything about the shark?" Steve asked.

"I can tell you a lot," Veronica said. "There are about eight species of shark likely to have ventured so close to shore, but only two that could have done this much damage."

The more Veronica talked, the calmer she became. Her breathing slowed and her hands stopped shaking. Danny Royal was becoming a subject instead of a corpse, something she could detach herself from. What she didn't know was that was one of the reasons Steve started asking her so many questions. He knew if he could distract her from the horror and shift her attention to the facts, to her expertise, her discomfort would evaporate.

He also knew it would give his father a chance to examine the body without interruption or too much attention from Kealoha or Veronica, which was what Mark asked for with his nod to Steve.

"This was done by a tiger shark," she said. "From my

measurements of the bite radius, I estimate it's about twelve feet long."

"How do you know it was a tiger shark?" Steve asked.

"The location of the attack, witness photographs of the dorsal fin, the shape of the wounds, and one more thing." She took a Baggie out of her pocket. It contained a shark tooth. "I found this stuck in the victim's pelvic bone."

"And you took it?" Kealoha asked, snatching the bag from her. "That's evidence. I said you could look at the body, not touch it. That's the medical examiner's job."

"What difference does it make?" she said. "We know what killed this man."

"We do?" Mark asked.

Kealoha looked at Mark as if he'd forgotten he was there, which, in fact, he had.

"You saw the shark get him. A hundred other people saw it, too," Kealoha said. "And if that wasn't enough, take a look at what's left of him. You could bury him in a shoe box."

"I have no doubt that Danny Royal was attacked by a shark," Mark said.

"Then what's your problem?" Kealoha asked.

"My problem," Mark said, "is that it happened *after* Danny Royal was murdered."

Steve groaned. His vacation was over and his father's had just begun.

Once again, Wyatt's thoroughness paid off in unexpected ways. He'd always planned to stay in Kauai for a few days after he'd killed Danny Royal, but he hadn't intended to follow the two men he'd seen at the restaurant.

Something about the long conversation they had with Royal at dinner bugged him. Why was Royal so friendly with them? Who were they? And how much did they know?

Wyatt didn't think they were a threat, but he was still curious. So after handling the Danny Royal situation and all the necessary cleanup, he'd decided to watch them, more as a way to kill time and remain sharp than anything else.

He expected them to grab their camcorders and take him on a guidebook tour of the island, to all the usual prepackaged, preheated, predigested attractions, restaurants, beaches, and stores, to have the usual prepackaged, preheated, predigested experiences. He didn't see the point of it all. Every airport gift shop sold "vacation videos" that had the same shots of the same places from the same angles as every home movie every tourist made. Didn't that tell anyone anything?

Guidebooks were a waste of time. They sent you on a well-traveled path with nothing left to learn or explore. Visiting landmarks, historical spots, and so-called natural wonders wouldn't tell you squat about a place or its people. You might as well go to Disneyland.

Wyatt believed if you wanted to really know a place, you had to seduce someone who lived there. Get inside them and then into their world. Sleep in their bed. Stay in their home. Go where they go. Eat what they eat. Shop where they shop. See what they see. Until you have their smell on your body, their taste on your lips, their clothes on your back, and it feels comfortable. Then leave.

That's how you visit a new place. That's how you get to know it, if you really care. Try finding *that* for sale in an airport gift shop on your way out of town.

But the two strangers didn't do what Wyatt expected. They didn't go to a luau. They didn't go look at Waimea Canyon. They didn't cruise the Na Pali coast. They didn't see the Spouting Horn.

They went to visit the police.

Perhaps it was a coincidence. Perhaps they'd had their wallets picked or their rooms burgled.

But Wyatt didn't believe in coincidences. It was one reason he was still alive.

Something wasn't right about this. And if he hadn't

stayed an extra day or two after the fact, he never would have known.

Thoroughness. That's what being successful in his work was all about.

A few minutes after the two men entered the station, Wyatt got out of his car and strode up the sidewalk to break into their rental car. It wouldn't be difficult. The crappy fleet cars rarely had alarms, and even if they did, they were ridiculously easy to disable within seconds. That wasn't an issue with their car. Wyatt picked the lock and was sitting in the passenger's seat in eight seconds.

He opened the glove box, took out their rental agreement, and photographed it with a miniature digital camera. Then he put the brochure back, locked the doors, and returned to his own vehicle.

The task took less than two minutes to accomplish and reaped enormous benefits.

Now he had a name, a home address, and a credit card number to go on.

That was all he needed. In a few hours, he'd know everything worth knowing about Mark Sloan.

Chapter Six

"I'm not a medical examiner, but I know sharks," Veronica Klein said, motioning with a nod to Danny Royal's savaged torso. "All this was definitely caused by a shark. Not by a knife, a gun, or some boat propeller."

"I agree, and I'm sure the medical examiner would as well," Mark said. "But the fact remains: Danny Royal was already dead when the shark attacked him."

Mark pointed at a wound with his scalpel. "I don't see any evidence of bleeding into the surrounding tissues. That means his heart had already stopped pumping and blood was no longer circulating through his body when these catastrophic wounds were inflicted."

"Wait a minute," Kealoha said. "You saw him swimming—everybody did." He turned to Steve. "Didn't you?"

Steve nodded. "Yeah, I did."

"Are you certain it was Danny Royal you saw in the water?" Kealoha asked him.

"Yes, I'm sure." Steve said.

"There you go." Kealoha turned back to Mark. "You trust your own son, don't you?"

"I do," Mark said. "And so did the killer."

"Are you saying your son was an accomplice?" Kealoha asked incredulously, an amused smile on his face. He really seemed to be enjoying himself. Steve couldn't blame him;

there probably wasn't much excitement for a homicide cop in Lihue.

"In a sense, we all were, every one of us on the beach," Mark said. "We all said we saw a man killed by a shark."

"If that wasn't what you saw," Veronica asked, "what *did* you see?"

"A show, pure and simple, designed to disguise a murder," Mark said. "And the killer might have gotten away with it, too, if I hadn't found this."

Mark took out the baggie containing the leaf that he dipped in the splatter on the inner tube and handed it to Kealoha.

The detective held the baggie up to the light. "A leaf covered with blood?"

"Sure looks like it, doesn't it?" Mark said. "Yesterday, Steve rescued a boy in an inner tube who was floating near Danny Royal when the attack occurred. This morning, I found the inner tube on the beach, covered with that stuff and swarming with ants. They were attracted to the splatter, which I'm certain is corn syrup mixed with red dye. Also known as movie blood."

"We saw a shark fin, we saw a struggle, and we saw blood, but we never saw a shark," Steve said, the whole deadly scenario clear to him now. "Our imaginations took over from there."

"So how was he killed?" Veronica asked, fascinated.

"Are you familiar with the legend of Kamaikaahu?" Mark asked.

"The monster who killed travelers and blamed their deaths on sharks," she said. "Turned out he was a man with a shark's mouth on his back."

"Metaphorically speaking, I think that's what we're dealing with here. I'm guessing Danny Royal was pulled under by a scuba diver, who then tore open a bag of movie blood while Danny struggled and drowned," Mark said. "Then the killer probably took the body by boat someplace where he knew sharks congregated, like the harbor or the mouth of a stream, and dumped it."

"Stuff like this doesn't happen here," Kealoha said, shaking his head. "Except on *Hawaii Five-0*."

"It does now," Steve said.

"I always wanted to be Steve McGarrett," Kealoha said with a grin. "K'den, guess I better start investigating. I'm going to send this red goop off to be tested, then visit Danny Royal's house." He glanced at Steve. "Wanna come along, brah, and show me the cool stuff they teach you at the LAPD?"

"Sure," Steve said.

"I'd like to stick around and observe the autopsy," Mark said to Kealoha. "If you and the medical examiner don't mind."

"Be my guest. I'll call ahead to Dr. Aki and let him know." Kealoha turned to Veronica. "I'd appreciate it if you'd keep this to yourself for a while. No sense alerting the killer that we're on to his sorry ass."

"Sure," Veronica said, a little stunned herself by the revelations. "This is just so incredible. Will you let me know what happens?"

"How about over dinner some time?" Steve asked.

"I'd like that." Veronica smiled, handed Steve her card, and walked out.

"Wait," Kealoha said. "Don't I get one?"

She didn't bother to turn around. Steve glanced at the card, turning it over in his hand.

"What do you know," Steve said with a grin, "It *is* printed on both sides."

Wyatt had his laptop plugged into his cell phone and was downloading all of Mark Sloan's credit card purchases for the last six months when Ben Kealoha and Steve Sloan emerged from the police station. He logged off, shut down the laptop, and started the car.

The two cops got into a Ford Taurus and headed toward

Poipu on the Kaumaulii Highway. Wyatt followed four cars behind, wondering just how much the men knew.

He reviewed every move he'd made in the preparation and execution of his job and couldn't see his mistake. But he knew that in his business, you rarely did until you had to kill it or it killed you.

Maybe it wasn't a mistake, just bad luck. A practical joke of cosmic proportions that put an LAPD homicide detective and his father, some kind of deductive genius, in the same orbit as Danny Royal a day before he was murdered.

Or it wasn't, and they were there by design, to get Danny Royal or flush out his pursuer.

Either way, it didn't matter now.

Wyatt's job wasn't finished yet, and he had to know whether he'd be looking over his shoulder for Dr. Mark Sloan while he completed it.

From what he'd already learned skimming through online newspaper archives, he knew the doctor was not to be taken lightly. Mark Sloan solved the Silent Partner killings, the Sweeney family bombings, and the mystery behind the crash of Pac Atlantic Flight 224. Any one of those cases would have been career-capping achievements for an ordinary cop or Federal agent. But those were just a few of the many high-profile cases Mark Sloan had solved over the years, and he didn't even have a badge.

If Mark Sloan was on to him, the doctor wouldn't give up or be distracted easily. That didn't worry or frighten Wyatt. He respected competence, especially in an adversary. It only reaffirmed his own skills and forced him to rise to a new level of proficiency. Wyatt was already several steps ahead of Mark Sloan and intended to remain that way.

The detectives drove through Old Koloa Town, a row of authentic frontier-style storefronts dating back to the 1800s, capped on one end of the street by a 1970s-era supermarket and a Chevron station on the other. The cops turned the corner onto Poipu Road, and Wyatt followed them past the dreary tourist trap to the resorts and the elegant homes that hugged the shore.

It was obvious where they were leading him, so Wyatt fell farther back, allowing his quarry to reach Danny Royal's house and get settled in. No sense risking detection when it was unnecessary. He pulled into the parking lot of the Kiahuna Poipu Shores and found a spot that afforded him a clear view of the house.

While he waited, he powered up the laptop and plugged in his cell phone modem. He had more research to do.

Danny Royal's house was like a scaled-down version of his restaurant: elegant and colonial, facing the beach, and gently shaded by tall palms. A wide veranda furnished with cushioned rattan furniture surrounded the white one-story house with a vaulted roof.

Steve Sloan and Ben Kealoha stepped up onto the veranda and followed it around to the back of the house, where floor-to-ceiling windows faced the beach. Nothing seemed to have been disturbed. Kealoha knocked once on the French doors, and when no one came, he slipped on a pair of rubber gloves and tried the doorknob. It was unlocked. Steve was surprised, but Kealoha took it in stride.

"Royal went out for a swim. He thought he was coming right back," Kealoha said, handing Steve a pair of gloves from his pocket. "Besides, who carries their keys with them in the ocean?"

"The house is on the beach," Steve said, putting on the gloves. "Anybody could have come in and robbed the place while he was swimming."

"Guess he was a trusting soul," Kealoha said.

They stepped into a spacious living room with a high, open-beam ceiling that was painted white. The house was immaculately clean, every surface gleaming.

"I'm making a mental note to question the cleaning lady," Kealoha said. "And ask her what she charges. Maybe she'd do my place pro bono."

Classical music played softly from hidden speakers, and the rooms were comfortably cool, chilled by the air conditioners that had kept humming through the night.

The furniture was high-end tropical rattan, in keeping with the Hawaiian colonial theme, arranged to offer an optimum view of both the beach and a massive fireplace made of lava rocks.

There were some issues of *Gourmet*, *Architectural Digest*, and other glossy magazines decoratively arranged on the glass-topped coffee table. The walls were adorned with expensive maritime art, including intricate models of ships in glass boxes on the koa-wood bookshelves.

To Steve, the books looked as if they'd been picked out by a decorator for their size and color rather than what they contained.

It was like visiting a Tommy Bahama store without the clothing displays, and about as personal.

"Hello?" Kealoha shouted. "Anybody home?"

"You notice anything unusual about this place?" Steve asked.

"It's like visiting a model home," Kealoha said. "One way out of my price range."

"But even model homes have family photos all over the place, to create some warmth and the illusion that someone lives there," Steve said. "Danny didn't even bother with the illusion."

"He lived here," Kealoha said, finding a leather wallet and a set of keys on the counter.

"Maybe he wasn't someone," Steve said.

Kealoha gave him a look. "Huh?"

"Never mind," Steve said, wandering into the master bedroom while Kealoha thumbed through Danny's wallet. Danny Royal lied to Steve and Mark about his past in New Jersey. After seeing this place, Steve wondered just how much of Danny Royal's life was false.

The master bedroom was as immaculate and impersonal as the rest of the house, except for a stack of puzzle magazines on the bedside table. Steve picked a couple of them up. They were all word games—crosswords, anacrostics, mixigrams, crosscounts, word staircases, and a dozen other kinds of puzzlcs he'd never heard of. He opened the magazines. The puzzles were either completed or nearly completed in pencil by the same hand.

Steve thought Mark probably had subscriptions to the same magazines. He put the magazines back and strayed over to a desktop computer in the corner. The work area was clean, as if the computer was an art object on display instead of a tool to be used.

He turned on the computer and let it boot up while he continued poking around.

Steve was going through the silk jackets and aloha shirts in the massive walk-in closet when Kealoha came in.

"The guy has a driver's license, a credit card, a gasoline card, a social security card, and that's it," Kealoha said. "My wallet is like a filing cabinet. How 'bout yours?"

"Looks like Danny Royal lived lean," Steve said.

"It isn't possible, bruddah." Kealoha stuck the wallet in an evidence bag and shoved it in his pocket. "Nobody lives this lean."

Steve knocked his knuckle on the floor, gauging the sound. The knocks had a slight hollow quality over a certain patch of floor. He took out a car key and pried it between two slats of wood. They popped up. With some room to maneuver his fingers, a dozen other slats pulled easily, revealing a floor safe.

"Maybe we'll find some answers in there," Steve said. He got up and glanced back in the bedroom. The computer was showing a password screen. "The computer may tell us even more. How long will it take to get your crew in here to open the safe and hack into the computer?"

Kealoha snortled. "What crew? That's major tech stuff. We don't have anybody does that, 'cept my eleven-year-old nephew. He could probably hack that in five seconds, then use it to break into Bill Gates' home computer."

"So what do you do in situations like this?"

"We never have sits like this," Kealoha said. "I gotta call in the big boys with the big toys from HPD."

"When do you think they'll get here?"

Kealoha shrugged. "Tomorrow afternoon, maybe. My luck, it'll be the moment I sit down to lunch."

As if on cue, Kealoha's stomach growled. "I knew we forgot to do something on the way here," he said.

Chapter Seven

The S-shaped counter in the tiny saimin noodle shack was so low, Steve had trouble fitting his knees underneath it. Perhaps that was why the handwritten sign on the wall implored customers not to stick gum under the counter—so people wouldn't leave with gooey knees.

The ramshackle restaurant in a warehouse section of Lihue had no tables, so Mark, Steve, and Ben Kealoha sat together at the far end of the crowded counter for a late lunch.

"I eat here for breakfast, lunch, and dinner," Kealoha told them.

"Why?" asked Steve, his question nearly smothered by the loud smack of the screen door snapping shut behind another customer.

"Because this stuff makes chicken soup look like tap water, bruddah," Kealoha said. "But mostly because the cheapest burger on this island is about nine bucks and I don't feel like blowing a day's pay on grub."

"Whatever they're cooking smells wonderful," Mark said, glancing at the menu on the wall. "What do you recommend?"

"The extra large special bowl," Kealoha said. "They empty the fridge into it. It's onolicious."

"Sounds good to me," Mark said.

Kealoha motioned to a waitress and held up three fingers.

A few minutes later, the three men were eagerly devouring their huge bowls of steaming saimin, a hearty combination of salty broth, fresh noodles, vegetables, thin slices of pork, cubes of Spam, and hard-boiled egg made by a sour-faced old Japanese woman they could see sitting on a stool in the kitchen.

After the first delicious mouthful of the wonderful soup, Mark flashed the cook his most winning smile, the one that had reassured countless patients and had been getting him out of all kinds trouble for more than sixty years. The old lady was unimpressed.

He shrugged and went back to enjoying his saimin, surely one of the best dishes he'd ever had. Mark could see why Ben Kealoha was addicted to it.

The three men didn't speak again until they'd consumed their bowls of saimin and each ordered thick slices of home-made liliko'i pie, an impossibly light passion fruit chiffon with a whipped cream topping. Between forkfuls of pie, Steve and Kealoha told Mark what they found, or rather didn't find, at Danny Royal's house. If it wasn't for the puzzle magazines, the house looked as though no one actually lived there.

"What you saw in his house fits with what we discovered in the autopsy," Mark said. "Danny Royal was an illusion. He had extensive plastic surgery, a chiseled nose and chin, implants in his cheeks, major orthodonture—the works. The shape and features of his face were radically altered."

"Maybe he had a bad accident," Kealoha said, "and they had to put his face back together."

Mark shook his head. "There was no evidence of that kind of trauma. This was definitely elective surgery. He gave himself an entirely new face. Based on what you saw at the house, I think he created a new identity to go with it. I seriously doubt anything about Danny Royal is what it seems."

"You don't go to those extremes unless you're running from something," Steve said. "Or someone."

"I'll have his wallet and his place dusted for prints," Kealoha said. "Maybe we'll get a hit."

"I have a feeling it's not going to be that easy," Steve said. "At least it never is for me."

"You're in paradise, brah," Kealoha smiled. "Everything is easy here."

"There's another way to go at this," Mark said. "Dr. Aki and I took detailed notes and photos of Danny's face. With your permission, Ben, I'd like to send them to a forensic anthropologist I know in L.A. It will take some time, but I believe she can use the photos and our data to create a three-D computer model of what Danny Royal's face looked like before his plastic surgery."

"Fo' real? Cool!" Kealoha grinned like a child opening Christmas presents. "Go for it, bruddah!"

Wyatt didn't bother following the two detectives when they left Danny Royal's house. He stayed behind in his parked car at the Kiahuna Poipu Shores because he knew all they'd found was what he'd intentionally left behind.

The wallet and house keys.

He'd copied the hard drive on Royal's computer and emptied the floor safe last night, keeping the $50,000 in cash and burning the two false passports he found inside. He sent the money this morning by Priority Mail to one of the many PO boxes he kept under false names throughout the country. If he ever needed money, there were substantial amounts of cash available within a few hours' reach of most major American cities, and he didn't have to go into a bank or use an ATM to get it.

Wyatt didn't erase Danny Royal's hard drive because he didn't want to raise any questions when somebody eventually showed up to settle Danny's affairs in the wake of his tragic, accidental death. He'd cleaned the safe out because he doubted Danny had told anyone the secrets it contained.

But now things had changed. Wyatt would have to do a much more thorough, and permanent, cleansing tonight.

In the meantime, he had to move forward. There was an urgency to his work now that didn't exist before.

It had taken Wyatt years, and extraordinary patience, to find Danny Royal. But in the end, it was Danny who revealed himself. It always was.

Royal's ex-wife and teenage son had been monitored electronically and visually from day one. Wyatt knew it was only a question of time before Royal contacted his kid again.

It finally happened on the boy's sixteenth birthday. The kid got an e-mail from his dad. The simple message had been cleverly relayed through servers around the world before hitting the kid's AOL mailbox. But Wyatt was able to trace it back to an Internet café in Kauai.

He'd fled to a tropical island. What a cliché. But it only made Wyatt's job easier. Searching for a small island certainly beat trying to find a guy in, say, France.

So Wyatt went to Kauai and hunted. Going to the best restaurants. The nicest stores. The exclusive golf courses and the fanciest resorts. And he watched people.

It was a given that Danny Royal had changed his face and identity. So Wyatt had studied videotapes of Danny Royal to memorize his body language, his gait, the way he used his hands when he spoke. He knew it was only a matter of time, skill, and luck before the paths of the hunter and the hunted would cross.

In the end, it didn't take that long and wasn't very hard.

Danny Royal had altered everything he could about his appearance, but it was the one thing he couldn't alter that gave him away.

His gimp leg.

Once Danny Royal was found, the question became the best way to kill him so that no one would suspect a murder. A shark attack in front of a couple hundred eyewitnesses was a true inspiration. Wyatt supposed he could have come up with something less elaborate, but one did have to find some pleasure in his profession or what was the point of doing it?

Perhaps that had been his mistake.

He couldn't afford any more. Nor could he afford the time and patience it took to find Danny Royal. There were new players involved now, creating a ticking clock.

In a way, he was pleased about it. He found it energizing and somehow less lonely. Playing poker is always more fun than solitaire.

He left his car in the lot, went into the hotel, and took the stairs to Mark Sloan's floor. It limited the number of people who'd see his face.

Breaking into the room was simple. It was a nice ocean-view suite. Nothing fancy, but still expensive. He went through the suitcase, the drawers, and searched all the furniture, careful to leave no visible sign of his presence.

There were a couple of grocery bags full of simple medical supplies and a doctor's bag containing a stethoscope, tongue depressors, an otoscope/ophthalmoscope, rubbing alcohol, ibuprofen tablets, steroid cream, antibiotic ointment, even a few Tootsie Roll suckers.

Mark Sloan was either a throwback to an earlier era, when doctors still made house calls, or was so dedicated to his work he couldn't leave it behind.

All he found that had anything to do with Danny Royal was a stack of souvenir recipe postcards from the restaurant, and they'd been in clear view on the writing table when Wyatt walked in. If Mark Sloan came here with the intention of meeting Royal, nothing in the room revealed it.

It's what Wyatt didn't find that was useful. There were no books to read or magazines to flip through. Not even a Hawaii guidebook, beyond the advertising-laden, throwaway crap the hotel left in every room. Wyatt concluded Mark was a man who didn't like distractions and who remained focused on his work, which explained the doctor's bag and the extra medical supplies. Mark couldn't leave the hospital behind, so he brought it with him.

But now that Mark Sloan had a murder to investigate, Wyatt was certain it would be getting the doctor's complete attention, even if it wasn't any of his business. The man wouldn't be able to help himself.

That was good to know.

Perhaps, Wyatt thought, there might be a way to manipulate that to his benefit.

The search of Steve Sloan's room took even less time than Mark's. There were guidebooks, magazines, and paperback books stacked on the nightstand. A six-pack of beer had been crammed into the tiny refrigerator. There was a bag of Doritos, some candy bars, and a bottle of Coca-Cola stashed on a shelf in the closet, along with souvenir shirts, caps, and flip-flops. And nothing in the room had anything to do with Danny Royal. Unlike his father, Steve Sloan was on vacation and open to any distraction that came along. Danny Royal wasn't one of them, and never would have been if not for Mark Sloan; Wyatt was certain of that.

As Wyatt left the room and went down the stairs, he decided it had been bad luck after all. Mark Sloan stumbled into Danny Royal's life, and Wyatt's job, by accident.

But the more Wyatt thought about it, the less it seemed like a problem. In fact, it began to look like a great opportunity.

By the time Wyatt reached the lobby, he knew exactly what to do.

CHAPTER EIGHT

Kamalei Moala, the hostess at the Royal Hawaiian, lived in a tiny bungalow in Hanapepe on the same overgrown property as her impossibly old grandparents, who sold homemade taro chips off their front porch to passing motorists, who were few and far between.

The elder Moalas fried the chips, made from taro roots and lightly seasoned with garlic, and sold them hot and fresh for $3 a bag. They'd been doing it as long as Mark had been alive. And then some.

Mark and Steve each bought a bag, just to be polite, but couldn't stop eating them as they talked to Kamalei, who sat at the picnic table in front of her bungalow.

Kamalei Moala looked very different here, away from the seductively low lights of the restaurant, wearing a simple floral sundress, nursing a glass of iced tea. She wasn't quite as exotic. Her eyes were bloodshot from crying, but she offered the Sloans a warm smile anyway.

"These chips are wonderful." Mark held up a bag. "I've never had anything quite like them. What is a taro, anyway?"

"It's similar to a potato and is an important part of Hawaiian culture. We use it to make poi, kulolo, squid luau, lau lau, and chips," Kamalei said. "Like corn for the American Indians, it has great spiritual, historical, and ceremonial significance besides being good to eat."

"Really?" Mark said, examining a chip. "Sounds much more interesting than a potato chip. And tastes better, too."

He stuck the chip in his mouth, savoring it, then offered the bag to Kamalei. "Would you like one?"

"No, thank you. I've had enough taro chips to last me a lifetime," she said. "I'm sure you didn't come all the way out here just to buy my *tutu*'s chips, Dr. Sloan."

"You remember us?" Steve asked.

"You came to the restaurant for dinner the other night," she said. "You're Danny's friends."

"Actually, we only met him on Saturday," Mark said. "We hardly knew him at all, but we'd be interesting in talking to people who did."

"You knew him as well as anybody," Kamalei said, without a hint of bitterness or sarcasm in her voice. She was simply stating a fact. "Danny didn't like to talk about himself."

"You didn't find that odd?" Mark said.

"People talk about themselves way too much, especially men. Danny was different. He liked to listen. Danny cared more about what other people had to say. That was his secret."

"We were wondering what it was," Steve said.

"It wasn't the food that kept bringing the customers back, it was Danny. They loved him. He made everyone feel as if they were the most interesting people in the world."

"Including you?" Mark asked.

"Danny was a nice man to work for," she said defensively. "Why are you asking all these questions?"

"Now that he's dead, we're trying to settle his affairs, contact his next of kin." Steve said. "But we don't have anything to go on."

"You're getting awfully involved for two people who never met him before," she said.

"We witnessed his killing and identified his body for the police," Mark said. "We've sort of been drafted into this. Besides, we're on vacation. We have time. It's the least we can do to repay his hospitality. We'd really appreciate your help."

"Did he have any close friends or lovers who might have known him better?" Steve asked.

"I was his lover," she said matter-of-factly. "Off and on. So were lots of women."

"Do you have their names?"

She raised an eyebrow. "I didn't keep track of them. Why do you ask?"

Steve shrugged. "Maybe one of them knows more about him than you do."

"He didn't see many local girls. Most of them were tourists, single women only here for a week or two," she said. "Nothing serious. Vacation romance. You know how it is."

"Oh yeah. Sure. Of course." Steve said in an offhand way, glancing at his dad. "Who doesn't?"

"I've known Danny since he opened the restaurant four years ago," she said. "He started out renting the old Outrigger House after it went bust. I was his first hire. I've been his lover, off and on, ever since."

"And you didn't mind sharing him?" Mark asked.

"Danny never snuck around behind anyone's back," she said. "He always made it clear up front that his relationships were casual—no strings, no baggage, just good times. And that was okay, because they were. Great times. Danny knew how to treat a woman."

"But it remained casual," Steve said. "You were never even tempted to leave your toothbrush?"

"He's my comfort guy, the one I go to when my romances crash and burn, which they always do."

The comfort guy. It sounded to Steve like something he could get into. He had a restaurant. He had beach house. How hard could it be? Steve wanted to ask Kamalei for some pointers, but instead he asked, "Did he ever talk about his past to you?"

"All I know is that he came from somewhere in New Jersey, where he ran some burger joints, and that he hurt his knee playing high school football."

"You weren't kidding when you said you knew him as well as we did," Steve said.

"Who he is now is what matters," Kamalei said. "What difference does his past make?"

"Interesting choice of words, considering . . ." Steve let his voice trail off, full of innuendo.

"Considering what?" she asked.

Steve just smiled. Unnervingly. Actually, he was still thinking about the possibilities of this Comfort Guy thing. But he doubted being the host of BBQ Bob's had the same allure as the Royal Hawaiian. Perhaps there was a recipe or two off those souvenir postcards he could re-create at his place.

"Did you ever see Danny treat anybody else the way he treated us?" Mark asked. "Perhaps someone he might have known outside the restaurant?"

"Besides the occasional liquor vendor or food rep? Just repeat customers, tourists visiting Kauai again and stopping in for another meal. Danny always made them feel like they were special guests who were sorely missed," she said, her eyes narrowing suspiciously. "Why do you want to know?"

Mark smiled reassuringly. "Like we said before, we're just looking for anyone who should be informed about his death, someone on the mainland, perhaps."

"Didn't he have a will or something?" Kamalei asked.

"Not that we know of," Mark said. "No lawyer or family members have come forward. Do you know who his attorney might be?"

"No, but I know his accountant, Earl Ettinger up in Kapaa, and his banker, Arliss Brewer. They come in for dinner all the time."

"Were they investors?" Mark asked.

"Not Mr. Ettinger—he just likes to eat at a discount. But Mr. Brewer and the First Bank of Lihue held the mortgage on the restaurant," she said. "Probably on Danny's house, too. I think he liked to see how their money was doing."

Steve tried to think of a way to ask his next question without putting Kamalei on guard, but there wasn't one, so he saved it for last. It was the question he asked so often in his work, he thought about having it printed on little cards to save him the trouble of asking it.

"Danny seemed like a wonderful guy," Steve said. "But everybody's got enemies. He must have had at least one."

"Just the shark," she said.

It was a little after 2:00 A.M. when the sirens woke Mark Sloan from a deep sleep. He immediately became aware of the light flickering on the other side of his closed drapes and the smell of something burning.

Mark got up, went to the window, and parted the drapes. A house on the beach was consumed by fire, flames licking out the windows and spitting embers into the night sky. Firemen were dousing the raging fire with multiple streams of water, but the house was a lost cause. The best they could hope to do now was stop the flames from spreading to other properties.

The phone rang. Before he answered it, he knew it was Steve. And he knew what he was calling to tell him.

Ten minutes later Mark and Steve were both dressed and hurrying across the parking lot toward the police line, where officers held back the distraught neighbors and a few hotel guests shaken from their sleep who came to watch Danny Royal's house burn.

After this latest incident, Steve figured he and his dad would be the only guests left in the Kiahuna Poipu Shores tomorrow.

Sgt. Kealoha spotted them immediately and waved them past the officers.

"Guess we won't be needing the HPD big boys after all," Kealoha said bitterly.

"I think that was the idea," Steve replied, noticing a grim smile on his father's face. "What are you smiling about?"

"This is a message," Mark said. "The killer knows we weren't fooled and that an investigation has begun. He's telling us that he's not going to sit back and let us come after him. He's going to make it as difficult for us as possible, leaving nothing but scorched earth behind, literally and figuratively."

Kealoha whistled. "The fire tells you all that?"

"This fire," Mark said. "And the other one."

"What other one?"

Just then, Kealoha's cell phone trilled, but he didn't make a move to answer it. Instead he stared at Mark with a look that fell somewhere between awe and disbelief.

"The restaurant, of course." Mark said.

Chapter Nine

Mark and Steve didn't bother to go see the Royal Hawaiian burn; instead they went back to their hotel rooms for a couple hours' more of sleep.

They met for breakfast at a little after 8:00 A.M. and, as Steve had predicted, the hotel seemed even emptier than it had the previous morning. More guests had left and no one new was checking in.

The news that Danny Royal's body had been found and identified was in the paper, but there was no mention of any police investigation.

"I wonder how the killer found out," Mark mused aloud.

Steve looked up from his stack of pancakes. "About what?"

"That his ruse failed. The only ones who knew Danny Royal's death was actually a homicide are the two of us, Ben Kealoha, Veronica Klein, and the medical examiner," Mark said. "Then again, news might have leaked when Ben asked the Honolulu Police Department to send a tech unit over here to crack Danny's safe and hack his computer. Anyone hearing about that could infer that an investigation had begun. Or perhaps Kamalei was involved in Danny's murder, and our questions spooked her."

Steve set down his fork and tossed his napkin on the table. He was about to say something when his dad, lost in thought, spoke again.

"There's another thing," Mark said.

"There always is," Steve said wearily.

"Maybe the killer burned down Danny Royal's house and his restaurant to send *two* messages. One to us, and one to someone else—a warning about what happens to people who do what Danny did. Or was doing. Or was about to do."

Steve looked at Mark. "What are we doing?"

"What do you mean?"

"I mean, why are we investigating Danny Royal's murder?"

"Why do we investigate anything?"

"I know why I do it," Steve said. "It's my job. But I'm on vacation here, and I'm not on the Kauai Police force, and this is their case."

"That never stopped you before."

"No, that's never stopped *you* before," Steve said. "I have plenty of work waiting for me back home without looking for more. I'm on vacation, remember? So I'm asking myself, What am I doing?"

"You're assisting the Kauai Police."

"They haven't asked for my assistance," Steve said.

"I distinctly heard Ben invite you to go search Danny Royal's house with him," Mark said.

Steve held up his hands in surrender. "Okay, I admit I was curious. But I've had a chance to sleep on it. This is a local homicide; there's no reason for me or for you to be involved anymore."

"I'm involved for the same reasons I get involved in any other homicide investigation," Mark said. "Either I'm asked for advice, or it's a case you're working on, or it involves one of my patients."

Steve held up three fingers, lowering one at a time as he made his points. "No one has asked you for advice. It's not a case I'm working on. And it doesn't involve one of your patients."

"That's not true," Mark said defensively. "Danny Royal was my patient. He came to me with his jellyfish stings."

"You're reaching. You want to know my theory?" Steve didn't wait for an answer. "For you, running around the island asking questions about a murder *is* your idea of a vacation. You're having a great time. I saw the look on your face at the fire last night."

"I don't take any pleasure in the suffering of others," Mark said.

"No, but you take a lot of pleasure in solving mysteries," Steve said. "And you can't leave this one behind."

"What would you like me to do, Steve?"

"Think about letting Kealoha do his job and the two of us enjoy the rest of our vacation."

Mark was quiet for a moment, considering what Steve said, then he nodded. "You're right, we came here for rest and relaxation. I should have fun."

"Finally, you're grasping the concept. Take it easy. Enjoy what Kauai has to offer."

"I will." Mark pushed his chair away from the table and stood up.

"So what do you have in mind?"

"I thought I'd go down to First Bank of Kauai for a look at Danny Royal's financial records and anything he might have in a safe-deposit box. Want to join me?"

"Sure." Steve sighed and got up.

Sgt. Ben Kealoha was waiting for them inside the bank with Arliss Brewer, the bank manager and chief loan officer, and Earl Ettinger, Danny's accountant. Kealoha was armed with a court order allowing them to see all of Danny Royal's bank records and to open a safe-deposit box, assuming he had one.

He did.

They found the usual mortgage documents, deeds, and insurance policies, as well as $100,000 in cash and half a dozen passports for Danny under a half a dozen different names and nationalities.

Stuck amid the mortgage documents for the restaurant

property, Mark found one of Danny's souvenir recipe cards, a tantalizing picture of lemongrass-seared island opah on one side, the recipe and a handwritten note on the other.

Re: Ideal Oven, Ask Jim Lowe. A loose, trendy cook.

The only other information on the card was the preprinted address and phone numbers for the Royal Hawaiian and, in almost microscopic type, the name and address of the company that made the cards.

Kealoha asked Brewer if he could borrow the bank's conference room to talk and to go over the cartons of financial information Ettinger brought and that the bank had collected for them.

Brewer agreed, and even offered to provide all the fresh-ground Kona coffee they needed. They gladly took him up on his hospitality, and, while Ettinger patiently waited outside, they interviewed the bank manager about Danny Royal.

Brewer was a man in his midforties with too much gel in his short hair. He looked quite comfortable in a coat and tie, despite the humidity and heat outside. Seeing a banker in typical business attire in Kauai somehow seemed strangely out of place to Mark.

"What can you tell us about Danny Royal?" Kealoha asked.

"Mr. Royal was a conscientious, dependable, hardworking businessman," Brewer said, sitting ramrod straight in his chair. "He came here with nothing and rose to become a pillar of the community."

"I've always wondered," Steve said, "what's it take to become a pillar?"

"He ran a successful business and took an interest in the community," Brewer said. "He gave money to local charities, donated services, promoted tourism, and was a member in good standing of the Chamber of Commerce."

"So basically, it's something you buy," Kealoha said.

"It's also about character, Sgt. Kealoha," Brewer said.

"And Danny had plenty of that," Steve replied, spreading the passports out like a poker hand. "At least half a dozen of them we know of so far."

"Mr. Brewer, you said Danny came here with nothing," Mark said. "What did you mean by that?"

"When he came here four years ago, he rented the Outrigger House property from us," Brewer said. "It was a poorly run restaurant that went under and defaulted on its mortgage payments, so we assumed ownership of the property and furnishings. Mr. Royal rented it all from us to start his own restaurant, slowly fixed the place up, and once the business took off, we sold the building to him."

"When did he open his account with you?" Mark asked.

"Shortly after he started renting the Outrigger property," Brewer said. "We deducted his payments directly from his accounts."

Mark took out a pencil and began taking some notes on a legal pad. "What was his balance?"

"When he first opened the account?"

"Yes."

"About nine thousand dollars," Brewer said, referring to some documents in front of him.

Kealoha covered his mouth as he yawned. Steve didn't know if it was because he was bored or because he'd been up all night at the two arson scenes. It was probably a little bit of both. Suddenly, Steve felt a yawn coming on, too.

Mark made a note on his pad. "Did Danny take out a loan with the bank to pay for the improvements he was making in the restaurant?"

"No," Brewer said, "He paid for that himself."

"Where was the money coming from?"

"I understood he had some family money or something," Brewer said. "The account shows that, for the first year or so, he received regular transfers of eight to nine thousand dollars every month."

"From where?" Mark asked.

Brewer referred to the paperwork again. "Numerous banks on the mainland and abroad."

"When you say *abroad*," Steve asked, "would you be speaking of the Cayman Islands?"

"One of the banks involved was situated there, yes," Brewer said.

Kealoha snickered. "And that didn't raise any alarm bells with you?"

"Sergeant, if I got alarmed every time we received a transfer from a Cayman Island financial institution, I'd have to shut down the bank," Brewer said. "It is not uncommon for people of substance to put money there to avoid excessive taxation."

"I'm confused, Mr. Brewer. I thought you said Danny started from nothing," Mark said. "People with nothing don't usually have accounts in the Cayman Islands."

"Perhaps what I should have said was that he didn't initially bring much capital into his business and that he lived modestly at first. As his business grew, he increased his investment and assumed debt accordingly," Brewer said. "He was a patient and careful man when it came to his money and ours."

"We heard he'd owned some restaurant franchises in New Jersey," Steve said.

"He might have worked in the restaurant industry before," Brewer said, "but I was always under the impression that this was the first business of his own."

"You don't check these things out before you loan a guy money?" Kealoha said. "Because if that's the case, I'd like to borrow some money before I leave."

"I don't know anything about his previous business endeavors," Brewer said, "beyond the fact that no red flags showed up when we checked his credit."

Mark glanced at the handwritten note on Danny's recipe card. "Have you ever done business with anyone named Jim Lowe?"

"The name doesn't sound familiar, no."

Mark asked a few more questions, Kealoha yawned a few more times, and then Brewer was excused. Steve noticed that Mark had filled three pages of his legal pad with notes and figures.

Earl Ettinger, wearing slacks, was invited in next. He was a short, balding, round-faced man wearing an untucked tan silk shirt with a mild floral pattern that gave him the illusion of being a little taller and thinner than he actually was. He was holding a thin leather briefcase that gave him the illusion of being more important and professionally occupied than he actually was. And he was smiling, giving the illusion that he was actually glad to be there.

"Good morning, gentlemen," Earl said.

"Thanks for coming down, Mr. Ettinger," Kealoha said.

"Call me Earl, please," Earl said, passing his business card all around before taking a seat and setting the briefcase beside him on the floor. "How can I help you?"

"We have some questions about Danny Royal," Kealoha said, yawning.

"Fire away," Earl said, smiling even bigger, giving the illusion that now he wasn't just happy, but thrilled to be there.

"From what Mr. Brewer told us," Mark said, "it seems that Danny was very frugal with his money when he first arrived here."

"Yes, indeed he was," Earl said. "Rented a little apartment in Waimea and drove a used car he bought off one of the rental agencies."

"He paid cash for both?"

"Yep," Earl said.

"I understand he was getting some money from other banks," Mark said.

"A little less than ten grand a month from other accounts he had here and there," Earl said.

"Here and there," Mark repeated, sorting through some of the bank account statements until he found what he was looking for. "That would include the five accounts he had in different banks here in Hawaii with balances of about nine thousand dollars each."

"Yes," Earl said.

"And then there were the occasional transfers from other banks for nine thousand dollars or less."

"Right."

"That didn't strike you as odd?"

"How so?"

Mark and Steve shared a look, then Steve asked, "How did you and Danny get together, Earl?"

"He came in and had me do his tax return," Earl said. "It was pretty simple that first year. He hadn't opened his restaurant yet."

"Did someone refer him to you?"

"No, he just walked in to the H&R Block at the Kukui Grove Mall," Earl said. "They open up a temporary outlet in one of the vacant storefronts around tax time every year. Lucky for me I was free when Danny came in."

"Lucky for both of you," Kealoha said, stretching in his seat, trying to stay awake.

"That was the day my own accounting firm really began," Earl said wistfully. "In a sense, Danny and I grew up together in the Kauai business community."

"He was a pillar," Steve agreed.

"How did Danny pay for the improvements he made to the restaurant?" Mark asked.

"He paid cash," Earl said. "Danny didn't want any debt hanging over his head, not until he had a steady, dependable cash flow."

"As opposed to the steady, dependable cash flow from all his other bank accounts," Kealoha said.

"He'd rather spend his own capital than take on risk," Earl said. "I thought that was sound financial thinking, and I proved to be correct. He incorporated, paid himself a salary, and loaned much of it right back into the business until the restaurant was a success."

"I see," Mark said. "And then he took out loans to buy the Outrigger property and his house on the beach."

"Yep," Earl said. "He didn't even trust himself with a credit card until a couple years ago, and then only one."

"Are you familiar with a vendor Danny might have dealt with named Jim Lowe?" Mark asked. "He might have sold Danny some ovens?"

"Doesn't ring a bell," Earl said. "But you're going back a lot of years. You'd have to look at the canceled checks."

"I'll do that. Thank you, Earl," Mark said. "You've been a big help."

Earl rose with a smile. "I hope you'll remember me at tax time."

He started to hand out his card again, but Steve stopped him. "You already gave us one."

Earl winked. "Give one to a friend."

Chapter Ten

As soon as the accountant left, Mark leaned back in his chair and sighed. "I think it's pretty clear what Danny Royal pulled off here."

"Maybe I'm just dead tired," Kealoha said, "and incredibly bored, but it isn't totally clear to me. I see the pieces, I'm just not sure how they all fit together."

"Let's start at the beginning. We know that Danny Royal was in hiding with a new face and a new identity," Mark said. "You can easily buy both."

"In L.A., you can buy good identities any day of the week on the sidewalk on Alvarado Street," Steve added. "Driver's licenses, social security cards, birth certificates—the works, for as little as a hundred dollars."

"But Danny had another problem that wasn't quite so easy to solve," Mark said. "He had a lot of money he'd taken from somebody that he had to put into play without raising any attention. Unlike most crooks, Danny was smart enough to know not to be greedy, that to avoid detection you have to be patient instead. You have to invest or leverage the money, replacing the cash with assets, little by little over time."

"You don't go out and buy a Ferrari, or go gambling in Vegas, or move into a mansion," Steve said. "You keep a low profile."

"Which isn't easy to do with a couple hundred large in

your pocket," Kealoha said. "Not that I'd know what that's like."

"The banks have to notify the federal government of any deposits over ten thousand dollars, so Danny opened dozens of accounts just shy of the limit, kept some cash on hand, and put the rest in the Cayman Islands," Mark said. "He used that money to rent an apartment, buy a cheap car, and to lease the space for his restaurant."

"The restaurant became the Laundromat for his money," Steve said. "He paid cash for everything he could, then once the place got going, he paid himself a salary, loaned the business money, basically funneling his money back through the restaurant any way possible."

"He paid his taxes, established credit, took out a mortgage, and within a few years the money was clean. He was finally making real money rather than laundering what he already had," Mark said. "He'd become legitimate. But he never stopped being afraid."

"How do you know he was scared?" Kealoha asked.

"The fake passports and cash he kept in his safe-deposit box," Mark said. "I'm willing to bet he had more cash and IDs hidden in his house in case he needed to make a quick escape."

"Odds are you're going to find out his social security number is legit," Steve said. "Probably belongs to some upstanding citizen who paid his taxes, never got in trouble with the law, and died five years ago. Or he's still alive in some rest home somewhere, not even sure what his own name is."

Kealoha stood up, yawned, and stretched. "So where do we go from here?"

"We go back to Los Angeles tomorrow," Mark said sadly, then adding hopefully, "unless there's something more you need from us here."

Kealoha shook his head. "You've already done more than enough. I'm going to grab some lunch, then start going through all this stuff."

"We could start on it for you," Mark said eagerly.

"No, thanks," Kealoha replied, much to Steve's relief. "I've lined up some detectives at the station to help me out. Stop by HQ on your way to the airport and I'll fill you in on what we've got."

Mark and Steve walked outside, pausing on the steps of the bank to take in the day, the warm sunshine, the sleepy pace of Lihue, a town that seemed architecturally trapped in 1977.

"You don't look happy," Steve said.

"We've hit a wall," Mark said. "The story ended here; it began somewhere else. We just don't have a clue where."

"It's not our problem, Dad."

"Then why do I feel this intense pressure right behind my eyes?"

"I'm not a doctor," Steve said, "but it sounds to me like you need a vacation."

There was nothing more Wyatt could do in Kauai, so he took the first flight out to Los Angeles. On the way, he turned on his laptop and browsed over the material he'd gathered on Mark Sloan and his son.

He'd analyzed their credit card statements, their phone bills, their DMV records, and managed to get a look at Steve Sloan's service record. Privacy no longer existed for anyone—except men like Wyatt, whose survival depended on it. Wyatt paid a high price for the sophisticated software and database passwords he'd acquired, but it was worth every penny to have unfettered access to bits and bytes of people's lives.

As soon as he landed at LAX in the late afternoon, he rented a car and drove to a storage unit he kept in Canoga Park, a bleak corner of the San Fernando Valley filled with auto body shops, apartments overstuffed with illegal aliens, and warehouses where porno films were shot.

The storage units were covered with gang graffiti and were protected by a live-in manager, who liked to tool around the property in his golf cart and had put rattrap boxes in every corner and alcove.

Wyatt walked up to his little closet. A cheap $10 padlock was all that protected his tens of thousands of dollars' worth of sophisticated electronics and unsophisticated weapons. Anyone who put expensive locks on their storage units might as well put a placard outside that said: GOOD STUFF INSIDE. COME AND GET IT!

He left the weapons, took the electronic goodies, and drove through Las Virgenes Canyon, down the Santa Monica Mountains, and into Malibu, the exclusive beach community for the very rich. Having just left Kauai, Wyatt was struck by the contrasts between the two iconic visions of sandy paradise.

They both had long beaches, palm trees, and almost endless sunshine. What Hawaii didn't have was a Berlin Wall of obscene houses, tall fences, and a traffic-clogged freeway cutting people off from the beach. And even if anybody got to the beach, what little sand that wasn't eroded away was covered with raw sewage, used syringes, and TV production crews hauling in fake palm trees, fake dunes, and swimsuit models to sell the world on a paradise that didn't exist.

But other than that, Hawaii and Malibu were virtually the same.

Mark Sloan lived on an exclusive stretch of Malibu across from the colorfully dated Trancas Market, where people with multimillion-dollar homes shopped for groceries in flip-flops, cutoffs, and sweatshirts and pretended they were beach bums.

Wyatt discovered in his research that Mark bought the house cheap in an auction held by the DEA, who'd taken the prime property from some drug dealer. Mark lived on the top floor and his son lived on the first floor. They shared a front door, but there was separate access to the bottom floor from the beach. That was the door Wyatt used to break in after he disabled the alarm.

Wyatt spent the next two hours methodically and efficiently infesting the house with electronic bugs. He opened up their computers and installed chips that would allow him to capture each keystroke and, when they were on-line, see whatever they saw in real time. The image would be transmitted to his computer and, if he wasn't there, would be captured on his hard drive for later viewing. He used another piece of electronic wizardry to clone their cell phones so he could eavesdrop on their calls at will or, when he wasn't around, have them recorded by his computer for playback.

All the devices he planted were energy parasites powered by their hosts. No need to worry about batteries. In all, he left close to $50,000 in electronics behind in Mark Sloan's house. He thanked Danny Royal for so kindly offsetting that unexpected expense out of petty cash.

When Wyatt finished with the house, he moved into the garage, bugged Mark's Saab convertible, and planted a satellite tracking device under the hood. Wyatt would rely on the Defense Department's array of satellites to pinpoint Mark Sloan's location at any time and relay it to his wireless handset.

Your tax dollars at work, Wyatt thought.

He wouldn't have to risk tailing Mark Sloan; he'd just listen to everything the doctor said and track all his movements from the safety, distance, and anonymity of a computer screen.

Whatever Mark knew or found out now, Wyatt would know it, too.

Mark Sloan's last night on Kauai was spent struggling to sleep, unable to quiet his thoughts, unable to stop thinking about the mystery of Danny Royal.

Who was Danny Royal?

A very smart, very cool-headed individual. Smart enough not only to take a great deal of someone's money, but to know how to disappear afterward.

A man who never relaxed, who never lowered his guard, never letting anyone into his life, living, in every regard, only on the surface. Even his house was utterly devoid of a personality, except for a few crossword puzzle magazines.

With that thought, Mark sat up, got out of bed, and turned on the lamp on the bedside table. He found the stack of recipe cards he took from the Royal Hawaiian, picked out the one that matched the card they'd found in the safe-deposit box, and wrote on it:

Re: Ideal Oven, Ask Jim Lowe. A loose, trendy cook.

It seemed pretty straightforward. A note about someone to contact about a piece of kitchen equipment and a chef. But what if it was something more? An anagram, perhaps?

So for three hours Mark tried reorganizing the letters of the first sentence into other possible sentences, but came up with nothing that made any sense.

Deliverance: I'm a Jello Owl.

We laced a vermilion jello.

Cleveland: Wire Joel a Limo.

We've corralled a mini jello.

Lo, a medicinal jewel lover.

A love Jew cleared a million.

A vile medical jello owner.

In frustration, he removed the *re:* from the mix, but still couldn't come up with anything any more sensible or even grammatical.

A Camino leveled Jill, Ow.

A clean evil willed mojo.

Jill menaced a olive owl.

A cajoled ill evil woman.

He had even less luck when he moved on to the second sentence of the note: *A loose, trendy cook.*

If Mark had a computer, he figured he could probably come up with a thousand more senseless combinations of words out of what was scrawled on Danny's recipe card.

Maybe the note wasn't a puzzle. It just was what it was—a note about a guy to call for a deal on ovens and a good chef—and he was obsessing over nothing.

Then again, Danny was referring to a trendy *cook* rather

than a *chef*. It seemed odd. The distinction between a chef and a cook wasn't major, and merely one of perception, but it would certainly make a difference to a man running an elegant restaurant as opposed to a diner. Wouldn't Danny Royal have preferred a trendy chef over a trendy cook?

Mark turned off the light, got back into bed, and tried to sleep. But again the questions kept coming.

What was Danny Royal running from? *Where* was he running from? *Whom* was he running from?

Whom? Now, there was an interesting question. Finding Danny couldn't have been easy, not if it took five years to happen. And that had to be expensive. So whoever it was had deep pockets, patience, and an infinite capacity for vengeance.

And what about the killer? Mark doubted it was the aggrieved individual. This had to be the work of a hired hand. A professional who wanted to make Danny's death look like an accident.

A shark attack, of all things.

So the killer was a professional who wasn't afraid of challenges. He probably relished them.

Whoever the killer was, he had to get scuba gear, a boat, a tiger shark fin. And he'd probably been on the island for a while, watching Danny and learning his habits. Somewhere along the line, the killer must have left some kind of clue, some trace of his existence and his movements. Nobody is invisible.

Mark made some notes on the hotel notepad, reminding himself of things to ask Kealoha to look into when they met for the last time tomorrow.

It wasn't going to be easy walking away from this mystery, but Mark had to concede, as he finally drifted off to sleep, that he'd run out of leads.

Chapter Eleven

Three hours before their flight back home, Mark and Steve stopped at the police station in Lihue to say good-bye to Sgt. Kealoha and see if there were any new developments in the case.

They walked in to find Kealoha and two other detectives going over the paperwork from the accountant and the bank. Kealoha was wearing the clothes he'd had on the day before and looked like he hadn't slept much, if at all.

Mark took a few sheets of paper, torn from his hotel notepad, from his shirt pocket. "I came up with some possible avenues of investigation and some questions you might want to look into."

"First, let me tell you everything we've found out since yesterday," Kealoha said, pointing to a blank dry-erase board mounted on the wall.

"That much?" Steve said.

"Impressive, huh? Turns out Danny Royal's social security number is legit. We traced the number back to Danny Royal of Summit, New Jersey, who was a law-abiding citizen and regular taxpayer right up until the time he died six years ago."

"Figures," Steve said.

"We got some clean prints off Danny's wallet and passports and ran them through AFIS, coming up blank,"

Kealoha said. "Whoever he was, he never served in the military, law enforcement, or spent time in the pokey."

Kealoha motioned to the two tired men behind him, both of whom were on the phone. "We've checked out Royal's credit card statements and phone bills. All he bought on the card were small things from local merchants—no plane trips or anything that might have given us a lead. Virtually all of his phone calls have been to suppliers or local hotels and residences, presumably to confirm dinner reservations."

"Did Jim Lowe's number show up in any of those calls?" Mark asked.

"Not so far." Kealoha said, "though he could work for one of the vendors, or be somebody who just came in to eat at Danny's restaurant one night."

"You get anything off the calls from Danny's house?" Mark asked.

"Almost all of them were to his restaurant or to local hotels."

"Any long-distance calls?" Steve asked.

"Only from the restaurant, and those we've tracked to vendors he was doing business with."

Steve nodded. "He was careful, all right."

Mark offered his notes to Kealoha again. "Perhaps we've let ourselves get distracted by focusing on who Danny Royal is rather than how he was killed."

"I'm going to contact dive shops, see if I can track who rented or bought scuba equipment over the last week, and check with the airlines, see who brought dive stuff along with them," Kealoha said. "I'm also checking every boat-rental place on the island and going over any reports of stolen or missing watercraft reported over the last two weeks. Plus, I'm talking to sport fishermen to see if anyone was asking about buying shark fins."

Mark crumpled up his notes and tossed them in a nearby trash can. "You're good, Ben."

"I don't often get a chance to shine," Kealoha said.

Mark held out his hand. "It's been a pleasure meeting you. Good luck on the case."

Kealoha shook his hand. "Ho, az nuts, Doc. Deah wooda be no case witout you, brah. An den da *akamai* killer wooda fooled us lolo mokes. We tanks planny." He grinned at Mark's blank look. "We owe you one, Dr. Sloan."

"That's what I thought you said." Mark grinned back. "Either that, or you said I had hazelnuts in my suitcase. I'll let you know as soon as those sketches come in from the forensic anthropologist."

Steve shook Kealoha's hand. "Gimme a call, brah. We'll talk story, shoots?"

"Shoots, brah, dun deal," Kealoha replied with a grin. Then he added, "You do realize you sound ridiculous trying to talk pidgin, right?"

"You think that's bad," Steve said, "you ought to hear me jive."

As they turned to leave, Mark gave Steve a look and whispered, "Do people still jive anymore?"

"Hell if I know," Steve replied.

The breakfast crowd at BBQ Bob's mostly tended to be people who looked like stereotypical truckers; thick-necked, heavyset men and women in jeans and faded shirts and baseball caps. They were drawn to a breakfast menu of eggs and potatoes served up with thick slabs of steak, bacon, ham, pork, or sausage, slathered in butter and grease, and, on request, ass-kicking barbeque sauce.

It wasn't the healthiest of diets, unless you happened to be a strict adherent of a low-carb, protein-rich lifestyle, which none of the patrons were.

Knowing all that, Dr. Jesse Travis often wondered if he was violating his Hippocratic oath by co-owning the place and serving heaping platters of cholesterol to people. He tried to appease his guilty conscience by adding granola, fruit cups, and cottage cheese to the breakfast menu, but so far the only people who ever ordered them were the waitresses and, occasionally, Dr. Amanda Bentley and Jesse's girlfriend, Susan Hilliard.

Of course, Amanda, being a pathologist and medical examiner, and Susan, being a nurse, both knew better than to eat up the "hot death" BBQ Bob's served.

"It's not hot death," Jesse corrected Amanda, who sat at the counter, sipping a cup of coffee and regarding the customers. "It's a hearty breakfast."

"It hearty all right," she said. "It goes straight to the coronary arteries."

"How can you say that? The cowboys and explorers and homesteaders and farmers who made this country great, who road horseback over mountain ranges, through snowstorms, and across blistering deserts, they ate like this."

"They also treated fevers by bleeding people and prescribed mercury as a laxative," Amanda said. "Should we still be doing that, too?"

It wasn't easy for Jesse to argue a medical point he didn't believe in. But as a businessman, he believed in catering to the culinary desires of his customers. He had a lucrative breakfast business going, something few barbeque joints could boast about, and he didn't want to lose it. His customers wanted meat, grease, and butter, and in large quantities, so that's what he gave them.

Besides, he hated it when Amanda lectured him. Especially when she was right.

Jesse admired and respected the bright, bubbly, African-American woman. She was a brilliant pathologist, a respected medical examiner, and an attentive single mother of a five-year-old boy, a feat she pulled off by being extraordinarily organized, practical, and focused. It was how she managed her life so efficiently and, in Jesse's opinion, how she tried to manage everyone else's.

"People like a breakfast that sticks to their ribs," Jesse said, hoping it didn't come out as defensive whining and certain that it did.

"And their waistlines and their butts," Amanda said,

barely stifling a smile. "Look at these people. It's sticking all over them."

"You know what you are?" Jesse wagged a finger at her. "A food prude."

"A what?"

"A food prude," Jesse said. "If people don't eat like you, if they don't graze on weeds all day and swallow handfuls of vitamins like peanuts, they're barbarians or fatsoes."

Amanda thought about it for a moment. "You swallow peanuts by the handful? No wonder you think you're serving a balanced breakfast here."

Jesse groaned in frustration and disappeared into the kitchen. Amanda grinned to herself and finished her coffee just as Mark and Steve came in, all tan and rested from their vacation.

Well, they were tan, anyway, Amanda thought. They didn't look very rested.

"Welcome back," Amanda said, as they slid onto stools on either side of her.

"Have you been giving Jesse hell?" Steve asked.

"I've been doing my part," Amanda said. "But I guess I can ease up a little now that you're back. How was the trip?"

"It was great for a while," Steve said.

"Especially toward the end," Mark said.

Steve snorted derisively. "Speak for yourself."

"What happened?" Amanda asked.

"He found a murder to investigate," Steve said.

"Why am I not surprised?" Amanda said. "What did he do, scan the paper each day looking for homicides he could intrude on? How many crime scenes did he show up at uninvited?"

"Why are you talking about me like I'm not here?" Mark said. "It's not like I go looking for murders to get involved in."

Steve and Amanda both turned and looked at him. Mark shifted self-consciously on his stool.

"Well, not this time I didn't," Mark said, motioning to Steve. "You could back me up on this."

"I could," Steve said, making no effort to do so.

Jesse emerged from the kitchen and broke out in a huge smile when he saw Steve and Mark at the counter. "Hey, how was the vacation?"

"It was murder," Steve said. "As usual."

Amanda could see Jesse was confused. "Mark got involved in a homicide investigation."

Jesse gave Mark a chastising look. "On your vacation? You just can't help yourself, can you? What were you *thinking?*"

Amanda held out her hand, palm open, to Jesse, who sighed, reached into his pocket, and handed her a crumpled $20 bill.

"You had a bet?" Mark asked, astonished.

She shrugged. "It was a sucker bet." Amanda smiled at Jesse. "And I found a sucker."

Jesse glared at Steve. "Why couldn't you control him? He's your father."

"To be fair," Steve said. "It wasn't entirely his fault. The guy was attacked by a shark right in front of us."

Jesse looked incredulously at Mark. "You were investigating a shark for murder?"

"It was a bit more complicated than that," Mark said.

"It already sounds complicated," Amanda said.

While Steve went back into the kitchen to get their breakfast order going, Mark began filling Amanda and Jesse in on their investigation into Danny Royal's murder and the dead ends they ran into so far. By the time his story was done, Mark and Steve had finished their breakfast and were sipping their coffee.

"Which forensic anthropologist did you give the photos and measurements of Danny's face to?" Amanda asked.

"Claire Rossiter," Mark replied.

"She's the best," Amanda said. "If it's okay with you, I'll

give Dr. Aki a call in Kauai, and see if he'll fax me his report. I'd like to work with Claire on this."

"I'd appreciate it," Mark said.

"Wait a minute," Steve said, pushing his empty coffee cup aside. "Now you're getting into this, too?"

Amanda frowned. "I'm just assisting."

"No one asked you to," Steve said, then glared at his father. "Or you either. It's not our case, it's a Kauai Police investigation, and they're handling it."

"What difference does it make to you if Amanda and Mark want to volunteer their time and expertise?" Jesse asked.

"Because it inevitably means I'm going to get dragged into it, too," Steve said. "I don't mind that if it's an LAPD case. Well, I *do* mind, but I've learned to live with it. This is actually meddling. You have no legitimate reason to be involved."

"Sgt. Kealoha doesn't have a lot of resources available to him," Mark said. "I don't think he'll care if we lend him some of ours."

"Ah ha!" Steve slapped the table. "That's exactly what I'm talking about. What resources did you have in mind?"

Mark tapped his head with an index finger and smiled. "Just what I was born with."

Steve narrowed his eyes accusingly. "What about Amanda? You've already got her going over the autopsy reports from Kauai and assisting the forensic anthropologist in a facial reconstruction."

"I volunteered," she said. "Remember?"

"Don't you see?" Steve said to her. "That's how it starts. Pretty soon you're devoting all your waking hours, and the hours you're *not* supposed to be awake, to chasing down his hunches. It's insidious."

"And it's fun," Jesse said, turning to Mark. "What can I do?"

Jesse was always eager to help, gladly volunteering what little free time he had between his ER residency and co-owning a restaurant, which didn't make his girlfriend, Susan, too happy, though he could usually talk her into helping Mark, too.

"A fresh cup of coffee would be nice," Mark said, sliding his cup toward him. "I'm afraid for now there isn't much else you can do. The case is at a standstill."

Mark glanced at Steve, who was quietly fuming. He understood Steve's reluctance to spend his Hawaii vacation investigating a murder, but his son had gone along with it anyway. But now that they were back home, Mark was surprised by Steve's unusually heated opposition.

Many years ago, when Steve first became a detective, he hated it when his father got involved in his cases. It embarrassed Steve to have his dad show up uninvited at crime scenes, offering unsolicited advice and looking over his shoulder. But his son had come to appreciate and rely on Mark's help, ignoring the jeers from fellow cops, and his case clearance rate soared. Over time, Mark and Steve developed a smooth and effective investigative rapport that they both enjoyed.

Or so Mark thought. What had changed?

Chapter Twelve

For the next week, it was business as usual for Dr. Mark Sloan. He went into Community General Hospital each day, treated his patients, consulted with other physicians on their patients, attended administrative meetings, and ate his lunches in the cafeteria. When he came home, he read through medical journals, did crossword puzzles, watched CNN, and tried each night, without success, to make a different Danny Royal recipe. He became convinced that Danny Royal, among his other as-yet-unknown crimes, purposely left key ingredients out of his recipes.

All week, Mark resisted the urge to call Ben Kealoha or Claire Rossiter, the forensic anthropologist, to see how their work was going. He did, however, look about a thousand times at the souvenir recipe card on which he'd replicated Danny's handwritten note: *Re: Ideal Oven, Ask Jim Lowe. A loose, trendy cook.*

There were three Jim Lowes in the state of Hawaii and he'd called all three, only to find that Sgt. Kealoha had as well. None of them worked in the kitchen appliance business, nor were they chefs, nor had they ever met Danny Royal. The Jim Lowes also wondered why a doctor from Los Angeles was calling and why they should answer any of his questions.

Mark got that reaction a lot over the years. He was used to it.

So, antsy and anxious, Mark pestered Steve about the homicides he was working on. Unfortunately, the cases weren't very perplexing, nor were the guilty parties hard to spot. Husbands killing wives. Gang members killing rivals. Stalkers killing the objects of their obsessions.

For Steve, it came down to paperwork. Lots and lots of paperwork, and Mark couldn't help him with that.

After just a week back, Steve was ready for another vacation. In a completely different sense, so was Mark. He needed something to challenge his mind, and his work at Community General wasn't enough.

Finally, he woke up early one morning to find an E-mail from Claire Rossiter waiting for him, with the digital files of Danny Royal's facial reconstruction attached. He downloaded them, and a face slowly appeared on his computer screen.

The face staring back at Mark on his computer monitor looked nothing like the Danny Royal he'd met. This man had a fuller, fleshier, more lived-in face, which made sense, since it approximated the one he'd actually been born with. Even though it was a computer-generated image, this face had imperfections rather than the airbrushed smoothness of a male model on a magazine cover.

Mark felt strangely disappointed. He'd expected to see something revealing in the face, something that betrayed Danny Royal's past or true character. Instead, the face was just that: another face. It conveyed neither intelligence nor malice nor anything else. Would a real picture, as opposed to a computer-generated image, have been more revealing? Would he have seen the qualities he'd been hoping for? He doubted it.

He forwarded the picture to FBI Special Agent Ron Wagner, an old friend at the Bureau he'd worked with on the Pac Atlantic Flight 224 investigation, and asked him to run the photo through their databases. He gave Steve a copy when he came up to breakfast and asked him to see if Danny's description matched any open cases at the LAPD.

"You could just forward this photo to Ben Kealoha," Steve said. "He could put it out on the wires himself."

"I've got contacts at the FBI he doesn't have," Mark said. "They'll get to it quicker if it comes through me rather than Ben."

"I'm sure Ron would have pushed it through as fast for a friend of yours as he would for you," Steve said. "Be honest, Dad, you just want to be involved."

"Okay, I confess, I want to solve this myself," Mark said. "I spent time with the victim. I saw his murder. I examined his corpse. I can't leave it at that. It feels personal to me now."

"It's not because you met Danny or saw his murder," Steve said. "It's because you figured out the shark attack trick. At that moment, in your mind it became a cat-and-mouse game between you and the killer, and you can't walk away from the playing field."

"You're right," Mark conceded. "And I won't stop until I catch him."

"Dad, there's no telling where this investigation will take you," Steve said. "Danny Royal could have come from anywhere. Unless it turns out to be an LAPD case, I'm not going to be able to back you up. It's not like I can call in any vacation days—I just used them up."

"I understand," Mark said.

"I'm not sure you do," Steve said. "You're chasing a professional killer. You get too close, he'll take you out of the game."

"It's not the first time I've faced that risk," Mark said.

"But it may be the first time you do it alone," Steve said. "If it comes to that, if it looks like you're going to be out there without me to watch your back, walk away from it. Don't die for this. I'd never forgive myself."

Now it all became clear to Mark. This was the reason Steve was so opposed to him continuing to investigate the case. Steve was worried he wouldn't be able to protect his father from harm.

Mark surprised Steve by giving him a hug. The Sloans weren't a very affectionate family, despite their devotion to each other. So whenever they touched, it came as a surprise and was unexpectedly emotional.

"Now you know how I feel every time you go to work," Mark said.

"There's a big difference, Dad," Steve said. "I've got a badge and a gun."

"It doesn't make you bulletproof," Mark said. "I still worry."

Steve considered that for a moment, then said, "This is why I don't have kids."

How touching, Wyatt thought.

He sat on his bed in his room at the Santa Monica Holiday Inn, looking at the facial reconstruction on his laptop and listening to the Sloans' sickly sweet conversation.

He was pleased that Mark considered this a contest between the two of them. This was a lonely profession, and to have someone out there, a dedicated adversary, was a new and exciting change for Wyatt. He retained his essential anonymity, and yet was actively engaging another individual in a game.

It was a game that Mark Sloan couldn't possibly win, not with Wyatt's unfair advantage. Still, it was fun.

Wyatt had to admire Mark Sloan's resourcefulness. This forensic anthropologist he'd found was first-rate. The facial reconstruction was a remarkably accurate recreation of Danny Royal's original face. Mark was well on his way to discovering the truth about the dead man.

Wyatt was pleased, because now the bugs and tracking devices would really start paying off, making his difficult assignment so much easier. Already he'd learned about Jim Lowe, though he had no idea where Mark had found the name or what its significance might be.

Wyatt had spent days compiling lists of Jim Lowes in every state in the nation. There were hundreds, and he was doing full background checks on each of them. It was tedious research, hours spent hunched over his laptop, but it was necessary. The key was not to let the tedium dull his senses, to make him blind to the revealing fact when it finally showed itself amid all that irrelevant data.

The fact hadn't emerged yet, but Wyatt was relentless. He'd find it.

If Jim Lowe was one of the others, then Wyatt had to find the man before Mark Sloan did.

And then Jim Lowe would have to die.

The Federal Building in Los Angeles was an unappealing monolith of white concrete rising from Wilshire Boulevard, directly across the street from the sprawling Veterans Memorial Cemetery. When viewed from the cemetery, the building looked like a gigantic tombstone. Mark wondered if that unfortunate effect was intended as some misguided architectural attempt at stylistic unity, or if it was entirely accidental.

Mark was at the Federal Building at the urgent request of FBI Special Agent Terry Riordan, with whom he'd recently worked on the Silent Partner serial killer investigation. All Terry would tell him was that the meeting regarded the inquiries Mark made to Agent Wagner in Virginia. But Mark was excited. The facial reconstruction must have meant something to the Bureau or he wouldn't have been summoned less than eight hours after he'd sent the file.

Terry Riordan was a big Texan with a gregarious smile and a bone-breaking handshake. Mark knew him to be an aggressive agent, not only when it came to his investigative approach but also in the way he played Bureau politics. Before the Silent Partner investigation, Terry hardly registered on the FBI radar. Now Terry was a player, and he didn't make a move without considering the political ramifications of his actions.

Mark figured Terry owed him a few favors, and he was prepared to cash them in.

The agent, in his usual presidential navy blue suit and red power tie, met Mark at the security checkpoint, gave him a clip-on ID badge, and led him into a conference room, where two other agents were waiting for them. Terry introduced Mark to Special Agents Sandra Flannery and Tim Witten, both from the Las Vegas office. Sandra was a too-thin, short-haired brunette in her early thirties with a cold, focused gaze. She wore a scoop-necked white shirt under a long, almost knee-length black jacket and matching pleated pants. Tim was rugged in a preppy, let's-go-sailing kind of way. He looked like he stepped out of the Abercrombie & Fitch catalog and straight into the FBI. Mark was willing to bet Tim's idea of casual was wearing a sweater over his shoulders, the arms tied loosely around his neck.

The introductions were barely over when Sandra held up a glossy print of Danny Royal's facial reconstruction.

"We want to know where, how, and why you found this man," Sandra said.

"I'll be glad to tell you everything I know," Mark said, "right after you tell me who that is."

Sandra glanced sharply at Terry, who smiled.

"Sandra, Dr. Sloan has helped the FBI out on several investigations," Terry said. "He's what you might call a friend of the family."

"He's a civilian," she said.

"Do you want to hear what Dr. Sloan knows or not?" Terry said, his smile fading.

She sighed and nodded to Tim, who cleared his throat, opened up a thick file in front of him, and stood up, as if delivering a presentation in class.

"The man in that picture is Stuart Appleby." Tim took a photo out of his file and held it up. It looked like a passport or ID photo, but it was clearly the same man. The resemblance to the computer-drawn image was almost perfect. "He's a fugitive, wanted on kidnapping, extortion, and murder charges."

"What happened?" Mark asked.

"We believe he was the point man in the kidnapping of eighteen-year-old Connie Standiford five years ago." Tim laid a picture of the teenage girl on the table in front of Mark. She was in her cheerleader's uniform, a buoyant smile on her face, her cheeks red and her eyes sparkling. "They were waiting for her at home when she came back from school. They cut off her pinkie and left it for her father as evidence that they had her."

"Her father was Roger Standiford," Sandra said. "The casino owner."

Mark was familiar with him. Standiford was widely credited with reinventing Las Vegas with his over-the-top, family-friendly, theme park casinos like the T-Rex and Gilligan's Island. Standiford certainly had the deep pockets to fund a prolonged hunt for the fugitives and pay for their demise.

"Roger Standiford got a call on his private line demanding 4.5 million dollars in cash in six hours or his daughter would be killed," Tim continued. "He did as he was told. He got the cash together and was given delivery instructions by cell phone. After the handover, they told him she was buried alive in a storage container in the desert beside his house."

Tim slid another picture in front of Mark. It showed the teenager, curled in a corner of the storage container, clutching a poorly-bandaged hand to her chest. She was obviously dead.

"Her father was too late," Tim said. "There was a pipe to the surface for fresh air, and the kidnappers left her with a couple bottles of water, but it was a hundred-plus degrees out there that day."

"We don't think they meant for her to die," Sandra said. "But that doesn't change the result."

Mark realized the kidnappers had made a crucial miscalculation. They'd assumed all she'd need was air and plenty of water.

They didn't take into account that her terror and pain would change her needs. Fear would have quickened her breathing, increasing the amount of oxygen she needed and carbon dioxide she was exhaling. Her rapid breathing would also have made her become dehydrated more rapidly, moisture escaping from her body with each frantic breath.

With no light in the container, and the claustrophobic horror she must have been enduring, Mark doubted she even touched the water. All of that combined with the suffocating heat, the pitiful airflow, and the buildup of carbon monoxide, and Mark doubted she would have survived more than a couple of hours.

It would have been a horrible death.

"You said 'they' didn't mean for her to die," Mark said. "So there are others."

Tim spread out a fresh array of photos in front of Mark. "Diane Love, William Gregson, and Jason Brennan. They were his crew."

"Are they also still at large?" Mark asked.

Sandra nodded. "It was an inside job. Within hours after the murder, it was apparent who the kidnappers were. Stuart Appleby was one of Standiford's assistants. Diane Love worked in the cashiers' cage at the T-Rex. William Gregson and Jason Brennan both worked for Standiford's construction and development company. They all disappeared the day of the kidnapping and haven't been heard from since."

"If Danny Roy—" Mark stopped and corrected himself. "I mean, if Stuart Appleby is any indication, these pictures are useless. They've all had extensive plastic surgery and are living quiet lives on their shares of the ransom money."

Mark explained how he met Stuart Appleby, the details of his murder, and how the fugitive established his new identity on Kauai. Sandra listened very carefully while Tim took notes.

"The puzzle magazines were a mistake," Sandra said.

"How do you mean?" Mark asked.

"Appleby used to love to do crossword puzzles in his free time," Sandra said. "That and his limp were the two things he couldn't shake."

"You can change your face, your name, and your identity, Agent Flannery," Mark said. "But you can't change who you are."

Terry looked at the two agents. "Looks like you're both on your way to Hawaii."

"I wouldn't bother," Mark said.

Sandra smirked. "With all due respect, Dr. Sloan, just because you spent a few days on the island asking questions and looking at some paperwork doesn't mean there isn't more to be learned. We intend to dig a lot deeper and a lot more thoroughly than you did vacationing."

"And while you're there, looking into Appleby's life as Danny Royal, the killer will be continuing to stalk the other fugitives," Mark said. "That's why he burned down Appleby's house and restaurant. He was sending them a warning."

"The murder may have had nothing to do with Appleby's past," Tim said. "It may have arisen out of some conflict in his new life as Danny Royal."

"Perhaps," Mark said. "But I doubt it."

Sandra and Tim shared a look. Clearly they didn't have much respect for Mark's opinion and didn't bother to hide their disdain.

"Really?" Sandra asked. "You're chief of internal medicine at Community General Hospital, is that correct?"

"Sandra," Terry said firmly.

"Hold on, Terry, I'm just getting some clarification here." Sandra looked Mark in the eye. "So in your professional opinion, Appleby couldn't have been killed for any reason except his involvement in this five-year-old kidnapping case."

"Yes." Mark said.

"That's helpful, doctor," Sandra said. "Maybe I should ask my chiropractor for his opinion, too."

"This is only the first killing," Mark said. "The other three kidnappers will be killed, too, their deaths made to look like accidents. It may not be this month, it may not be this year, but this man will find them."

"Not before we do," Sandra said.

"He beat you to Appleby when the Bureau gave up years ago," Mark said. "What makes you think he won't beat you to the others?"

Mark got up and walked out. His odds weren't much better than the FBI's as far as finding the others before the killer did, but at least he knew it. The FBI's arrogance may have been one of the obstacles to its success.

He wondered again what mistake Appleby had made.

How did the killer find him after so many years? What did the killer know and what resources did he have that the FBI didn't?

Mark was committed to the hunt now, but had no idea where to begin or how to develop some kind of edge over his clever adversary.

Terry Riordan caught up with Mark as he was leaving the building.

"I apologize for Agent Flannery's attitude," Terry said. "They just flew in from Vegas and walked in five minutes before you did. I didn't get a chance to brief them. She doesn't know you. She isn't familiar with your track record in this arena."

Mark nodded. He didn't really care what the agents thought about him. He cared about stopping more killings.

"I'd like to take a look at the file on the kidnapping," Mark said, "and anything you have on the four suspects."

Terry snorted. "I'm sure you would, but we aren't a library."

"You just finished complimenting me on my abilities in this arena," Mark said. "What do you have to lose?"

"You mean besides my career?" Terry said. "I know your experience and your abilities. But you're still a civilian as far as the FBI is concerned. Unlike the Silent Partner investigation, you have no standing in this case."

"There wouldn't be a case now if I hadn't discovered the shark attack was a trick, and if I hadn't asked Claire Rossiter to work up a facial reconstruction."

"And we appreciate the effort," Terry said. "We'll reimburse you for what you paid Rossiter. I'll even send you an official commendation on FBI stationery if it will make you feel better."

"What would make me feel better is to catch this killer before he kills another one of the kidnappers," Mark said. "Whoever he is, he's a skilled professional who doesn't come cheap. It took a lot of time, talent, and money to track down Appleby."

Terry pulled Mark aside. "Can I give you some advice? Let it go. We're on the job. We're the FBI. Believe it or not, we're pretty good at what we do."

"Not as good as he is." Mark started to walk away, but Terry stopped him.

"Wait," Terry said, then lowered his voice to barely more than a whisper. "We've been hearing rumors for years, nothing we can substantiate yet, about a man who approaches wealthy families who've lost a loved one to an unsolved violent crime and offers them closure."

Mark felt a chill creep up his back. "He offers them vengeance for a price."

"He says he'll do what the law won't."

"Has he?" Mark asked.

Terry shrugged. "You tell me."

Chapter Thirteen

It wasn't easy getting a call through to Roger Standiford. Mark didn't actually succeed, but his message got to the man nonetheless.

As soon as he got back home, he called Standiford's office. Mark couldn't get past the hotel magnate's impenetrable front line of executive assistants, so he left his name, number, and a simple message: *I saw Stuart Appleby die.*

Fifteen minutes later, Mark got a call back offering him an appointment with Standiford at noon the next day. That wouldn't be a problem for Mark. Las Vegas was only a forty-five-minute plane ride from L.A., and flights left from Los Angeles International Airport on an almost hourly basis. Mark made a reservation on the 8:00 A.M. flight and got a return ticket for 8:00 P.M. the same day. He wanted to allow himself plenty of time to talk and snoop around a bit.

Mark knew he'd find Steve at BBQ Bob's, so he drove over to the restaurant for dinner. Business was light, which disappointed Steve and Jesse, but Mark didn't mind, even though he had some money of his own tied up in the place. The slow night gave him a chance to fill Steve and Jesse in on what he'd learned without too many interruptions for delivering ribs to customers or checking on things in the kitchen. He told them about Danny Royal's true identity, the Standiford kidnapping, and the FBI's suspicion that a professional killer was offering wealthy families vengeance for a price.

When Mark finished telling them everything, including that he had an afternoon meeting lined up with Roger Standiford, both Steve and Jesse seemed troubled.

"You're being manipulated," Steve said. "The only reason Riordan told you about the professional killer was so you'd run with it. And you are, just like he knew you would."

"What does Agent Riordan expect me to do that the FBI can't?" Mark asked.

"Get in to see Roger Standiford and press him about the contract killer," Steve said. "The Feds haven't made any progress investigating his daughter's kidnapping and murder. Standiford is probably so disgusted with them that he won't let them in the door, and he certainly won't see them to hear accusations that he hired some hit man. But Riordan knew if he teased you with details of the kidnapping and gave you the lead about the hit man, you'd do his job for him."

"I don't see the downside for me," Mark said.

"You're being used." Steve said, "Isn't that enough?"

"Not if it helps me find the other kidnappers before Standiford's hit man does," Mark said. "The FBI is concentrating on backtracking Stuart Appleby's life in Hawaii."

"Who is Stuart Appleby?" Jesse asked.

"Danny Royal," Steve said. "Try to keep up."

"The FBI isn't going to get anywhere following that trail," Mark continued. "Riordan gave me something I could use with Standiford. I have a chance to make some real progress."

"Which Terry Riordan will find some way to use for his own political benefit in the Bureau," Steve said. "Even if it means screwing you along the way."

"I don't have anything at stake here," Mark said.

"I've noticed that," Steve said. "Which is why I keep asking why you're doing this."

"Because there's a killer out there hunting these kidnappers down, and he's going to murder them one by one unless someone stops him," Mark said. "And it doesn't look like the FBI is up to the task."

"And you are, Rambo?" Steve asked.

"I don't intend to do it alone," Mark said. "When I find the kidnappers, I'll call in the authorities to make an arrest. And if I can figure out who the hit man is, I'll do the same thing."

"Okay, so here's what I don't get," Jesse said. "Who gives a damn?"

"Excuse me?" Mark asked.

"Let me see if I got this straight," Jesse said. "Danny Stuart Royal Appleby kidnapped and killed Standiford's daughter and ran off to Hawaii with a million bucks. Standiford hires a hit man who finds Royal Appleby and kills him."

"That's the working theory," Mark said.

"So the guy who's murder you're trying to solve was a kidnapper and a killer."

"Yes," Mark said.

"Now you want to find the other kidnappers before this hit man finds them and kills them."

"Yes," Mark said.

"Why? The police and FBI are on the case, and if they're too late . . ." Jesse shrugged, letting his voice trail off and his implication hang in the air.

"You're condoning murder, Jesse."

"They kidnapped a girl, cut off her pinkie, and buried her alive," Jesse said. "I'm saying no one is going to shed a tear for Danny Stuart Royal Appleby or any of them. The FBI couldn't catch them, so Standiford simply found someone who could."

"But this guy isn't catching them," Mark said, "he's *killing* them."

"Is there any question they're guilty?" Jesse asked.

"It's still murder," Mark said. "I don't have any sympathy for the kidnappers or killers, but I believe they should be tried, convicted, and punished under the law."

"And while that is going on, the Standiford family has to relive the tragedy again in excruciating detail and the taxpayers have to foot the bill," Jesse said. "Seems to me Standiford is seeing justice gets done."

Steve studied Jesse. "Have you been watching the *Death Wish* marathon on channel five again?"

"I'm just saying it's hard to get worked up over whether these guys live or die," Jesse said. "They're scum."

"So the rich and powerful get a free pass at murder," Mark said, "as long as the victims deserve what they get."

"Some might call it justice," Jesse said.

"Charles Bronson, for instance," Steve added.

"It isn't justice," Mark said. "Murder is murder."

"That means as far as you're concerned, the guy who took out Danny Stuart Royal Appleby and is hunting down the others is no better than the people he's after," Jesse said, "and is deserving of the same punishment."

"It's not as far as I'm concerned, Jesse. It's as far as the law is concerned."

Jesse looked at Steve. "Does that seem right to you?"

"Not really," Steve said. "But it's the law, and I guess if we start letting people kill anyone they think is guilty of a crime, where will it end? The American Heart Association can take a contract out on us for the food we serve."

Jesse narrowed his eyes at Steve. "You've been talking to Amanda."

Steve jerked his head toward Mark. "Where do you think Amanda gets it?"

"Speaking of food, I think I'm ready to eat." Mark picked up the menu and scanned it. "What low-fat, high-fiber items do you have on the menu?"

"Just the menu." Jesse set the salt and pepper shakers in front of Mark and smiled. "Enjoy."

* * *

Las Vegas was like an aging starlet hopelessly addicted to plastic surgery. Construction cranes were the only feature of the skyline that never changed.

The city no longer matched the image its name conjured in Mark Sloan's mind. The Rat Packers were all dead. The Dunes Hotel was blown up for a TV special. High rollers arrived in Lincoln Navigators stuffed with kids. Casinos weren't casinos anymore; they had become "vacation destinations." The hotels were no longer just buildings but rather an urban floor show of performance architecture.

The romanticized Las Vegas that Mark remembered, if not from experience then from countless movies, would never have included a casino like Roger Standiford's T-Rex, with its gigantic mechanical dinosaurs stomping along the strip out front, roaring their mechanical roars.

Mark parked his rented Ford beside a dozen other rented Fords in the T-Rex's enormous parking structure and hoped he'd remember that his car was located somewhere in row four of the Triassic Age. He took a steep escalator down through a waterfall to the casino floor, walked past the mighty *Tyrannosaurus rex* that loomed over the Jurassic Buffet, and approached one of the "reservation consultants" behind the faux chiseled-stone counter in the cavernlike lobby.

Five minutes later, Mark was studying the stalactite-styled lights on the ceiling when Nate Grumbo, Standiford's head of security, came to greet him. With his vaguely Neanderthal features, Grumbo could easily have moonlighted as one of the cavemen who battled dinosaurs in the nightly floor show.

"Good morning, Dr. Sloan. Welcome to the T-Rex." Grumbo's voice sounded as if it came from a throat filled with gravel. "Please come with me."

Mark followed Grumbo to a private elevator hidden behind the rain forest foliage of Dinosaur Grotto. Grumbo pressed his meaty paw against some kind of touch screen, which lit up for a moment as it scanned his hand, and then the elevator doors opened with a hiss.

Grumbo motioned Mark inside the richly paneled mahogany car, a stark contrast to the garish prehistoric décor of the rest of T-Rex. As the elevator car ascended, Mark glanced up and noticed a tiny camera aimed at him with the same undivided intensity as Grumbo's cold gaze.

Mark then noticed narrow beams of laser light moving between the slats of wood paneling, crisscrossing his body in a rapid, gridlike pattern. He assumed he was being searched, x-rayed, and scanned for weapons, electronic devices, biological agents, and maybe even smuggled snacks. If they tried to take away his protein bar, he'd say he didn't see the signs that said NO OUTSIDE FOOD ALLOWED, which would be the truth.

He smiled amiably at Grumbo. "Tight security you have here."

"It's necessary," Grumbo said.

"Yes, I suppose it is," he said, just to be saying something. Grumbo's stony silence was unnerving, which, Mark supposed, it was intended to be.

Something beeped in Grumbo's jacket. He reached into his pocket, glanced at something that looked like a PDA, and then put it away.

"Could I have the cell phone that's in the inside breast pocket of your jacket?" Grumbo said, no doubt specifying which pocket to impress Mark with the invasiveness of the security measures. "It will be returned to you when you leave."

Mark reached into his jacket, pulled out his slim cell phone, and gave it to Grumbo, who looked at it for a moment as if he was trying to decided whether to crush it or eat it, then put it in his pocket instead.

The elevator doors opened to a huge outer office that was overwhelming in its open space and sparse furnishings. The room was a vast oval with a two-story-high curved ceiling. There were three assistants working at their ovoid desks, spaced far apart from one another. The walls were almost concave, off-white, and unadorned with any art. Two slanted, steel-and-leather chairs, shaped as if they were about to pounce, were arranged in the center of the room. The floor was marble, and as Mark and Grumbo walked across the expanse their footsteps echoed through the space, somehow making it seem even larger.

The outer office felt like something out of an early James Bond movie, one of those volcano bases the cat-stroking villains liked so much. Mark wondered if the similarities were intentional, and decided they had to be.

Grumbo led him toward an enormous pair of double doors that opened into Standiford's office as they approached.

After everything he'd seen so far, Mark expected Roger Standiford to be a man as garish, aggressive, and obnoxious as his buildings, but he was wrong. Standiford had a deep, even tan and was dressed casually in slacks and a monogrammed silk shirt. He smiled warmly at Mark and walked toward his guest with a casual, friendly gait that seemed wrong against the grandiose design of his office, which was almost entirely made of glass, giving him a commanding view of the entire city from his desk, a steel-and-glass work of contemporary art.

"It's a pleasure to meet you, Dr. Sloan." Standiford shook Mark's hand and led him to a pair of facing chairs identical to those in the outer office. As Mark sat down, he realized that somehow Grumbo had silently slipped out and closed the doors behind him, leaving the two men alone.

"I've done some reading up on you and the astonishing number of homicides you've solved," Standiford said. "You're a remarkable man."

"I'm afraid I haven't read much about you," Mark said. "But you have quite an office here, so I assume you're doing well. I have to ask, though . . . With a desk like that, where do you put your paper clips and breath mints and little sticky pads?"

"I see you're not a man who's easily intimidated," Standiford said. "Or impressed."

"That's not true. I met a lady a few months ago who swam in the freezing water off Antarctica wearing only a regular bathing suit and cap. Anybody else would have died of hypothermia in minutes, but she can swim for hours in intensely cold waters without any ill effects. She's one of only two people we know of on earth who can do that. I was impressed with her abilities and intimidated by how much more there is to learn about the human body than we already know."

"I'm sure there's a moral in there somewhere, but it's lost on me," Standiford said. "I'd rather hear about the guy you met who swam in much warmer waters."

"You mean Danny Royal. I was vacationing in Kauai with my son when I met him on the beach," Mark said. "He'd been stung by some jellyfish during his daily swim. I helped him, and he invited us to dinner at his restaurant. The next day I was on the crowded beach when he took his swim and I saw him get attacked by a shark."

"What happened?" Standiford said.

"I saw a fin in the water behind him, then he was pulled under," Mark said. "There was a lot of splashing, a lot of blood, and panic on the beach. It was like a scene out *Jaws*. In fact, it was *exactly* like that. It was totally make-believe."

"You seem to be the only one who thinks so," Standiford said. "They closed beaches. People are afraid to go in the water. The newspapers say it was a particularly vicious tiger shark."

"What they don't say is that the blood was fake," Mark said. "And that Danny Royal was dead before he was attacked. They also don't mention his real name was Stuart Appleby and five years ago he killed your only daughter. They don't want to alert the killer that they are on to him, but I'm certain he'll know very soon."

Standiford met Mark's gaze. "You're certain it was Appleby."

Mark nodded. Standiford's face betrayed nothing. A perfect poker face for a man who made his living off people who played cards.

"I guess I've made it a lot easier for your man," Mark said.

"My man?" Standiford said.

"The guy you hired to hunt down and kill Appleby and the others," Mark said. "Now he doesn't have to prove to you that he got the right guy. I've done that for him."

"Do you expect me to feel sorry for Appleby? After what he did to my daughter? To my life?"

"No," Mark said.

"All I want is for justice to be done."

"Then you won't mind giving me the same information you gave your man."

"I don't understand."

Mark sighed. "You've screened me for listening devices and I'm sure this office is secure, so let's be honest, shall we? It's just the two of us here."

Standiford just looked at him, so Mark went on.

"Let me see if I can guess what happened. A year or so after the murder, when the FBI investigation had stalled, you were approached indirectly by someone who offered to find the kidnappers and make them pay. He told you that no one would ever know they'd been dealt with except you. He told you it would take a lot of time, but he would be relentless. All you had to do was wire a large sum of money to an offshore account somewhere, then more when the assignment was successfully completed."

"Do you know what they did to my daughter, Dr. Sloan?" Standiford asked. Mark nodded. "They didn't just kill Connie, they terrorized and tortured her. And after she was dead, the torture didn't end. My wife was haunted by what happened. She tried to kill herself twice. First Emily blamed herself for what happened, then she blamed me. Our marriage disintegrated."

"I'm not defending the killers or what they did," Mark said.

"Then what the hell are you doing, Dr. Sloan?"

"I want the same thing you do," Mark said. "I want justice. There doesn't need to be any more killing for that to happen."

"I won't help you go after him," Standiford said.

"Because you don't want to be charged as an accessory to murder."

"Because I don't think what he's doing is wrong."

"Fair enough," Mark said. "But you know who I am and what I can do. If it's justice instead of vengeance that really motivates you, you'll help me find Diane Love, William Gregson, and Jason Brennan before he does."

"What difference does it make to you?" Standiford said. "Did you know my daughter? Do you know the people who killed her?"

Mark shook his head. "I was on the beach when Appleby was murdered. I want to be sure innocent people don't get hurt."

"He doesn't work that way," Standiford said. "He never kills an innocent."

"If I hadn't been there, he would have," Mark said. "There was a panic. People ran out of the water in terror. One man was slammed against the rocks by the waves and nearly bled to death. There were kids on that beach who will be traumatized forever by what they think they saw. They did nothing to you or your family. Is that your idea of justice, Mr. Standiford?"

He studied Mark for a time, then stood up slowly. "Mr. Grumbo will give you everything we have on the kidnappers."

Standiford turned his back on Mark and focused his gaze out at his unobstructed view of the city.

The meeting was over. Mark got up and headed for the door, which opened automatically as he approached it to reveal Grumbo facing him on the other side. Just as Mark stepped through the doorway, Standiford looked over his shoulder.

"Where were you five years ago, Dr. Sloan?"

Mark turned as the doors closed. In his final glimpse of Standiford, Mark saw an expression of such startling anguish and pain on his face, he was certain the next thing he'd hear was the scream of a man leaping to his death.

But there was no scream; it died inside Roger Standiford, along with everything else.

Chapter Fourteen

Roger Standiford was still standing at the window when Nate Grumbo returned to the office twenty minutes later.

"Did you give Dr. Sloan the files?" Standiford asked.

"Yes," Grumbo replied. "Do you think he'll be able to find the others?"

"Dr. Sloan is a very resourceful man. It's quite possible that he will," Standiford said. "Have we heard from the hired help?"

"One minute after Dr. Sloan left the office," Grumbo said. "We received an E-mail requesting the remainder of funds owed on Stuart Appleby."

It had taken years for Standiford's avenger to prove himself, but now he was definitely living up to his reputation. The hired help knew about Mark Sloan and, as the doctor predicted, was even using him as his unwitting messenger. Standiford wondered what other surprises his employee had in store for him.

"Wire the money to his Swiss account immediately," Standiford said. "Add a ten percent bonus."

Standiford turned and could see something in Grumbo's implacable expression. Perhaps it was an infinitesimal crinkle at the edge of his mouth, or a slight dilation of the pupil. Whatever it was, Standiford registered it unconsciously, because it was nothing anyone would have noticed with the naked eye.

"Is something bothering you, Nate?"

"The scanners in the elevator picked up something," Nate grumbled. "The circuitry of Dr. Sloan's cell phone was altered. I think somebody's put a bug or a tracking device in it."

"Do you think Dr. Sloan knew?"

Grumbo shook his head.

Standiford nodded and allowed himself a little smile. He didn't have to wait long for the hired help to surprise him again.

"Things are going to get interesting."

"You're a doctor?" Patsy Durkin asked groggily, standing in the doorway of her apartment at the Desert Sunrise.

"Yes," Mark said. The doorbell had awakened her and she still seemed a bit dazed, her eyes puffy, her lips dry. Patsy wore a faded, oversized, sleeveless T-shirt and baggy sweats, and her breath smelled of alcohol and cigarettes.

"Is Jason sick?" Patsy Durkin was a showgirl at an off-the-strip hotel, and she worked three shows a night and slept through much of the day. Five years ago, she had been Jason Brennan's girlfriend.

"I don't know," Mark said. "I'm trying to find him. I think he could be in some danger."

"From, like, a disease or something?"

"No," Mark said. "Nothing like that."

The Desert Sunrise was a two-story, L-shaped block around a parking lot and a tiny fenced-off pool. The place was a motel that had been converted to apartments. It appeared to Mark that the conversion mainly involved scraping the word MOTEL off the sign and replacing it with APTS. The faded image of the old letters still remained under the new ones.

"It's about the kidnapping and murder of Connie Standiford," Mark said. "I'm assisting the police in their investigation."

"So you're like a doctor private eye," she said, adding with a smile, "Dr. Barnaby Jones."

Mark wanted to get past the introduction and get to the point of his visit, so he gave up.

"Yes, that's it," he said.

"My parents loved *Barnaby Jones*, though I couldn't figure out how that old guy could chase anybody without croaking on the spot. No offense."

"None taken," Mark said. "Could I come inside and talk with you for a few minutes?"

She shrugged and let him in.

The air was stale and smelled of old cigarettes and beer. Beyond that, the tiny, boxy apartment was surprisingly neat. There was a kitchenette, a linoleum-floored dining area, and a doorway in the back leading to what looked like a small bedroom and bath. Mark took a seat at the Samsonite dinette table. In the center of the table was an arrangement of plastic fruit and fake flowers.

"I understand you were living with Jason at the time of the kidnapping."

She sat down across from him and rubbed her eyes with the index finger and thumb of one hand. "Not here, that was back in the day."

"The day?"

"When I was still dancing at the MGM Grand. Jason was working construction, so the money was good," she said. "We had a nice place in Summerlin. They had a pool and a hot tub there."

"Do you ever hear from him?" Mark asked.

Patsy shook her head. "Every year or so the lady from the FBI comes and asks me the same question. Nope, haven't heard from him since the kidnapping."

"What do you know about his family?"

"They thought I was a slut," she said.

"Who did?"

"His stuck-up sister," Patsy said. "Lived in Chicago, married an insurance salesman, had a couple bratty kids. She doesn't hear from him either."

"How do you know?"

"A, because he hated her prissy guts, and B, because the FBI lady told me," Patsy said. "Jason came out here to get away from his family, so I don't think he ran back there with his million bucks."

Most of the details about Jason's life could be found in Standiford's files. Mark was looking for something else; he just didn't know what it was. For now, he was just adding color to the stark facts in the files, hoping that somewhere down the line he'd hear or see something that would bring the disparate pieces of information together into a clue about Jason's new identity.

"What did he like to do when he wasn't working?" Mark asked.

"You mean besides lay around with me?" She scratched under an armpit while she thought about it. "Well, Jason liked to drink beer and watch sports or *The Simpsons*. He liked going to buffets a lot, especially ones with fried chicken. Sometimes he'd play basketball with his friends."

"Any characteristic behavior?"

"Huh?" She gave Mark a blank look.

"Things he'd do that were uniquely Jason," Mark said. "The little things that define a personality."

"He pissed like a horse twenty times a day and never put the toilet seat down," Patsy said. "He'd pick food out of his front teeth with the edge of a piece of paper. Didn't shave on weekends. Chewed his nails when he was upset. He was thirsty all the time, always had a Big Gulp in his car. Liked to put catsup on rice, which is pretty disgusting, if you ask me. And he wore lots of tank tops and sleeveless shirts."

"Which leads me to my next question," Mark said. "How would you describe him physically?"

"Great," she said.

"Could you be more specific?"

"Buff, tight, in good shape," she said. "How much more specific do you want me to get?"

"Any defining characteristics?"

"Oh yeah," she said, grinning.

"I meant tattoos, scars, birthmarks."

"He had a little scar on his forehead from a construction accident," Patsy said, scratching under her armpit again. "A few two-by-fours fell on his head. Other than that, he had dry skin and calluses on his hands from working. Jason hated putting on skin lotion, but I wouldn't let him touch me with those sandpaper hands."

"What did he dream about?"

"Me," she grinned.

"What else?"

"Me with big knockers," she said, "which he missed, because I didn't get the implants until after he left."

Mark may not have known what the information was that he was looking for, but he knew that wasn't it. "What I meant was, how do you think he would have spent his share of the ransom?"

"He didn't spend any of it on me, as you can see," she said, with a sweep of her hand to take in the apartment and her existence in it. "He probably did what all men would do with big bucks. Bought a sports car, a Playboy Playmate, and a penthouse apartment someplace."

If he'd learned anything useful, Mark wasn't aware of it. All he wanted to do was leave. He smiled and rose from his seat. "Thank you, Miss Durkin. You've been a big help."

She got up, too. "You said you're a doctor, right?"

"Yes."

"My armpit won't stop itching. Do you mind taking a look?" She raised her left arm and leaned toward Mark, making sure he got a nice close-up view. "My medical insurance is kind of nonexistent right now."

There were worse places she could have asked him to look, so Mark figured he was getting off easy.

"Sure," Mark sighed, taking his glasses out of his pocket. "Let's see what the problem is."

After examining Patsy and determining she was suffering from an allergic reaction to one of the deodorants she was using, he advised her to change brands and buy a simple over-the-counter cortisone cream to ease her discomfort.

He then drove out to Henderson, an endless sprawl of new tract homes and big box stores just outside Las Vegas. The town had no main street or discernible character; its identity, if it had ever existed to start with, was subsumed in favor of the sterility and sales-tax revenue provided by Costco, The Home Depot, Sportsmart, Wal-Mart, and Barnes & Noble. What those stores were to shopping, the Lost Trails Hotel & Casino was to gambling.

The Lost Trails was as big as any other casino, without the bloated, amusement park vulgarity or vacation-resort aspirations. Architecturally, it looked like a massive reinterpretation of the Mediterranean-style tract homes and condos that surrounded it, which seemed at odds with the Western theme of the casino. The parking structure wasn't filled with rental cars but with down-market SUVs and sensible mid-sized family sedans with bumper stickers like PROUD PARENT OF A VIEWPOINT SCHOOL HONORS STUDENT! The casino didn't have a showroom, a circus-in-residence, or any fancy restaurants to entice guests through its doors. Instead, it had a twelve-screen movie theater with stadium seating and a twenty-four-hour Chuck E. Cheese outlet.

Mark met Karen Cooper, during her break, at a table in front of Panda Express in the Lost Trails "Chuck Wagon" food court. All the restaurants storefronts, from Sbarro Italian to Mongo's Mongolian BBQ, looked like covered wagons, in keeping with the "Wagon Train of Good Eatin'" motif. Little placards on the tables offered free slot machine spins, movie tickets, and VIP player status to people who cashed their paychecks at the casino.

Five years ago, Karen had been a cashier at the T-Rex

with Diane Love, her best friend. Now Karen Cooper worked as a cashier at the Lost Trails. She was dressed in her frontier cashier uniform, a red-checked cotton shirt with the Lost Trails logo stitched on the chest and a pair of denim jeans held up with a Lost Trails imitation silver belt buckle.

"I couldn't stay at the T-Rex after what happened," Karen said, idly moving her chow mein around her plate with her fork. "I just couldn't face the people there."

"But you had nothing to do with the kidnapping," Mark said.

"With Diane gone, who were they gonna take it out on? Me. Her best friend, her roommate. The one who should have known."

"Did she ever express any resentment toward the Standifords before?"

"She resented anyone with money because she never had it herself," Karen said. "It always struck me as kind of ironic she ended up counting cash all day."

"Did Diane ever tell you anything about her past?"

"You mean about her old boyfriends and stuff?"

"I'm more interested in her family."

"She grew up in Vegas. She was an only child. Her mom was a maid at the Trop. Her Dad was a pool man. Supposedly, there's lots of work for a good pool man in Vegas."

"Was he a good pool man?"

"I suppose so," Karen said, studying the orange chicken chunks on her plate as if they were rare gems. "But he was a lousy card player. Diane said he was always in debt to somebody, until he just disappeared one day. Her mother told her he ran off, but Diane always thought some pissed-off loan sharks planted him in the desert somewhere. She'd read in the paper about some new housing development breaking ground and would say, like a joke, 'I wonder if they'll find Dad.' I never thought was very funny. Kinda sad, actually."

Mark looked past Karen at the gamblers. The majority were middle-class whites, with a scattering of retirees.

There were a few people in wheelchairs parked in front of the slot machines, pumping in quarters. He knew these weren't tourists. These people lived here. And instead of depositing their paychecks in a bank like everybody else, they thought it was a good idea to cash them at a casino instead. After all, the bank didn't give them free movie tickets or a VIP player membership card. Mark wondered how many men like Diane's father there were in the casino, feeding their mortgage into a dollar slot machine.

"Where's her mother now?" Mark asked.

"Not driving around in a Mercedes, if that's what you're getting at," Karen stopped her exploratory poking at her orange chicken and switched to shaping her fried rice into a neat square with her fork. "Last I heard, she was still cleaning rooms."

"What were her relationships with Stuart Appleby, William Gregson, and Jason Brennan like?"

"I didn't know she had relationships with any of them until the FBI knocked on my door and told me what they'd done," Karen said. "I couldn't believe it. I was in a state of shock for days. Connie Standiford was a good kid. How could anyone, how could *Diane*, do that to her?"

"Did you know any of the kidnappers?"

"Sure, I knew Stuart," she said. "He was Standiford's flunky at the T-Rex. We'd see him around. But I never heard of the other two. Diane had this whole secret life. The woman I knew was just a lie. The only thing about her I know was true was the stuff about her parents. I gave the things Diane left behind to her mom. You know, like the stereo, her clothes, a TV. Her mom was just devastated by the whole thing."

Mark looked at the perfectly arranged, neatly segregated portions of her untouched combination plate. The conversation had ruined her appetite but not her sense of order. She was probably a great cashier.

"Did Diane ever talk to you about her dreams?"

"How do you mean?" she asked.

"I'm looking for something that might point me toward where she is today and who she might be," Mark said. "If she could reinvent herself as somebody, who would it be?"

"She loved to ski, water or snow, didn't matter," Karen said. "So I suppose she'd find some way to make a living off it. Maybe she's in Tahiti or the Alps. She dreamed about going to both those places someday."

Mark asked Karen a few more questions, and learned that Diane had a scar from a dog bite on her left hand, and wore glasses for nearsightedness.

He left the Lost Trails Hotel & Casino feeling no closer to finding Diane Love than he'd been before he got there.

Karen Cooper was wrong. Diane Love did send her mother some money. Every year on her mother's birthday, Diane sent $5,000 in cash in a manila envelope. Wyatt knew this because every year he intercepted the parcel before it was delivered and kept the money.

Actually, he intercepted all of her mother's mail before it was delivered, passing it on only after he'd screened it for any clues to Diane's whereabouts. So far, he hadn't found anything that might help him locate the fugitive.

The money was sent from a different major American city each year. Seattle. San Francisco. Phoenix. Boston. New York. Wyatt doubted Diane was moving that frequently. He assumed she traveled to those cities simply to mail the parcel from a spot as far away from her actual location as possible.

Wyatt had scoured airline, train, and bus manifests covering the two or three days of arrivals to each city in advance of each postmarked parcel, looking for any names that recurred among the thousands on the lists. Of course, she also could have driven to each of the cities, but there was no way he could think of to track that.

He found a few recurring names on the airline and train manifests and spent a few weeks searching those people out. He followed the women and sifted through every detail of their personal lives until he was absolutely certain none of them was Diane Love.

During the time Mark talked with Karen Cooper, Wyatt was sitting a few tables away, his back to them, eating a slice of pizza and eavesdropping on their conversation through an earpiece that received transmissions from the listening device in Mark's cell phone. He'd kept his eyes on the gamblers, never turning to look at the man he was following.

Wyatt had known, of course, that Standiford's security system would detect the devices he'd put in Mark's cell phone. He also knew that they wouldn't tell the doctor anything about it. The discovery would only underscore to them that Wyatt was on the job and earning every cent that he was being paid.

Although Wyatt didn't hear what Standiford told Mark, he knew everything that the grieving father could possibly say. The only thing Wyatt didn't know was whether or not Standiford would reveal that he'd hired someone to do what the FBI had failed to accomplish.

It didn't make a difference to Wyatt one way or another. Mark Sloan already knew somebody was out there and who was paying for it or the doctor wouldn't have arranged the meeting. And Standiford didn't know who Wyatt was, where he came from, or what motivated him to pursue his line of work. There was nothing Standiford could say that could harm him.

So far, Mark hadn't learned anything Wyatt didn't already know. Wyatt was deeply disappointed. His expectations of Mark Sloan, especially after the doctor's performance in Kauai, had been high. Unfortunately, since Mark returned to the mainland, he'd been bumbling around aimlessly, learning nothing even remotely useful.

Wyatt was beginning to wonder whether his surveillance of Mark Sloan was a valuable use of his time, if he might get closer to Diane Love, Jason Brennan, and William Gregson using his tried-and-true methods.

Then again, as far as those three targets were concerned, Wyatt's methods hadn't produced any results.

He decided he had nothing to lose by sticking with Mark Sloan for a few more weeks.

Wyatt was a patient man. It was just a matter of time before justice would be done.

Chapter Fifteen

United Furniture occupied a busy corner on a street it shared with Garrett's Furniture, Thomasville Furniture, Ethan Allen, Kales' Furniture, Levitz Furniture Showroom, and Ron's Bar Stools & Dinettes.

If there was a furniture war in Nevada, this was the front line.

Mark parked in front of United Furniture and walked into the store, where he was assaulted by blasts of cool air and elevator music so intense he wanted to run back to his car. But he bravely soldiered on, down the long row of recliners, to a huddle of salesmen who looked like they'd bought their suits a Wal-Mart. One of the salesmen, a pudgy, slightly balding man in his forties, peeled off from the rest and approached Mark, his arm outstretched, an impossibly large, joyous smile on his face. It was as if Mark had walked in with the cure for cancer in one hand and a signed agreement for world peace in the other.

"Good afternoon, sir," the man said, taking Mark's hand and shaking it enthusiastically. "Welcome to United Furniture Company. How can I help you today?"

You can start by shutting off the music and turning down the air conditioner, Mark thought. But he said, "I'm looking for Victor Gregson."

The man's smile widened even more, a feat Mark

wouldn't have thought was physically possible. Mark got an unwanted look at all the salesman's gleaming capped teeth.

"It's Vic to my friends, amigo," he said. "Let me know which satisfied customer referred you, and I'll send him a gift certificate worth ten percent off any item in the store."

"Roger Standiford," Mark said.

Vic Gregson's smile diminished in size to something that would no longer interest the *Guinness Book of World Records*. "Who are you?"

"I'm Mark Sloan. I'm helping the FBI and Roger Standiford find your brother."

It wasn't exactly a lie, but it wasn't the truth either. Mark neglected to mention he was a doctor because he didn't feel like explaining or justifying why the chief of internal medicine at a Los Angeles hospital was hunting down wanted fugitives. He did enough of that at home. Thankfully, Vic Gregson didn't press him on it.

"Why the sudden interest?" Vic asked.

"Someone wants to kill him," Mark said. "We'd like to catch your brother before the killer does."

Vic nodded and wandered over to the widest, tallest, most garish recliner Mark had ever seen. It was about the size of a golf cart, its bloated cushions upholstered in black leather with burled walnut trim along the overpadded armrests.

"We call this the Captain's Chair," Vic said. "It's the recliner for the new millennium."

"I'm not really interested in a recliner," Mark said.

"I'm not really interested in my brother," Vic replied. "This is a sales floor, Mark. You're taking me away from incalculable potential business."

Mark glanced around the store at row after row of recliners. He didn't see a single customer.

"I'll make a deal with you, Mark. I'll answer your questions about Bill if you'll let me tell you about this amazing step forward in recliner technology, styling, and comfort."

"Okay," Mark said.

Vic motioned to the chair. "Sit down, Mark. Experience the opulence and serenity of the Captain's Chair."

Mark sat down in the chair and sank deep into its plush pillows. He was enveloped in warmth, the chair wrapping itself around him like a hug. The recliner felt like his bed first thing in the morning after a nice, long, peaceful sleep. How could something so ugly feel so comfortable?

The salesman beamed, as if reading his mind. "That's comfort-tech engineering, Mark."

"Really?" Mark said, leaning back, the footrest popping up to support his legs. "Tell me about your family."

"We grew up in Kelso, Washington, where my dad had a furniture store. My uncle had this store, and was doing gangbuster business, and invited my dad to join him, so we moved out here," Vic said. "Business was great. Of course, the big boys in furniture noticed and decided to squeeze us out. We went from being the only furniture store in the area to competing with a dozen national chains and major discounters. So we developed a niche, and you're sitting in it. Recliners."

What he'd shared with Mark was the history of United Furniture Company, not the story of the Gregson family. But the more Mark thought about it, perhaps Victor had told him a lot about the Gregsons. The family was all about the furniture business.

"Where did Bill fit in to that?" Mark asked.

"He didn't," Vic said. "He didn't have an affinity for furniture. You're either born with it or you're not."

"I wasn't aware of that," Mark said.

"Frankly, Mark, he didn't have a flair for sales or my natural people skills, either. He'd sit around in the back room, playing with the computer. I had to fire him."

"And that's when he went to work for Standiford Construction?"

"I figured after a few months earning a living doing physical labor, he'd finally appreciate the furniture trade and return to the store, eager to work," Vic said. "Instead, he kidnapped Standiford's daughter."

Something dark passed over Vic's face. Whether it was sadness, pain, or fury, Mark wasn't sure. Whatever emotion it was, Vic quickly pushed it aside with a gargantuan smile and a burst of renewed sales vigor.

"You know why we call this the Captain's Chair?" Vic asked. "Because it puts you in total command of your relaxation."

"Aren't I anyway?"

"You only think you are, Mark." Vic flicked an armrest switch and a thousand "fingers" beneath the supple leather began kneading Mark's muscles. "With this chair, the dream becomes reality."

Mark's tense muscles, from his head to his toes, were loosening up, which was pretty amazing to him because until the massage started, he had no idea his muscles *were* tense.

"Did Bill have any unusual physical characteristics or behaviors?"

"He started going bald in his twenties," Vic said, "and had the annoying habit of picking his nose in public."

Now all Mark had to do was find a bald millionaire with a finger up his nose. How hard could that be?

"Did you ever meet Stuart Appleby, Diane Love, or Jason Brennan?" Mark said.

"I heard their names for the first time when news broke about the kidnapping," Vic said.

"Kidnapping and murder," Mark corrected.

"Whatever," Vic said, the dark look passing over his face again. He forced a smile. "This recliner is also a multimedia, multitasking experience. You've got a universal remote, a built-in CD player with surround-sound speakers, and a full range of ports and jacks for your Game Boy, headphones, cell phone, and laptop computer."

"Do you ever hear from your brother?" Mark asked.

"The only reason he'd ever call is to ask for money, and

he has plenty of that now, so what would be the point? I'd hang up on him, anyway. He's dead to me," Vic said, then motioned to the other armrest. "Did you notice the cup holders, Mark?"

No, he hadn't. In fact, Mark was having trouble noticing anything anymore. It was taking all his willpower just to stay awake.

"Did Bill have any aspirations?"

"Making money without having to work for it," Vic said. "What happens if you run out of beer or chips while sitting in the chair?"

"It gets them for you?"

"Almost, Mark. You press this button here," Vic said, and suddenly his voice was amplified throughout the store. "And you activate the hidden loudspeaker. No matter how far away the kitchen is, they'll hear you when you call."

Vic hit the switch again, turning off the loudspeaker. "You want to know my favorite feature of this remarkable piece of furniture?"

"There's more?" Mark asked.

"You almost never have to leave its soothing embrace," Vic said. "Touch that knob and see for yourself."

Mark touched a knob on the console with his index finger and the chair moved forward with a soft, electric hum. He pushed the knob to the right, and the chair moved in that direction. The recliner wasn't just the size of a golf cart, it traveled like one, too. Mark felt a smile on his face.

He glanced up at Vic. "How much is it?"

Mark left Las Vegas, feeling frustrated and angry with himself, on the 8:00 P.M. flight to L. A. He'd learned more about the recliner than he had about Diane Love, Jason Brennan, or William Gregson.

Rationally, he knew he shouldn't be too hard on himself. What did he expect he'd accomplish in so short a time? The FBI had been on the case for five years; did he really think he'd stumble on a huge revelation in just eight hours? Did he actually believe he was that much smarter than everyone else?

No, he didn't.

But like everyone who goes to Vegas, he went thinking he'd get lucky. Instead of drawing the winning poker hand or landing the winning spin on a slot machine, he'd hoped he'd ask the right question and yield the perfect clue.

That didn't happen.

What did he learn? Patsy Durkin told him her ex-boyfriend Jason Brennan went to the bathroom all the time and never put the seat down. Karen Cooper told him her former best friend Diane Love dreamed of skiing the Alps. And Vic Gregson revealed his brother, William, liked to pick his nose.

The information, if he could even call it that, was hardly worth the time or airfare.

He had to face reality. The chances that he'd find the three fugitives before Standiford's hit man did were slim. For one thing, the hit man had a five-year head start on him. Mark hadn't made any progress, while his resourceful adversary could already be closing in on one, or all, of his prey.

As the plane lifted off the runway and into the night sky toward Los Angeles, Mark tried to get comfortable in his aisle seat and went over again what little he knew about the case.

Five years ago, four of Roger Standiford's employees kidnapped his daughter, Connie, and buried her alive, thinking she'd be fine with some water and a tube for air. They were tragically wrong.

Standiford paid the $4.5 million ransom and was told where to find his daughter. But he got there too late. She was dead.

That's when the FBI entered the investigation.

Meanwhile, the fugitives divided the money and fled, underwent massive plastic surgery, and created new identities for themselves. They successfully eluded the FBI, and the investigation stalled.

As the months wore on, the Standiford case became less and less of a priority. The agents moved on to more pressing cases, revisiting the Standiford case only when time allowed or new developments came up.

But there were no new developments, at least not that the FBI knew about.

At some point, perhaps a year or two down the line, Roger Standiford was contacted by a professional hit man who offered his specialized services to wealthy victims of violent crime. The hit man offered to find the fugitives and kill them, making their deaths look like accidents. Standiford hired him, and somehow this death merchant found one of the fugitives, Stuart Appleby, living in Hawaii under the name Danny Royal.

The hit man tried to make Appleby's murder look like a shark attack and, when that failed, burned down Appleby's house and his restaurant to eradicate any clues and send a warning to the remaining fugitives. In doing so, the killer boldly announced his presence.

Mark had only two clues to go on, neither very promising. One was Steve's observation that Appleby liked puzzle magazines. The second was the discovery of a souvenir menu postcard from the restaurant with a note written on it: RE: IDEAL OVEN, ASK JIM LOWE. A LOOSE, TRENDY COOK. Was the note significant or just a meaningless reminder Appleby had written to himself?

Out of desperation, Mark tried to track down Jim Lowe and, based on the puzzle magazines, even tried arranging the words on the card into others sentences. Neither effort had led anywhere.

That was all he had to go on.

The more he thought about it, the more he realized he didn't really have anything at all.

Mark's initial strategy had been to try to find the fugitives before Standiford's hit man could. But now he could see that wasn't going to work.

He needed a new strategy. There was only one.

Instead of chasing the fugitives, he'd chase their pursuer. The downside was he had even less to go on and, like the hunt for the fugitives, he would be taking a path that had already been well traveled by the FBI.

Even so, Mark started thinking about how he might begin. First, he'd contact Sgt. Ben Kealoha in Kauai and see what, if anything, the detective's investigation into the staged shark attack had revealed. Then he'd see if Steve could help him compile a list of violent crimes involving wealthy families, the killer's client base. It would take time, but once Mark had that list, he could question the families one by one, see if they'd been contacted by the hit man, and hope a lead would turn up.

It occurred to Mark that there was another approach he could take that might yield faster results.

If Mark could find a recent violent crime involving a wealthy family, he might be able to establish contact with them before the hit man did. If he could do that, it might be possible to trap the hit man when he came calling.

That was a lot of ifs, and there were no guarantees any of them would pan out before the hit man found the three fugitives and killed them.

It almost seemed futile.

Mark asked himself why he was putting in so much effort to save the lives of three killers, and almost immediately felt guilty for the thought.

Roger Standiford and Jesse had asked him the same question, and Mark didn't think twice before answering. He didn't doubt the strength of his convictions before, so why was he now?

Weariness and frustration, he told himself. That was all it was. A good night's sleep and some genuine progress in the investigation would erase any thoughts of giving up.

In the meantime, he decided to give his mind a rest, to

think of something else besides the case. So he glanced to his right, past the passenger beside him, to the view out the airplane window.

There was no view. Only darkness. Mark sat up in his seat, trying to peer down at the landscape below. More darkness.

So much for a distraction.

That's when Mark noticed, for the first time, the man sitting beside him. He was a young man, perhaps in his late twenties, dressed casually in khaki pants and a sand-colored Tommy Hilfiger sweater over a white T-shirt. The man was slumped in his chair, staring intensely at a Bellagio cocktail napkin on his open tray table. A woman had written her name across the top and her phone number below it, the Las Vegas area code included.

Mark glanced at the man's troubled face.

"Is she pretty?" Mark asked.

"Indescribably," the man answered, his voice tinged with longing and sadness.

"Did you click?"

"Like crickets," the man said.

"Is that good?" Mark said.

The man grinned. "Oh yeah."

"So why aren't you thrilled that she gave you her phone number?"

The man sighed and glanced at Mark. "I'm getting married next week."

Mark nodded. "Oh, I see."

"I didn't go looking for this. I came into town on business. I was sitting in the hotel bar, having a drink, and we just struck up a conversation. I wasn't even trying. It never happened like that for me before."

"That's probably why it happened so smoothly. You were just being yourself."

"She was the most beautiful woman I've ever seen," the man said. "It was as if she'd stepped out of my fantasies."

"My name is Mark Sloan." Mark offered his hand. The man shook it.

"Joey Tremont."

"Do you love your fiancée, Joey?" Mark asked.

"Yes," Joey said.

"You're a week away from the biggest commitment of your life," Mark said. "I didn't see this woman you met, but I'm guessing her allure went beyond her physical appearance and sparkling conversation. She represented freedom, excitement, possibility, and youth—everything you fear you're giving up by getting married."

"Aren't I?"

"Of course not," Mark said. "You're about to embark on a personal adventure far more exciting and full of possibilities than anything you've experienced before."

"You don't understand," Joey said. "This woman was like something out of the *Sports Illustrated* Swimsuit issue."

"Your life is about to change, whether you marry the woman you love or pursue this woman you just met. The question is, which change is going to make you a better person, give you lasting happiness, and offer you the chance to explore all your untapped potential?"

"That's a loaded question," Joey said. "It's obvious which choice you think I should make."

"It's not my life," Mark shrugged. "Either way you choose, this woman could easily become the biggest regret of your life."

"That's a big help."

Joey stared at the napkin for a long moment, then crumpled it up and stuffed it into the ashtray in the armrest between the two men.

"Now I'll always have something to fantasize about," Joey said with a grin. "The road not taken."

"Every life has one or two, Joey."

"Maybe I should tear it up so some other guy doesn't find it and give in to temptation," the man said, glancing out the window. There were lights below as they passed over Victorville, a mining town ninety-seven miles northeast of Los Angeles.

Mark felt that sudden, breathtaking thrill of revelation when one of the blurred notions in his head unexpectedly sharpened into a clear, undeniable truth. The picture was still taking shape as he picked the napkin out of the ashtray.

The man turned and looked at Mark incredulously.

"Don't tell me you talked me out of it just so you could call her," Joey said. "Nothing personal, but I don't think you're her type. Or age."

But Mark wasn't listening. He lowered his tray table, spread the napkin out in front of him, and stared at it. The woman's name was across the top, her area code and phone number written underneath. Her name was two words. Her phone number was ten numbers, spaced in groupings of three, three, and four numbers.

"What are you doing?" Joey asked.

"Solving a puzzle," Mark replied. "It's a word game I've been struggling with. The name and phone number on your napkin gave me an idea how to figure it out."

He took out his pen and wrote *Re: Ideal Oven* on one line and then, below it, wrote *Ask Jim Lowe.* And below that he wrote *A loose, trendy cook.*

And then Mark smiled to himself.

"Well?" Joey asked. "Did you find a hidden message?"

"No," Mark said. "I found a hidden person."

Chapter Sixteen

How could he have not seen it before? It was a puzzle, and a simple one at that. *Ideal Oven* was two words, an anagram for a person's name. And there was a V in the name of only one of the fugitives: *Diane Love*.

And in the sentence below, the letters were spaced in groupings of three, three, and four, just like a phone number.

Mark took out his cell phone and matched the letters in the phrase *Ask Jim Lowe* with the numbers they represented on the keypad.

275 546 5693.

It didn't look to him like a valid phone number, but he knew he was on the right track. The numbers had to be scrambled in some way. He wasn't even sure those were the right numbers. What if Appleby had to incorporate a 1 or a 0? There were no letters associated with those numbers on a telephone keypad, so what work-around would Appleby have used?

Mark wasn't a mathematician, but he guessed there were thousands of possible combinations for those numbers. How could he narrow down the possibilities?

That was the question that nagged him for the rest of the short flight and on the forty minute drive from LAX to Malibu.

As soon as he got home, Mark rushed straight to his laptop computer, turned it on, and opened his word processing program. He typed down what he knew:

Ideal Oven = Diane Love
Ask Jim Lowe = 275-546-5693.
A loose, trendy cook = ?

He studied the remaining undeciphered phrase as he picked up the phone and dialed the number he'd come up with from *Ask Jim Lowe*. Before he finished dialing, his call was interrupted by a recorded message:

"We're sorry, your call cannot be completed as dialed. Please check the number and dial again."

Mark hung up the phone and stared out at the beach. He couldn't see the surf in the darkness, but he could hear the waves breaking against the shore. It was the same way he felt about the message on the screen in front of him. He couldn't see the answer yet, but he was certain it was there.

Steve came up the stairs from the first floor, where he had a bedroom, a bathroom, and a small kitchen. Both his bedroom and his kitchen opened directly onto the beach. The second floor, where Mark lived, had two bedrooms, two baths, a gourmet kitchen, and a large deck that faced the ocean. The beach house was, in essence, a duplex linked by a staircase in the entry hall. This allowed Mark and Steve to share the same house but have separate spaces to call their own. Even so, Mark's kitchen had become their meeting place, and Steve usually came and went through the front door, unless he brought home a date.

"I thought I heard you come back," Steve said, then noticed the open laptop. "Couldn't wait to check your E-mail?"

"I think I broke the code on the recipe card we found in Danny Royal's safe-deposit box," Mark said. "I mean, Stuart Appleby's safe-deposit box."

"I know what you meant," Steve pulled up a chair beside Mark. "What have you got?"

Mark explained what he'd deciphered and the riddles still left to unravel. Steve looked the numbers.

"There must be ten thousand possible combinations of those numbers," Steve said. "Where do we start?"

Mark tapped the screen below the remaining undecoded phrase. "Right here."

A loose, trendy cook.

Mark decided to play a hunch. "If the first line is a name and the second line is a phone number, maybe the third line is a place. A city separated from the state by a comma."

"It's worth a shot." Steve took a pencil and wrote the phrase across the top of a legal pad with plenty of space between each letter. Then, below it, he made a list of the fifty states.

Together, Mark and Steve tried to match the letters of the phrase with the name of a state. Twenty minutes later, they succeeded.

Colorado.

"It fits with something I learned while I was in Las Vegas," Mark said. "Diane liked to ski. It makes sense she'd settle in Colorado."

Mark went to his bookshelf, pulled out an atlas, and looked up the state of Colorado.

"What letters do we have left?" Mark asked.

"O, T, E, N, K, Y, and S," Steve said.

Mark compared the list of cities and towns in Colorado with the remaining letters he had left. He found a match almost immediately.

"She's in Keystone, Colorado," Mark said.

Steve moved the laptop to face him, called up an Internet search engine, and typed in *Keystone, Colorado*. A moment later, he had hundreds of Web sites that mentioned the town. He clicked on one of them and smiled.

"Keystone is a ski resort community," Steve said, "about an hour and a half outside Denver."

"What's the area code?"

Steve scrolled through the pages on the screen until he found a phone number.

"9-7-0," he replied.

Mark returned to his seat and looked at the numbers he'd deciphered from *Ask Jim Lowe* on the napkin.

"I can find the 9 and 7, but not the zero," Mark said.

"It has to be there," Steve said. "I know we've got the right place."

"So do I," Mark said. "But there are no letters represented by a zero on a telephone keypad."

"He must have gotten around it somehow," Steve said.

Mark mulled the problem for a few minutes, staring at the keypad of his telephone, and came up with a possible work-around.

"What if Appleby used the letter O as a place holder for zero?" Mark said. "In that case, Appleby would have used the number 6, which corresponds with O on the telephone keypad."

Steve looked at the numbers they'd decoded. There were two sixes. If they allocated one for the zero, that left them with the numbers 5, 2, 5, 4, 5, 6, and 3.

"That's still too many numbers and possibilities," Steve said. "It would take months to track them all down."

"I think we can whittle the list down a bit more." Mark picked up the phone, called Information, and asked the operator for a list of telephone number prefixes for Keystone, Colorado.

Armed with that, Mark and Steve were able to unscramble the remaining numbers into two dozen possible phone numbers. They looked at their short list.

"One of these numbers belongs to Diane Love," Mark said, "who is somewhere in Keystone, Colorado, hiding behind a new face and a new identity."

"So what are you going to do now?"

"Book a flight to Denver for first thing tomorrow morning," Mark said, rising from his seat. "And then I'm going to drive up to Keystone and find her."

"All by yourself?"

Mark smiled. "You're welcome to join me if you'd like."

"I wasn't thinking about me," Steve said. "I was thinking about Terry Riordan."

Mark's smile faltered. "You want me to call the FBI?"

"Dad, it's their case," Steve said. "They have the resources and manpower to take it from here."

"It hasn't helped them so far."

Steve leaned back in his chair. "So now this is a competition between you and the FBI? A race to see who can solve the case first?"

"Of course not."

"Then what's stopping you from calling the FBI?" Steve said. "You have information that could lead them to a fugitive wanted for kidnapping and murder."

"I don't want to be cut out of this investigation," Mark said.

"So you leverage your information. If they want it, they have to keep you involved. Terry Riordan is a politician first, an FBI agent second. He'll make the deal because this is his chance to grab credit for closing a case the FBI has been working for five years. But you already knew all that. What's really holding you back?"

"I don't know." Mark shrugged and looked out the window. All he saw was his own reflection in the glass. He didn't like what he saw.

Steve got up, walked over to the window, and stood beside his father. "Yes, you do."

"I wanted to do this myself," Mark said quietly. "I wanted to beat the hit man on my own."

"Man to man," Steve said.

Mark nodded.

"But it's not about you and the hit man," Steve said. "It's about Connie Standiford and getting justice for what happened to her. You have to take your ego out of it. Calling in the FBI isn't a sign a weakness. It's the right thing to do."

Mark sighed wearily. "When did you get so smart?"

"I had a good teacher." Steve put his arm around his father's shoulder and they stood there in silence, trying to see past their own reflections into the darkness beyond.

The early morning was Stella Greene's favorite time of day. She was alone on the mountain, skiing swiftly down the steep, narrow ribbon of virgin powder between the trees.

Stella was trim and deeply tanned, with short black hair, strong hands, and not an ounce of extra body fat, despite having given birth to two children. Her formfitting ski suit flattered her near-perfect physique, and that was intentional.

She was acutely aware of how others saw her. When they looked at her, they saw a strong woman, physically and emotionally, seemingly born in the outdoors, totally at ease with herself and her environment.

Stella Greene was exactly the woman she always wanted to be, that she always knew she *could* be, long before she was.

Her morning ski run reinforced that self-image, reassuring her that everything she knew about herself was true, strong, and abiding. The mountain was her church, and skiing was her form of worship. She became one with the mountain, the snow, and the earth. The rhythm of skiing became fluid and instinctive. She fell into something like a trance, her body perfectly tuned to the changing terrain beneath her skis. Freed from having to concentrate on skiing, she reveled in the invigorating speed, the cold air whipping off her bare cheeks.

The double-black-diamond run was full of sudden drops that guaranteed big air, the giddy sensation of flying into the sharp blue sky, before landing again on the snow and rocketing down the glade. To Stella, catching the air was pure freedom, like nothing else on earth. She nearly shrieked with joy every time it happened.

It was those moments that she craved during the rest of the day as she taught the basics of skiing to the tourists. It was those moments that she dreamed about late at night, lying in bed beside her husband, her kids asleep in their rooms. It was those moments that she lived for, that she killed for, and that, very soon, she would die for.

Because while she was lost in her personal reverie, at one with the mountain, she was totally unaware of the figure in black traversing the glade behind her, coming up fast. She didn't know he was there until he intentionally clipped her, breaking her cherished rhythm, destroying her perfect balance, hurtling her out of control and screaming into the line of trees.

Her body smacked against a tall pine with a sharp crack. She wasn't sure if the sound was the snap of wood or bone or both. All she was truly aware of was her body sliding and spinning through the snow. It was if she was riding her body instead of inhabiting it, disconnected from pain or feeling of any kind until she finally came to rest against the base of another tree.

Stella wasn't sure which came first, the overwhelming pain or the horrifying sight of her legs twisted beneath her at unnatural angles, jagged bone sticking out through her torn clothing. Blood dripped from her wounds like oil leaking from a car.

He approached her now, his eyes obscured by frosty goggles, his face covered with a ski mask.

Wyatt studied her for a moment. She was still alive, simpering in the snow. Finding her hadn't been too hard once he had the dozen phone numbers. He just took a drive on the information superhighway. Wyatt pulled the phone records for each household and checked to see if anyone had ever called the Royal Hawaiian restaurant in Kauai. Only one household had. The Greenes. Then he checked the Greenes' credit card statements and found a cluster of charges in New York around the time the $5,000 was mailed from the city to Diane Love's mother. Game, set, and match.

"Help me," she whimpered.

He shook his head no. He didn't feel any pity. He didn't feel anything at all.

"Who are you?" she said, her slight voice cracking with fear.

"No one you know."

"Then why?" she asked pleadingly.

Wyatt looked around for something to finish the job. He found a heavy branch. He picked it up and hefted it in his hand. It would do.

"There are four and a half million reasons, Diane," he said.

Wyatt saw the realization flicker across her eyes, the instant of horrified understanding, just before he clubbed her with the branch. Roger Standiford would have appreciated that.

Chapter Seventeen

Mark called Agent Terry Riordan at a little past eight in the morning. Three hours later, they were both sitting side-by-side in cramped economy seats on an overbooked commercial flight to Denver.

There was a time when they would have taken an FBI jet, but that was before a faltering economy and huge budget deficits forced the Bureau to cut back and impose harsh restrictions on resources. The Bureau jet, much to Terry's chagrin, was reserved only for high-priority, ticking-clock situations, and, with the FBI focusing on homeland security, a long-dormant kidnapping case just didn't qualify.

"Special Agents Sandra Flannery and Tim Witten will fly in from Kauai today," Terry said, sipping from his plastic cup of Diet Coke. "They'll meet us in Keystone sometime tomorrow."

"That's good," Mark said, "because I don't know what we'd do without them."

The tone of his own voice surprised Mark. He didn't realize just how much he'd resented the way he'd been treated by Agent Flannery.

"Officially, it's their case. They've been on it since day one," Terry said. "It's a shame they were in Hawaii when this broke."

Mark glanced at Terry. "Which means you've been given responsibility for the case."

"Yeah," Terry said. "But I'm glad to pitch in."

"I'm sure you are," Mark said. If Terry caught the sarcasm in his voice, he didn't show it. The agent was concentrating on opening his tricky bag of peanuts. "Have Flannery and Witten discovered anything in Kauai?"

"They've been able to backtrack some of the money to offshore accounts," Terry replied, tugging on the bag, unable to get it open. "They're trying to determine if Gregson, Brennan, or Love might have used the same banks to hide their shares of the ransom."

"Does it look promising?"

"Not yet," Terry said. The bag suddenly ripped apart, spraying his tray table, Mark's lap, and the aisle with nuts. The agent cursed.

"Think they'll make it back in time for the arrest?" Mark asked and dropped a few spilled nuts on Terry's tray table.

"I doubt it," Terry said, carefully picking a nut out of his Diet Coke and tossing it in the aisle. "We're moving very fast on this. With luck, they'll be able to sit in on the interrogation."

Mark was sure Terry Riordan's urgency was motivated less by a desire to arrest the fugitive than to do it before he had to share the spotlight with Sandra Flannery and Tim Witten. Even though it was Mark who'd generated the leads, Terry Riordan would reap the career benefits within the Bureau. Terry would be seen as the aggressive agent who finally closed the case after Flannery and Witten toiled fruitlessly on it for five years. He'd move up the ladder, and they'd fall down a few rungs. The only way things could possibly go better for Terry politically was if Mark wasn't along for the ride. Terry had, of course, tried to talk Mark out of coming, but to no avail.

"The Denver office has pulled the names and addresses that go with the phone numbers," Terry gathered the salvaged nuts on his tray table together into a tiny pile. "About half are businesses, the others are residences. We're putting them all under immediate twenty-four-hour surveillance.

We're doing background checks on as many of the individuals as we can, but we're dealing with a lot of potential suspects. It's especially hard without a face or fingerprints to work with."

"I'd concentrate your efforts on the residences first," Mark said. "You might want to pull their phone records, see if any of them have ever called Danny Royal or his restaurant."

"We're already on it. The answers should be waiting for us on arrival in Denver." Terry ate a few nuts, then asked, as casually as he could: "So you got any ideas where William Gregson and Jason Brennan might be?"

"I'm thinking about it," Mark said.

What Mark was thinking was that he was completely out of clues. The souvenir recipe card with the note written on it had been Mark's only tangible lead, and the only fugitive it pointed to was Diane Love. And unless she had something to share, or they found some leads at her house, Mark had nothing left to go on.

He settled in for the remainder of the flight, excited by the prospect of apprehending one of the fugitives and worried that they might not find the others until they showed up on morgue slabs.

There was a time when a chopper would have been waiting for them, blades whirring in anticipation, on the tarmac at the Denver International Airport, instead of a mud-caked Ford Explorer idling outside baggage claim.

Terry cursed the economy that robbed him of enjoying the exciting perks that FBI agents before him once enjoyed, symbols of strength and authority that reinforced the importance of your duties, that proved you represented the most powerful law enforcement agency in the world.

Now the Bureau had been downsized and economized and bureaucratized into mediocrity. There wasn't all that much left in terms of status, power, or really nice toys to separate them from their law enforcement brethren in the

DEA, ATF, or the even the local police. It was downright dispiriting.

On the long drive up to Keystone, the lead Denver agent, Barton Feldman, briefed them on the information that had been gathered so far. Feldman was in his late fifties, graying and paunchy, and was what Terry Riordan considered a backwater agent, a nonplayer waiting out retirement and pushing paperwork. Terry didn't tell Mark his feelings about Feldman, but they came out anyway in the dismissive tone of voice he used when talking to the elder agent.

Feldman and the driver were up front; Mark and Terry sat in the backseat. Two other agents sat in the cramped pop-up seats in the cargo area and talked constantly on their cell phones, making it difficult at times for Mark to clearly hear what Feldman was saying.

Of the half dozen residential listings among the phone numbers, two looked especially promising. Both were women in their early thirties who had moved to Keystone within the last five years. One was Stella Greene, who worked as a ski instructor and whose phone bill showed two calls to the Royal Hawaiian in the last two years. The other was Adele Urich, an interior decorator, who was vacationing in Hawaii and had been there for several weeks.

Terry immediately called Hawaii and was able to catch agents Flannery and Witten before they boarded their mainland flight. The two agents would remain in Hawaii and chase down Adele Urich.

Mark could tell Terry wasn't very pleased at the possibility the action might be in Hawaii after all and, to be honest, neither was he.

Feldman ran through the list of other possible suspects, but either Greene or Urich were clearly the most likely to be Diane Love.

Stella Greene was married with two kids, a four-year-old boy and a two-year-old girl. Her husband, Chester, worked as a real estate agent. They lived in a modest house in a wooded area on the outskirts of Keystone. Stella didn't exactly match the profile for a fugitive kidnapper and killer, but neither did Sara Jane Olsen, the Symbionese Liberation Army member who participated in kidnapping, bank robbery, and murder and transformed herself into a churchgoing housewife and devoted mother. Olsen fooled everyone, baking cakes and arranging play dates for twenty years, before being apprehended. Her loving husband and kids never suspected that the only things she made better than cookies were pipe bombs.

The FBI had the Greene residence under surveillance, agents poised to move in as soon as the search warrant came through.

Mark and Terry were taken to River Run Village at the base of the Keystone ski area. The village was a recent development but the storefronts, restaurants, and condos had been built to resemble a nineteenth-century Colorado mining town. The architects used exposed stone, artificially weathered timber and rusted corrugated tin roofs to give the manufactured village its prefabricated history and carefully premeditated character. In a strange way, the detailed recreation reminded Mark of Las Vegas. While the River Run architecture was not quite as over-the-top, it was just as calculated. He wasn't surprised the Las Vegas native felt comfortable here.

The Ford Explorer was met by two agents in navy blue parkas with the letters *FBI* emblazoned in bright yellow on their backs.

That was Mark's first indication that something was very wrong.

He knew how much FBI agents loved to put on their logo wear at the slightest provocation, but this wasn't a situation where it made sense to advertise their presence. The last thing they'd want to do was spook their target. So why weren't they concerned about that now?

"She's gone," said one of the parka-clad agents as Terry and Mark emerged from the Explorer.

"What do you mean she's gone?" Terry snapped.

"She never showed up for work and her husband hasn't heard from her since she left around 7:00 A.M. this morning," the agent said. "The gondola operator remembers taking her up at eight. Alpine search and rescue teams are on the mountain now, and we've got a chopper up, as well."

"Damn!" Terry said. "Is there any way she could have been tipped that we were closing in?"

The agents shrugged.

"Damn!" Terry said again. "Seal this village up tight. No one comes or goes. Get all the skiers off the runs and lock them down in the lodge or whatever. I want each one of them questioned. Pick up Greene's kids at school, her husband at work, and take them to their house. Keep them there, get a warrant, and bug their phones. You got all that?"

The agents nodded. That's when Terry noticed the cold and the snow, and that every agent except him had somehow managed to slip into an FBI parka while he was talking.

"And where the hell is my parka?" Terry said, his face red with fury.

Mark declined the offer of an FBI parka and the opportunity to go up the mountain to question skiers. He opted instead to wait at the Inxpot, a coffee house and bookstore in the village.

It felt like he was sitting in someone's comfortable, book-lined living room in a woodsy Alpine lodge. A roaring fire crackled in the hearth and the air was rich with the soothing aroma of hot coffee and fresh-baked muffins. It was a very pleasant place, and under ordinary circumstances he'd have enjoyed his time there. But the inviting atmosphere did little to ease his anxiety.

Mark sat on a couch, picking nervously at a blueberry muffin and sipping a cup of La Vita Espresso, which the chalkboard menu behind the counter described as "a flavorful blend of three coffees from South America and Africa."

He killed time by reading the local paper, browsing through some of the books, and staring into the fire. The minutes ticked away like hours. The hours passed like days. He had another muffin and two more cups of coffee. There was enough caffeine coursing through his veins to keep him awake for a month. He had a feeling he'd need it.

"I booked my condo months in advance, flew five hours to get here, and what do I get on my first morning? An absolutely perfect day. Fresh powder, clear blue sky, a skier's dream. I couldn't wait to get out on the slopes."

Mark turned to face the man who was speaking. The man sat at the counter, sipping a cup of coffee. He was tall and lean, with an angular, sharp face, and wore a heavy gray wool sweater, jeans, and pair of Timberland hiking shoes damp from the snow.

"There's just one problem," the man said. "They've closed the place. Can you believe it?"

"At least the coffee is good," Mark said.

"I can get coffee at home," the man replied. "What are you reading?"

Mark was holding a paperback copy of *A Confederacy of Dunces*, a novel he'd often thought about reading but had somehow never gotten around to. He handed the book to the man, who fanned the pages, not really interested.

"I was just browsing," Mark said.

"This one of those Civil War books?" the man asked. "I like those."

"I'm afraid not," Mark said. "It's a different confederacy."

The man shrugged and slid the book back to Mark. "I didn't know there was another one."

"The title comes from a quote by Jonathan Swift," Mark said. " 'When a true genius appears in the world, you may know him by this sign, that the dunces are all in confederacy against him.' "

The man smiled. "Who doesn't feel that way sometimes?"

"I guess that makes us all geniuses," Mark said, putting the book back on the shelf.

"Just means we all *think* we are," the man said. "Like the genius who thought it was a good idea to close down a ski resort on a perfect day for skiing."

As if on cue, Terry Riordan finally came in, his face tight. "We found her."

Chapter Eighteen

"It looks like she wiped out and skied straight into the tree," Agent Terry Riordan said, standing behind Mark, who knelt beside Stella Greene's body.

Her face was like alabaster, her eyes like glass, tears frozen on her cold cheeks like streaks of wax. She didn't seem real. In many respects, Mark was pretty certain she wasn't.

"That's what it looks like," Mark agreed, rising to his feet. "But that's not what happened."

"You mean she didn't do a Sonny Bono?" Terry asked.

"She hit the trees," Mark said. "But those injuries aren't what killed her, though they might have eventually if she'd been left alone. But the killer didn't want to leave anything to chance."

"The killer?" Terry said. "What makes you think this wasn't an accident?"

"I read the snow. She hit that tree over there, and slid to a stop here," Mark motioned to her body and the blood around it. "You can see how the blood beneath her has pooled where she came to rest. But the wound by her head is different. There's blood spatter on the snow. You don't get spatter without impact."

Terry crouched beside her and examined the snow around her bloodied head. "Someone whacked her *after* she hit the trees, while she was lying here defenseless."

Mark nodded. "We were too late. He got her before we could."

"I wasn't aware it was a race."

"You are now," Mark said.

Terry rose to his feet and motioned over Agent Feldman, who had been standing with a handful of other agents, sipping coffee out of insulated mugs and comparing parkas with the search and rescue team. As Feldman trudged over, Terry surveyed the mountainside. Several snowmobiles were parked haphazardly along the tree line. The snow had been well trampled. Whatever signs the killer might have left were gone now. He sighed wearily.

"This is now a crime scene," Terry told Feldman. "I want this area secured and a forensic team up here right away. Get your lazy agents off their asses and tell them to start looking for a murder weapon. Have them talk to every skier at the lodge—maybe somebody saw something. Crack the whip, Feldman. The clock is ticking, and the hands are dripping blood."

Feldman nodded and trudged back through the snow to his men. Terry turned back to Mark.

"Now what?"

Mark stared down grimly at Stella Greene. "We see what story she has to tell."

Wyatt finished his coffee at the Inxpot a few minutes after Mark Sloan left with Terry Riordan, then he casually strode out to his rental car.

He hadn't booked a room yet and he needed a place to stay while he remained in Keystone, observing Mark's investigation from a safe distance.

Ordinarily, that distance would have been a lot farther than a bar stool away, but Wyatt hadn't intended to run into the doctor at the coffee house. It had been pure fate. Wyatt would have been foolish not to take advantage it.

Seeing the doctor sitting there, looking so old and impotent, he couldn't help saying something to the poor man.

While he engaged in meaningless small talk with Mark, Wyatt recalled the conversation he'd overheard the night before between Mark and his son. Mark had talked about his desire to catch Wyatt on his own, his belief that this was a contest between the two of them that the presence of the FBI might ruin.

It was laughable, Wyatt thought.

If Mark Sloan knew just how outmatched he really was, the doctor would have welcomed the FBI into the game. But even with the Bureau behind him, Mark Sloan still didn't have a chance at winning.

Even so, Wyatt admired the doctor's tenacity and instinct for the hunt. He wished he could congratulate Mark on unlocking the puzzle written on the recipe card. The discovery was a shock to Wyatt, who doubted he would ever have recognized, or deciphered, the puzzle himself.

The surprising turn of events, rather than making Wyatt feel inadequate, simply reaffirmed how wise he'd been to maintain his surveillance of Mark Sloan and use him as an unwitting ally.

Wyatt appreciated the sweet irony of it all. He wondered if Mark Sloan would be kind enough now to finish the job for him and lead him to the others.

It was almost too much to hope for.

When all this was over, Wyatt would have to send Mark a thank-you card, though he doubted Hallmark had something appropriate for the occasion.

Terry Riordan met Mark in the hallway outside the Summit County coroner's office four hours later. Mark had observed Stella Greene's autopsy while Terry remained on the mountain, looking for clues. They didn't find any. He was hoping Mark Sloan had had better luck.

Mark came out in bloody surgical scrubs. "I can't prove at this point that Stella Greene was Diane Love, but whoever she was, she had extensive plastic surgery. Her face was totally reshaped, her hair was colored, her teeth capped, and she had breast implants."

"You've just described the majority of the actresses in Hollywood," Terry said. "But if you had to make a guess, what would you say? Is she Diane Love?"

"Yes, I think so," Mark said. "We'll know for sure after Claire Rossiter arrives and gives us a computer sculpture of Stella's original face."

"You brought Rossiter into this?" Terry said. "We have our own experts."

"She's the best in her field, and she'll be on the next plane out," Mark said. "In the meantime, we were able to get a serial number off Stella's breast implants. That should lead us to the surgeon who did the work. If we're lucky, it's the same surgeon who worked on Stuart Appleby and the others. I've asked Amanda to check it out."

"You brought Dr. Bentley in on this, too?" Terry asked with a chastising tone. "I'd like to keep this in the family."

"It is," Mark said. "You've worked with Amanda and Claire before. They have my complete trust."

"I don't care. This is an FBI investigation," Terry said. "We have our own lab and our own experts. We don't outsource."

"What do you call me?"

"Damn lucky to be tagging along."

"You wouldn't have a case without me," Mark said, a slight edge to his voice. "So you might want to rethink who is tagging along with whom."

Terry sighed. "I appreciate everything you've done, but any information you develop from here on goes directly to me. If you want to play with the big boys, you play by our rules. Understood?"

Mark considered what the agent said. It was the FBI's case now; he couldn't pursue it as if it was a personal investigation any longer. At least not while he was riding along with the FBI.

"Understood," Mark said reluctantly. "But it works both

ways. I need to know everything you turn up and see all the evidence you gather."

"Fair enough," Terry said.

"What have you got?"

"Nothing."

"No wonder you think the arrangement is fair," Mark said. "I wonder how you'd feel if the situation was reversed."

"You'd be shut out," Terry said. "Flannery and Witten have called in from Hawaii. They've been interrogating Adele Urich. They don't think she's the one, but they're still checking into her story."

"See if she will voluntarily submit to facial X rays," Mark said. "If she hasn't had plastic surgery, we can immediately rule her out."

"Good idea," Terry said. "Meantime, we've got Greene's husband, Chester, on hold at his house. We've taken his kids over to stay with a family friend so we can search the place without rattling them. We're also checking Stella Greene's bank accounts to see if we can find out what she did with the ransom money."

"What have you told Chester?"

"That his wife's been killed in a skiing accident," Terry said. "I thought I'd hit him with the rest a little later."

Mark nodded. "Which is when?"

Terry glanced at his watch. "Right about now."

Mark changed out of his borrowed scrubs and drove out with Terry to the Greene's rustic A-frame, nestled among tall, snow-covered pines. The house was surrounded by FBI and police vehicles, bathing the house and the snowscape in multicolored flashes from their swirling dome lights.

Inside the house, FBI agents in parkas were searching every room for anything that might tell them something about Stella Greene's past. Terry went straight to the kitchen to talk with Chester, who Mark glimpsed briefly at the dining table, hands covering his face, his body convulsing with sobs. Mark decided to hold off on meeting the grieving husband for a few minutes, and instead headed for the master bedroom.

Being a doctor, Mark went immediately to the medicine cabinet in the master bathroom. He believed there was no better way to get a quick assessment of a person than to look at their medications.

Stella and her husband shared a sink. The medicine cabinet turned out to be a medicine drawer, secured with a firm child-safety latch. He lined up the meds on the counter and grouped them by whom they were prescribed for. Stella was taking Ambien for trouble sleeping, Xanax for anxiety, and Vicodin for pain, most likely from some kind of skiing injury.

With the dark secrets Stella had, Mark wasn't surprised she was riddled with anxiety and had problems sleeping at night. It probably got much worse once she had kids of her own and could imagine one of them enduring what she'd help do to Connie Standiford.

Her husband, Chester, was taking desmopressin acetate as a nasal spray, once a day, which meant he suffered from fatigue and dehydration from a pituitary insufficiency. Chester probably drank water by the gallon and knew where to find every bathroom in Keystone.

The kids had both been prescribed amoxicillin and Tylenol liquid, so Mark knew they'd each suffered ear or throat infections recently, just like millions of other normal, healthy kids their age. That was about to change. Soon they would learn that their mother was dead, and that she was a murderer. He could only imagine what damage that news would do to them emotionally and how it would shape the rest of their lives.

That was the legacy of violent crime. It was never an isolated, contained event. The consequences of murder could often be felt for decades after the act.

The rippling echoes of the Standiford kidnapping and murder were now profoundly affecting the lives of people who weren't even born when it happened. That, to Mark, was the greatest tragedy of all.

With that in mind, Mark went to the kitchen to meet another victim, someone who'd not only suffered a profound loss but was about to discover his life was built on a carefully constructed foundation of lies.

Mark tried to drift unobtrusively into the kitchen so as not to interrupt the flow of Terry Riordan's interview with Chester Greene.

Terry and Chester sat across from each other at the kitchen table. Chester's eyes were bloodshot and his face tear-streaked, but he was no longer sobbing. He was in shock, his voice calm, his eyes staring past Terry into some unfathomable distance.

Mark stood behind Chester and glanced at the magnets, notes, drawings, and school lunch menus stuck on the refrigerator.

"Why would anyone want to murder Stella?" Chester asked, his face drawn in anguish and disbelief.

"Your wife wasn't the person you thought she was," Terry said. "She had another life before she met you."

"Of course she did," Chester said. "Everybody has a life before they get married."

"Not everybody's includes kidnapping and murder," Terry said.

Mark gave Terry a look, surprised at the harshness of the agent's comment. Then again, it may have been the only way to knock Chester out of his shocked daze. If that was Terry's intention, it worked. Chester's eyes focused on Terry with a look of pure loathing.

"What the hell are you talking about?" Chester said.

"We think her murder was an act of revenge."

"My wife wouldn't hurt anyone. She's a gentle, loving person. She didn't have a single enemy. Not one."

"Were you aware that your wife had extensive plastic surgery?"

"She was in a bad car accident when she was a teenager,"

Chester said. "She was nearly killed." His voice caught, and he almost didn't finish the sentence.

Terry shook his head. "Forensics show the surgery was recent, that it was done within the last five years."

Mark hadn't told Terry that, but it was true. The agent was clearly basing his assumptions on Stuart Appleby's autopsy.

"So what?" Chester said.

"Your wife lied to you," Terry says. "Doesn't that mean anything?"

"Someone just killed her," Chester yelled. "Do you think I give a damn right now whether she lied to me about when she had her nose job? Why aren't you out there looking for her killer instead of trying to smear her?"

Mark noticed a tiny plastic file box on the kitchen counter engraved with the word RECIPES. He opened it. It was stuffed with clippings torn out of magazines and recipes written on index cards. He began to sort through the papers.

"Don't you want to know why she was killed?" Terry asked.

"You're not going to find that out talking to me," Chester said. "Or accusing her of a crime she couldn't possibly have committed."

Stuck amid all the other recipes in the menu box, Mark found a postcard folded in half. He unfolded it. There was a color picture of seared swordfish in a roasted macadamia nut–lobster butter sauce on the front, the recipe for the entree on the back.

It was recipe card from the Royal Hawaiian restaurant. There was no note. Just the address of the restaurant and, in smaller type, of Roswell Imaging, the printer.

"Do the names Stuart Appleby, William Gregson, or Jason Brennan mean anything to you?" Terry asked.

Chester shook his head.

"What about Danny Royal?" Terry asked. "Ever heard of him?"

"No," Chester said. "What do they have to do with what happened to Stella?"

"Five years ago your wife lived in Las Vegas and her name was Diane Love," Terry said. "She got together with Appleby, Gregson, and Brennan, kidnapped an eighteen-year-old girl, buried her alive, and ran off with a four-million-dollar ransom."

"My wife would *never* do that," Chester said.

"The crime happened five years ago, about the same time Stella got herself a brand new face," Terry said. "Think about it."

"No, you think about it," Chester said. "Take a look around. Stella's a mother, a *terrific* mother, with two wonderful kids she loves more than anything. Stella couldn't harm someone's child. Don't you see? She couldn't possibly be the person you're describing."

"You're right. Five years ago she wasn't Stella Greene, loving wife and mother," Terry said. "She was Diane Love, kidnapper and killer."

"You're making a horrible mistake," Chester said, his voice cracking.

"Have you ever met your wife's family?"

"Her parents are both dead," Chester said. "She has no other living relatives."

"Uh-huh," Terry said. "Doesn't that strike you as unusual?"

"That's your evidence?" Chester asked incredulously. "That she was alone in the world?"

"We have more." Terry said when, in fact, he didn't. At least not yet. Until the forensic anthropologist worked up a rendering of what Stella's face looked like before the surgery, everything they had was strictly circumstantial. But neither Mark nor Terry doubted they had the right woman. Neither did her killer.

"Then let's hear it," Chester said. "Because you haven't said anything yet that makes the slightest bit of sense."

"Have you ever been to Hawaii, Mr. Greene?" Mark asked gently.

Chester twisted around in his seat, noticing Mark for the first time. "No. What does that have to do with anything?"

Mark held up the recipe card to show the picture of the seared swordfish entree. "I was wondering where you got this."

The only one who seemed to react to the card was Terry Riordan, who smiled with satisfaction. The FBI agent now had one more piece of evidence, albeit circumstantial, with which to make his case.

"I don't keep track of where Stella gets her recipes," Chester said, then turned to Terry accusingly. "Now you're investigating what she *cooks*? What's the matter with you people? Have you gone insane?"

"It came from the Royal Hawaiian restaurant, Mr. Greene," Mark said. "It was owned by Stuart Appleby, one of the other fugitives. Your wife has called him on several occasions."

"It's a coincidence." Chester saw the doubt in Terry's eyes. "You don't understand. She loves experimenting in the kitchen. She likes to try unusual recipes, even though she screws most of them up. I don't mind, but it drives the kids nuts. They'd be happy eating Kraft Macaroni and Cheese every day. You know what Kenny told her once? She should ask Mrs. Kraft for recipes, because there's a lady who really knows how to cook."

A dark look passed over Chester's face. He glanced from Mark to Terry, then stared at a point somewhere beyond the kitchen, the house, and the world closing in around him. They were quiet. The only sounds came from the shuffling of FBI agents moving through the house and the steady hum of the refrigerator.

"She can't be dead," Chester said, his eyes glazing over, his voice dropping to a whisper. "This can't be happening to us."

Mark felt terrible for Chester Greene and his family. It

was only going to get worse for them before it got better, and even then it wouldn't be much of an improvement. The unspeakable betrayal, the unanswered questions, and the lasting pain would linger with the Greenes forever.

There was no joy for Mark in finding Diane Love. Not now. Not this way.

The crime that Appleby, Gregson, Brennan, and Love committed five years ago had just claimed three new victims.

Mark set the recipe card on the table in front of Terry Riordan and walked out of the house.

Chapter Nineteen

Adele Urich, the suspect in Hawaii, voluntarily submitted to an X ray to reveal whether she'd had major plastic surgery done to her face. She hadn't, which ruled her out as their fugitive. It was no surprise to Mark Sloan or anyone at the FBI. They knew Stella Greene was Diane Love. The question now was how to find Jason Brennan and William Gregson before Roger Standiford's hit man did.

The next day moved slowly as evidence was sorted at the FBI's temporary field headquarters, two adjoining rooms at a low-budget motel off the I-70, a few miles from Keystone.

It frustrated Terry that the FBI wouldn't even pop for a decent room at the Keystone resort, but even the cheapest rates were well above the approved daily spending limits. Terry tried to get an "FBI discount" from the desk clerk, who looked at him like he had a third nostril or something. He tried appealing to her sense of patriotism and justice, and got back a bunch of drivel about it being "high season" and them being at "full occupancy," which he didn't believe for a second. The clerk and her entire staff could look forward to being audited by the IRS.

Mark Sloan didn't care what their accommodations were. He would have felt cold and frustrated and uncomfortable wherever they were staying. The crime scene unit turned up nothing at the murder scenes. So far, agents hadn't found any anything unusual about the Greene's finances, nor any obvious indications that Stella had been in contact with Gregson or Brennan.

Claire Rossiter arrived the previous night and was hard at work on her computer sculpture of what Stella looked like before her surgery, but there wasn't much suspense surrounding her work. They all knew what the face would look like. The only person Rossiter's rendering would shock was going to be Chester Greene. Once the picture was done and could be compared to pictures of Diane Love, any hope Chester had that the FBI was making a big mistake would be lost.

Agents Flannery and Witten were still in Hawaii. Terry had deftly convinced them there was little they could accomplish in Denver and that there was far more valuable work for them to do on the island. The key clue could still be in the financial paper trail, he told them. You can't go wrong following the money. It works almost every time.

Perhaps it did, but Mark didn't think it would in this case. Then again, he had no idea what would. He'd already used up the one clue he had: the note on the recipe card. When he'd discovered another Royal Hawaiian recipe card in Stella's kitchen, for an instant he'd felt relief, certain they'd have another anagram to decipher that would lead them to the other fugitives. But when he unfolded the recipe card and saw that there was no note written on it, his heart sank. They were back to zero.

Still, it bugged him that she had a Royal Hawaiian recipe card. Did she save it for Appleby's phone number and address? If so, why did she only have information on him and not the other fugitives? And if she did have information on how to reach Gregson and Brennan, where was she hiding it?

Those questions in turn raised others in Mark's mind. Why did Appleby bother to encode and save contact information on Diane Love in his safe-deposit box and not the others? Then again, Appleby might have. The encoded information about how to contact them might have been among the clues lost when the hit man torched Appleby's house and restaurant.

At least Mark could find some solace in the fact they got to Greene's house before the killer could cleanse that home of any clues, too. Not that it was helping them now. If the clues were there, so far Mark had missed them all.

He spent most of the day going through the Greene's family photo albums, hoping to spot something among the people they met and the places they went. There was a nice picture of the Greenes grouped around Mickey Mouse at Disneyland, all smiles. Maybe it was Gregson in the mouse costume. Or Brennan. Or Amelia Earhart.

Mark slogged through more photos, then went through Stella Greene's jewelry, clothing, and books, hoping something would jump out at him.

Terry Riordan was obviously hoping that would happen, too. He kept staring at Mark, as if waiting for him to leap up and scream "Eureka!" at any moment.

Mark had a lot of faith in his unconscious mind to assimilate and sort random bits of information like pixels, and he knew that it often took time for a clear picture to emerge, but he couldn't help feeling he was falling behind in the race. The killer was out there pursuing the same targets and having a lot more success at it.

It wasn't until late afternoon that a break finally came their way. Mark got a call from Amanda on his cell phone. She'd traced the breast implant to a Beverly Hills plastic surgeon, Dr. Morris Plume.

Five minutes later, Mark Sloan and Terry Riordan were on their way to Denver International Airport to catch the first available flight back to L.A.

That day Roger Standiford received a fax from Denver. It was a copy of an article clipped from the back page of the local newspaper. The story was about the murder of a ski instructor named Stella Greene on the slopes of Keystone, Colorado.

The article said the FBI was investigating the homicide, but a spokesman for the Bureau wouldn't comment on their involvement in the case. The victim, according to her coworkers, was a popular instructor at the resort for the past five years.

The fax was followed, almost immediately, by an E-mail request for the balance of funds owed on Diane Love. A photo, showing Dr. Mark Sloan and an FBI agent outside the Summit County coroner's office, was attached to the E-mail.

Standiford wired the funds to the hit man's account. If Mark Sloan was in Keystone, Diane Love was surely dead.

Two of the people who'd killed his daughter had been punished, but Roger Standiford wasn't feeling the joy or satisfaction he thought he would.

It didn't matter what he felt. What mattered was that Stuart Appleby and Diane Love wouldn't be feeling anything anymore.

Then again, he wasn't sure they ever did.

Dr. Morris Plume's clinic was near the corner of Olympic and Robertson, as far south as he could possibly go and still call himself a Beverly Hills plastic surgeon.

His offices were on the second floor of a two-story office building that had been built in the late 1980s and looked like a Rubik's Cube with underground parking.

The waiting area had the requisite aquarium and a selection of in-flight airline magazines. The most recent copy was six months old. The only interesting reading material Mark found, as he and Terry waited for the doctor, was a slick, colorful brochure listing all the procedures available to patients.

If it wasn't for the pictures of nearly naked female models, the brochure could have been mistaken for a restaurant take-out menu. Each procedure was listed like an entree, with glowing descriptions of the wonderful results followed by the cost. Tummies could be tucked, noses crafted, pecs endowed, foreheads lifted, eyelids firmed, ears tweaked, buttocks enhanced, and lips swelled. Breasts could be lifted, shaped, enhanced, firmed, sculpted, augmented, contoured, and reduced. Dr. Plume also offered BOTOX injections, Cymetra injections, fat injections, collagen injections, and thorough dermabrasion.

The brochure promised "everything for a new you," and Mark couldn't argue with that. Dr. Plume had certainly fulfilled the promise for Diane Love and, Mark guessed, the other fugitives, as well.

Mark slipped the brochure in his pocket as Dr. Plume stepped into the waiting room to greet them. Dr. Plume was a fit man in his midthirties who had apparently sampled just about everything on his own menu. His face was unnaturally smooth, his forehead tight, his nose sculpted to a slender point. He seemed extremely alert, his eyes wide, his ears pointed like a hound's. His chin was prominent and so were his cheekbones, his broad smile revealing two rows of gleaming, perfectly white teeth.

"Sorry to have kept you waiting," Dr. Plume said, shaking their hands. "I was just finishing up a tricky mastopexy. What can I do to help the FBI?"

"Do you recognize these people?" Terry opened a file and extracted a sheet with pictures of the four fugitives on it. He handed the sheet to Dr. Plume, who glanced at it quickly and gave it back to him.

"Nope, not offhand," Dr. Plume said. "I see so many faces in here."

"They would have come in five years ago." Terry took another sheet out of his file and held it out in front of the doctor. "Two of them left looking like this."

The sheet had pictures of Stuart Appleby and Diane Love as, respectively, Danny Royal and Stella Greene. Dr. Plume's smile faltered a bit at the edges.

"We traced the serial numbers on her implants back to you," Mark said, exaggerating the truth just a bit. "We know you worked on them."

"Yes, I recognize these two," Dr. Plume said. "I have a

better memory of my own work. An artist remembers his paintings, not the blank canvases. Perhaps if you showed me what the other two look like now, I might remember them."

"That's what we're here to find out," Terry said. "We want to see the files on all four of them."

"I wouldn't know where to look."

"We'll start at A and work our way through," Terry said.

"I'm afraid I can't let you do that," Dr. Plume said. "I promise my patients strict confidentiality. I treat a lot of celebrities who wouldn't like their cosmetic histories revealed. I'm sure they'd mount a vigorous legal challenge against any effort you made to ransack my files."

Mark doubted Dr. Plume had any celebrity clients, but it would still be difficult to get any judge to sign off on a blanket search warrant of all the files.

"Besides, you say these surgeries were done five years ago?" Dr. Plume said.

"Yes," Terry said.

"That's a shame," Dr. Plume frowned, which wasn't easy, considering how tight his cheeks were. "Those files are long gone."

"Gone," Terry said flatly, narrowing his eyes.

"We had a flood."

"You're on the second floor," Mark said.

"We had a leak in the roof one particularly rainy weekend. The entire office got drenched," Dr. Plume said. "We lost hundreds of files."

"You better hope the insurance company confirms that," Terry said.

"I didn't inform the insurance company," Dr. Plume said. "I knew it wouldn't be covered so I paid for the repairs myself."

"Who was the roofer?"

"It was so long ago, who remembers that kind of thing?" Dr. Plume let his voice drift off. "You know how it is."

"What I know is that you gave new faces to four fugitives

wanted for kidnapping and murder," Terry said. "That makes you an accessory."

"I'm fully licensed to perform plastic surgery on anyone who wants it, and I am under no obligation to run background checks on my patients," Dr. Plume said. "Now, if you will excuse me—"

Dr. Plume started to go, but Terry grabbed him by the arm.

"Have you ever had a butt enhancement procedure?"

"No, I haven't."

"Then it's your lucky day, because you're about to get one, courtesy of the FBI. We're going to put a man outside your building on permanent and obvious surveillance, taking pictures of everyone who comes and goes from this office. We're going to scrutinize your tax returns, interview your patients, and go over your entire life with an electron microscope. And that's just for starters. We'll be on your ass night and day until we get what we want."

Terry released Dr. Plume, who seemed to have lost a little of the color underneath his tanning-parlor complexion. Without saying a word, the doctor turned his back on them and scurried back into his office.

"I'm sure they weren't the first wanted felons he's worked on," Mark said.

"So am I," Terry replied. "We'll crack him, it's just a question of when."

Mark shook his head. "No, the question is whether Brennan and Gregson will still be alive when we do."

The late-night FBI surveillance of Dr. Morris Plume's office was inconvenient for Wyatt, but at least they did him the courtesy of making themselves obvious about it. The two agents were parked in a Mercury Grand Marquis sedan across the street from the building, drinking Starbucks coffee and casually watching the building.

Wyatt drove up the alley behind the building in a Pacific Bell service truck he'd stolen earlier that afternoon. He got out, wearing a PacBell uniform and utility belt, pulled a ladder off the side of the truck, and propped it up against the building.

He climbed the ladder to the roof, disabled the alarm system, and picked the lock on the access door. Two minutes later, he was standing in Dr. Plume's office, staring angrily at three hefty bags filled with shredded files. He opened a bag. The paper was like confetti. Dr. Plume had invested in a very good shredder.

Wyatt destroyed the shredder out of spite, then removed the hard drives from all three computers in the office, though he doubted he'd find anything useful on them. For a moment he toyed with the idea of paying a visit to Dr. Plume's apartment in Marina Del Rey. Wyatt was sure he could easily torture the doctor into talking, assuming Dr. Plume had anything useful to reveal. But Wyatt couldn't do that without killing Dr. Plume afterward.

It just wasn't Wyatt's style. Although Dr. Plume was probably guilty of dozens of crimes, he was still technically an innocent. It was a subtle distinction, even for Wyatt, but enough to save the doctor for now.

Even so, Wyatt wouldn't forget Dr. Morris Plume. The doctor's day of reckoning would come.

Chapter Twenty

The overwhelming impression Josephine Candella gave to everyone who met her was one of roundness. Round face, round belly, round shoulders, and a round mouth that always seemed in the midst of saying "Oh!"

Josephine was on a bed in the ER, clutching her husband, Phil's, hand, looking desperately at Dr. Mark Sloan with her big round eyes. "What is it, doctor? Gallstones? Appendicitis? Stomach cancer?"

"It's none of those things, Mrs. Candella," Mark said to the woman, who'd been rushed in from work that morning complaining of severe abdominal pain. He flashed her a big smile. "You're pregnant. Congratulations!"

Josephine and Phil Candella stared at Mark in shock.

"That's not possible," Josephine said. "Are you sure it's not something I ate?"

"Not unless you swallowed a ten-week-old baby whole."

"Oh," she said, then mumbled to herself, "I thought I was putting on a little weight."

"You don't understand," her husband said to Mark. "She can't be pregnant."

"She most certainly can," Mark said. "And she is."

"But I'm sterile," Phil exclaimed.

Now it was Mark's turn to say "Oh." Josephine Candella flushed guiltily and looked like she might say "Oh," too. Then again, she always looked that way.

"Maybe you're not as sterile as you thought. Life is full of surprises," Mark edged back toward the door. "Someone will be down from obstetrics to talk to you both shortly. Congratulations again."

Mark slipped into the hall and took a deep breath. He'd have to warn the doctor from obstetrics that she might be stepping in the middle of a major marital battle.

"Dr. Sloan, could I have a word with you?"

Mark turned to see Clarke Trotter, Community General's legal counsel, approaching him from down the hall.

"What's up, Clarke?" Mark said.

The attorney patted his considerable belly as if he was also carrying a ten-week-old child. "How was your vacation in Hawaii?"

"Eventful," Mark said, making some notations in Mrs. Candella's file and dropping it off at the nurse's station. "But I'm glad to be back."

"That's what I wanted to talk with you about," Clarke said. "Since you returned, you've worked one week and then went off again for three days."

"Something important came up," Mark said.

"Another homicide investigation, perhaps?"

"What are you getting at, Clarke?"

The attorney patted his stomach and tugged on his red tie. It was his tell. Bad news was coming. "You're supposed to be chief of internal medicine at this hospital."

"Isn't that what I'm doing?"

"Not when you're gallivanting around indulging your hobby," Clarke said.

"Gallivanting?" Mark said. "Do people still say that?"

"With all due respect, doctor, we aren't paying you a salary to solve crimes," Clarke said. "We're paying you to practice medicine."

"Clarke, how many vacation days have I taken in the last ten years?"

"I don't know offhand," Clarke said. "I'd have to check."

"Zero," Mark said. "How many sick days have I taken?"

"Dr. Sloan, you're missing my point."

"I understand what you're saying," Mark said. "But I think I've earned a little flexibility with how I choose to allocate my hundreds of days of accumulated vacation time and sick leave."

"Have you considered taking an extended sabbatical instead?" Clarke said. "Or have you given any thought to retiring?"

"No, I haven't." Mark said, an edge to his voice.

"This isn't personal, Dr. Sloan. I'm merely voicing the board's concern," he said. "It would be one thing if your outside time was devoted to medical research or something of that nature. But the activities you've chosen don't always reflect well on the hospital."

Mark looked Clarke Trotter straight in the eye. "One of our board members spends most of his time *gallivanting* from one European or tropical medical conference to another, all his expenses paid for by pharmaceutical companies we do business with. I don't think that reflects well on this hospital. Another board member is *gallivanting* with one of our young nurses behind his wife's back. I don't think that reflects well on the hospital, either. Shall I go on?"

"That won't be necessary," Clarke said.

"I'd be glad to have this discussion with the board," Mark said. "Why don't you pencil me in on the agenda and we can get all this gallivanting on the record."

"There's no need to do that," Clarke said. "I'll convey your sentiments privately to the board. Please think about what I've said. We can talk about this again another time."

"I'd rather not," Mark said.

Clarke smiled as if he hadn't heard and waddled away.

It wasn't the first time Mark had clashed with hospital administrators over his work assisting the police with homicide investigations, and he knew it wouldn't be the last. The criticism had waned for many years, but ever since a mad bomber he had pursued blew up half the hospital, the board had, not surprisingly, taken a much dimmer view of his investigations.

But Mark had to concede that Clarke Trotter had a point. The truth was that paperwork was piling up on his desk. Since returning from Hawaii, Mark had been totally preoccupied by the investigation. It was even worse now that the leads seemed to have dried up. He was having trouble sleeping at night, unable to stop going over the details of the case in his mind.

Mark resolved to move that paperwork off his desk and dive into his administrative duties at the hospital. But first, he decided to stop by the path lab on the way to his office to see if Amanda had anything to report.

Amanda was finishing up an autopsy when Mark came in. She draped a sheet over the dead body and greeted him with a smile.

"I was just about to call you," she said, stripping off her gloves and heading for her desk.

Mark motioned to the corpse. "Suspicious circumstances?"

Amanda glanced back at the autopsy table. "Him? No. Died of natural causes, but because he lived alone, his body wasn't discovered for a few days. I was going to call you about this." She handed Mark a computer rendering of a woman's face. "This came in from Claire Rossiter. She sent you a copy in case the FBI wasn't in a sharing mood. This is how Stella Greene looked before plastic surgery."

Mark recognized the face immediately. "It's Diane Love."

The rendering was even better than the one Rossiter had done of Danny Royal, which made sense, since she had the actual face to work with instead of photos and measurements. Mark had to give Dr. Plume credit. He'd made Diane Love completely unrecognizable and did so without making her look like she'd obviously had lots of cosmetic work done. It was unfortunate for Dr. Plume that his skill wasn't shared by the surgeons he allowed to work on him.

"Your investigation is definitely on the right track," Amanda said.

"Only we're several laps behind," Mark said. "For all we know, the other two fugitives are dead already."

"Take it easy on yourself, Mark. The other guy has a five-year head start on you. Look at the remarkable progress you've made in just a few weeks."

"Unfortunately, you can measure that progress in corpses," Mark said. "It's all for nothing if we don't apprehend the fugitives alive."

"Even if you don't get to them in time, the hit man is still out there," Amanda said. "You're going to catch him."

"I won't rest until I do," Mark said.

"Which means neither will I," Amanda said. "And just so there's no misunderstanding, that's not a complaint. That's a commitment."

Mark smiled. "I appreciate that, Amanda."

He turned to go when Terry Riordan marched into the lab, clearly enraged.

"I'm glad to see you, because I want you to hear this," Terry said to Mark. "Dr. Bentley has seriously compromised our investigation."

"Are you talking about this?" Mark held up the rendering from Claire Rossiter.

"No, but it proves my point," Terry said, snatching the paper from him. "Your circle of friends can't be trusted. Your forensic anthropologist buddy is E-mailing FBI evidence to everyone in her address book—"

"I think you're exaggerating just a bit," Mark interrupted.

But Terry continued, ignoring Mark's interruption.

"And God knows how many people know the serial number of the breast implants, thanks to you and Dr. Bentley."

"I only talked to Mark and the manufacturer of the implant," Amanda said. "No one else."

"Then maybe you can explain why last night somebody broke into Dr. Plume's office, shredded his files, and stripped his computers."

"I thought you had the clinic under twenty-four-hour surveillance," Mark said.

"That's beside the point," Terry snapped defensively. "The fact is, someone else knew we'd traced the implant back to Dr. Plume. And now we have nothing."

"How did you find out about the break-in?" Mark asked.

"Dr. Plume's lawyers showed up screaming at my office this morning, accusing us of doing it," Terry said. "I wish we had."

"How do you know Dr. Plume didn't do it himself?" Mark said. "Maybe he faked the break-in to cover up destroying any evidence that he's helped felons create new identities for themselves."

"Witnesses saw a Pacific Bell service van in the alley behind the building last night," Terry said. "The van was reported stolen before we had our meeting with Dr. Plume, which means whoever took it knew what we were after before the doctor did."

"Unless the doctor was alerted before we got there that we were on the way," Mark said.

"Which brings us right back to this office," Terry said, glaring at Amanda. "And the shoddy handling of evidence."

"Did it occur to you that the leak might be somebody in the implant manufacturer's office?" Amanda said, glaring right back at him. "Of course, if your agents were better at surveillance, we wouldn't be having this conversation. You'd be talking to whoever broke in to the clinic."

"Good point," Mark said.

Terry shifted his anger to Mark. "I warned you about keeping this in the family. Now you know why. Thanks to you, our best hope of tracking down the fugitives is lost."

"We know who did the break-in," Mark said. "It was either Standiford's hit man or someone working for him."

"Which is why I'm flying to Vegas in half an hour to meet with federal prosecutors," Terry said. "We're going to offer Standiford a deal."

"He won't take it," Mark said.

"Then he can look forward to spending the rest of his life in prison," Terry said firmly. "We're redirecting our efforts in this case. Standiford is now the focus of our investigation. We're going to squeeze him until he talks."

"He never will," Mark said. "You're wasting your time."

"Thank you for your input," Terry said, "but we won't be needing it anymore. You and your friends are no longer part of this investigation. We'll call you when it's over."

And with that, Terry Riordan walked out.

Chapter Twenty-one

Steve took a slice of pizza from the Domino's box on the kitchen table and carried it back to the living room, where Amanda, Jesse, and Mark were eating.

Mark had just finished summarizing the latest developments in an investigation that he was no longer part of, which was, as it turned out, the latest and most interesting development.

"So if you're no longer involved in the case," Steve said as he sat down, "why are we all gathered here this evening?"

"Because he didn't mean it," Mark said.

"He sounded pretty clear to me," Amanda said.

"I'm always getting thrown off investigations," Mark said. "Ask Steve."

"The LAPD is thinking of printing up a form letter detectives can hand him to save them the hassle of telling him," Steve said.

"I'm only welcome on an investigation when I have something unique to contribute," Mark said. "I don't at the moment. But as soon as I do, they'll welcome me back as if I'd never left."

"I don't know why you'd want to go back," Jesse said. "Riordan is just using you when it suits him to further his own career."

"Unfortunately, it's not a question of what Dad wants,"

Steve said. "The FBI is in charge of the case. He has an obligation to go to them when he discovers any new leads."

"I have an obligation to go to the authorities," Mark said. "Whether or not it's Terry Riordan or the FBI remains to be seen."

"Have you come up with something?" Steve asked.

"Not yet," Mark said. "But I think I know how we should approach the investigation."

"Terry threw you off the case," Steve said. "You cross his path, he'll come down hard on you."

"That's not a problem, because we're on different paths," Mark said. "He's in Las Vegas, betting on Standiford to crack, and that's not going to happen. Jason Brennan and William Gregson kidnapped and killed Standiford's daughter; there's nothing Terry Riordan can threaten to take from him that he hasn't already lost."

"There's his freedom and his wealth," Jesse said, browsing through Dr. Plume's plastic surgery brochure.

Mark shook his head. "It means nothing to him compared to what he's lost. It's only a means to get him what he wants, which is vengeance."

"So what's your new take?" Steve said.

"It's not new," Mark said. "I've actually been considering it for a while. I'm just not sure it's going to work. There are a lot of variables we can't control. Instead of chasing the fugitives, we'll chase the hit man."

"Isn't that what the FBI is doing?" Jesse asked.

"Terry is squeezing Standiford," Mark said. "We're going to ignore Standiford and concentrate on other wealthy relatives of violent-crime victims."

"You want to find another rich family the hit man has contacted," Amanda said, "find out what they know, and see if they can lead us to him."

"I want to do more than that," Mark said. "I want to find his next client before he does and set a trap for him."

"You mean," Jesse said, "that you want to find a grieving

family with deep pockets who are pissed off at law enforcement for not finding whoever killed their loved one."

"Yes," Mark said.

"And then you want to convince them to help us nab the one guy who can get them the vengeance they want," Jesse continued.

"Yes," Mark said.

"No problem," Jesse sighed. "How hard could that be?"

"I know it's a long shot," Mark said, "but I don't see any other alternative."

"It could take months, Mark," Amanda said. "Maybe longer. We might never find the right family."

"He manages to," Mark said. "It's how he makes his living."

"I meant a family willing to set this guy up," Amanda said.

"We could get lucky," Mark didn't sound very convincing.

"Does this mean you're giving up on beating him to the other two fugitives?" Amanda asked.

"No, I'm still going to try," Mark said. "I can't help myself. It's keeping me up nights. The problem is, I don't have the slightest idea where to begin. Terry was right—Dr. Plume was our last, best lead. We're fresh out of clues."

They all sat quietly for a long moment, listening to the waves, thinking about the arduous task in front of them.

"Look at the boobs on this lady," Jesse said, pointing to a woman in the brochure. "They could probably qualify as flotation devices." The others looked at Jesse, who shrugged. "I'm just studying the evidence at hand."

"Now that you mention the evidence," Mark said, "there is one thing that's been bothering me."

"Just one?" Steve asked.

"That's usually a good sign," Amanda said.

"You mean that it's just one thing," Jesse asked her, "or that something is bothering him?"

"Keep looking through that brochure," Amanda replied. "Maybe Dr. Plume offers a brain enhancement."

"Why did Stuart Appleby go to the trouble of making a note of Diane Love's location, putting it in an anagram and locking it away in his safe-deposit box?" Mark said.

"He must have liked her," Jesse said.

"But why not keep track of the others, too?" Mark said.

"Maybe he did, but he kept that information at home," Steve said. "And it went up in smoke."

"I thought about that," Mark said. "But why would he keep one at the bank and the others at home? And another thing, why did Diane have a recipe card, too?"

"Isn't it obvious?" Amanda said. "So she'd know where to find Appleby."

"How hard would it be to remember the name of his restaurant?" Mark said. "Did she really need a recipe card for that?"

"Maybe she liked the recipe," Jesse said.

Amanda glared at him.

"And why didn't she keep track of the others?" Mark said.

"Maybe she did in some way, and nobody has found out how yet," Steve said. "Or maybe Appleby and Love didn't like the others and didn't care what happened to them."

"There's something we're missing," Mark said.

"There's a whole lot we're missing," Amanda said.

"Have you ever read *Highlights for Children* magazine?" Jesse asked.

Amanda glared at him again. "You're not helping."

"It used to be in my orthodontist's waiting room," Jesse said, undeterred. "My favorite part was the hidden pictures. You'd have to find the fish or the toothbrush or whatever was hidden in a bigger picture."

"What are you getting at?" Amanda asked irritably.

"Maybe there's something in the pictures on the recipe," Jesse said.

"You may be on to something," Mark said, getting up

from his chair and going to his desk, where he kept the stack of recipe cards he took after his dinner at the Royal Hawaiian.

"I also highly recommend Goofus and Gallant," Jesse said. "Everything I know about right and wrong I learned from those two."

"Where did you learn about medicine?" Amanda asked. "From *Rex Morgan, M.D.?*"

"That's where I learned about sex," Jesse said with a sly grin.

"They never had sex," Amanda replied.

"But those women," Jesse said. "They were hot."

Mark returned and spread the recipe cards out on the coffee table in front of them, the photographs of the meals facing up.

"Here they are," Mark said. "What do you see?"

"That I could never have afforded a meal at that place," Jesse replied.

They spent the next two hours scrutinizing the pictures, looking for any hidden images or words. They didn't find a toothbrush or anything else.

Mark typed the recipes into his computer and ran them through an anagram program he found on the Web, but couldn't turn them into anything even slightly resembling a name, address, or phone number.

At midnight, everyone gave up and called it a night.

Everyone except Wyatt.

He sat in his hotel room, where he'd followed along with Mark and the others, searching for hidden messages in the pictures of mouthwatering Pacific Rim entrees and in their complex recipes.

He didn't find anything, either, but it sure beat what he'd been doing all day, which was scouring Dr. Plume's hard drives for information on Brennan and Gregson. Wyatt found out more than he wanted to know about the payments received for boob jobs and face-lifts and BOTOX injections from a bunch of C-list character actors and has-been stars, but nothing about the fugitives he sought. It appeared, though, that Dr. Plume was operating a mostly cash operation, with little financing or credit and few insurance claims. Most of his clients paid in full and in cash, which led Wyatt to believe that most of the plastic surgeon's business came from people hiding from something or someone.

Something like murder and someone like him.

Contrary to what Mark Sloan believed, at the moment Wyatt was no closer to finding the other two fugitives than was the doctor or the FBI. But Wyatt enjoyed hearing about the FBI's laughable plan to crack Standiford and Mark's hopelessly elaborate effort to lay a trap for him.

Wyatt did have some lines in the water. William Gregson's one true love was single again and living in Memphis, and Wyatt was watching her movements, her mail, and her phone bills. There was always the possibility that Gregson, with a new identity and a fat bank account, might make another run for her. Jason Brennan had been very close to his grandmother, and she was dying of cervical cancer. Her death might bring Brennan out of hiding, if only to visit her grave. Wyatt had a number of long shot leads like that, but nothing that promised quick results.

For that, he was counting on Mark Sloan. But the doctor's winning streak seemed to have come to an end.

Mark spent the morning at his desk at Community General going through paperwork, which managed to distract him from the investigation for a few hours. He might have been able to keep his mind off it for the rest of the day if not for an unexpected phone call from Ben Kealoha of the Kauai Police.

"Ho bruddah, howzit goin'?" Kealoha said.

"It's good to hear from you," Mark said, genuinely pleased. Kealoha's energetic voice and boyish enthusiasm brought an immediate smile to his face. "I miss Kauai already."

"Fo' what? There aren't enough murders to solve in La-La Land?"

"I'm still stuck trying to figure out what happened to Stuart Appleby," Mark said.

"Who's that?"

Mark was silent for a moment. "The FBI hasn't told you?"

"Oh, they told me plenty," Kealoha said. "They told me to give them everything we had on Danny Royal. They told me they were handling the investigation now, and that I could go surfing or to a luau."

"What has the FBI been doing?"

"They spent a lot of time at the bank and talked to everybody on the island, 'cept me, of course."

"I owe you an apology, Ben," Mark said. "I should have called you myself and briefed you on everything."

"No worries, bruddah. I know you been on the hunt," Kealoha said. "Let's talk story."

So Mark did, filling Kealoha in on the Standiford kidnapping and murder, the true identities of the fugitives, and everything that had happened since he left the island. A half hour later, when Mark was done, Kealoha let out a slow whistle.

"We never get cases like that here," Kealoha said. "Which is a good thing, because I don't think I'm smart enough to solve them."

"It doesn't look like I am, either."

"I thought about doing like they suggest—go surfing, kick back—but I couldn't let go of the case, you know?"

"I know too well, my friend."

"So I hung back, watched the FBI dudes. They were real interested in Danny Royal's money," Kealoha said, "and not so interested in Kamaikaahui."

It took Mark a moment, and then he remembered what Kealoha was referring to: the Hawaiian legend about a man-beast who killed travelers, devoured them, and blamed their deaths on sharks.

"So I figured I could work on that and never bump into them," Kealoha said.

"Funny," Mark said, "I was thinking the same thing."

"Here's what I did. I guessed we're dealing with a guy in good shape, maybe in his thirties, early forties. I figured this moke needed three things to do his *Jaws* bit: a boat, diving equipment, and a shark fin. We found the boat pretty quick—it was stolen the day of the murder from a slip at Nawiliwili Harbor. The boat was cleaned real good, but the CSU guys found a hair and a spec of blood we were able to match to Danny Royal, anyway."

"Anything from the killer?"

"Only other evidence on the boat pointed back to the boat owners," Kealoha said. "So me and the boys here, we went to every single dive shop on the island, pulled their security-camera videos, and made stills of every guy who came to buy or rent equipment. We showed the pictures to every sport fisherman we could find to see if maybe one of these guys in the photos was asking around for shark fins."

"That's an amazing amount of legwork," Mark said, impressed.

"Hey, we don't get to play *Five-0* very often," Kealoha said. "It's nice to actually be a detective who detects for a change. One of the fishermen thought he recognized one of the guys, so we took that picture to hotels and rental-car places to see what we could get."

"What did you get?"

"About five different names, credit card numbers, and driver's license numbers for this moke, though he paid cash for just about everything," Kealoha said. "Funny thing is, everybody who ID'd him said the picture was a bit off. Like, 'He had a mustache before,' or 'Yeah, I recognize da guy, but he's lost weight.' "

"It makes sense that he'd alter his appearance," Mark said. "And use multiple identities."

"We pulled photos of the guy off the security cameras at

the hotels and rental-car places, too. So that's where we're at," Kealoha said. "You want to see this guy's pretty face?"

"Absolutely," Mark said, and gave him his E-mail address.

"It's on the way," Kealoha said. "I'll also send you his aliases. Good luck, brah."

"Thanks for everything, Ben. I owe you a big favor."

"Nail the bastard," Kealoha said. "Then we can call it even."

As soon he hung up, Mark logged on to his computer and saw the message from Kealoha was already waiting for him with a file attachment. He opened the message and, while he read it, downloaded the file containing the photos.

The killer had called himself Chase Lancaster, Cameron Colabella, Mel Aronsohn, and Antoine Killian. None of the names were familiar to Mark, nor had he expected them to be. But it was nice to know something, no matter how meaningful, about his adversary.

He called up his picture-viewing software and clicked open the file Kealoha sent. A half dozen grainy pictures appeared on screen like mug shots.

The man's appearance was subtly different in each shot—his clothing, the style and color of his hair, and the presence or absence of a beard or mustache. But when the different versions were laid out side-by-side, the basic shape of his face came through clearly. It was a plain face, one that could belong to an accountant or a soldier, that betrayed nothing of the soul of the man who wore it. The face of a mannequin, its plainness making it versatile, useful in any guise. It was that very emptiness, that unnatural sameness, that shone through and remained unchanged despite the disguises.

Mark didn't expect to recognize the man, so it came as a shock when he did. He'd been close to the killer and never even realized it.

He stared at the pictures for a long moment, trying to decide the best way to do what had to be done. After careful consideration of all the options and possible outcomes, he picked up the phone and made a long-distance call.

The voice that answered sounded bone-tired and world-weary. "FBI, Agent Feldman speaking."

"Agent Feldman, this is Dr. Mark Sloan."

"Agent Riordan isn't here, Doctor." Feldman said. "Last I heard, he was in Vegas."

"I know," Mark replied. "I called to talk to you."

"What for?"

"A favor," Mark said.

"No can do," Feldman said. "I can't tell you anything about the investigation."

"I was thinking the other way around."

"I don't get it." Feldman said.

"I want to tell *you* some new information about the case," Mark said.

"This should really go to Riordan."

"I don't want to give it to Riordan," Mark said. "I want to give it to you. What I have is a long shot, and it might not lead to anything, but if it does, the credit will be yours."

"What do you get out of it?" Feldman asked suspiciously.

"The satisfaction of doing the right thing," Mark said, "and whatever information you develop off what I'm going to tell you."

"This is my career we're talking about," Feldman said.

"Which could get a significant boost if this lead pans out," Mark said.

"Or I could get fired for telling you anything about the case," Feldman said. "Maybe even prosecuted."

"I don't want you to tell me anything about the case," Mark said. "Just what you find out from this lead."

"What happens after that?" Feldman asked.

"That's up to you," Mark said.

Feldman thought about it. Mark could almost hear the agent's synapses firing, which was more than they were doing when the call began.

"What've you got?" Feldman asked.

"I met Diane Love's killer," Mark said. "I actually spoke to him at the bookstore–coffee house in Keystone."

"The Inxpot," Feldman said. "How do you know it's the guy?"

"The Kauai police got a picture of a possible suspect," Mark said. "They sent it to me and I recognized the face. What are the odds that the same guy would be on Kauai the day Stuart Appleby was killed and in Keystone when Diane Love was murdered?"

"Does Riordan know about this?" Feldman asked.

"Nope," Mark said.

There was silence on the line as Feldman thought some more. Mark waited.

"All you have is a picture," Feldman said. "What do you think I can do?"

"The killer touched a book, *A Confederacy of Dunces* by John Kennedy Toole, and I put it back on the shelf. It was the only copy the store had," Mark said. "If it's still there, we might be able to get his prints off it."

"You want me to drive all the way up to Keystone, obtain the book, and bring it back here to be dusted," Feldman said.

"Yes," Mark said.

"And if by some miracle we get his prints and he's in the system, you want to know his story."

"That's right," Mark said.

"Then what?"

"I don't know," Mark said. "I suppose we'll talk and work something out."

"What's to stop me from taking this straight to Riordan and telling you squat?"

"Nothing at all," Mark said. "But what would you gain from that? Riordan will run with it and leave you behind. Is that really what you want?"

"Why didn't you take it to Riordan?"

Mark chose his words carefully. "We no longer have a productive relationship."

"And I'm the only agent you know in Denver," Feldman said.

"I'll E-mail you the picture of the guy," Mark said. "So will you do me the favor?"

"Sure," Feldman said.

Chapter Twenty-two

Mark sat on his deck with a glass of lemonade and faced the beach. The sky was cloudless and a brilliant blue, the water smooth and dotted with sailboats and, in the far distance, freighters moving slowly up and down the coastline. It was the view entertainment-industry people spent millions of dollars to enjoy, hoarding the sand of the Malibu coast for themselves and fighting interest-group lawsuits demanding access to the beach.

But Mark wasn't looking at the view. His gaze was in front of him on the page of photos depicting the various guises of the killer during his business trip to Hawaii.

For too long, his adversary hid in the shadows, the corpses he left behind the only proof of his existence. Now Mark had a face to look at and the memory of their brief meeting in Colorado. It brought the man to life for him and made the unspoken challenge between them even more real.

Mark felt more pressure to find Brennan and Gregson now, even though nothing had actually changed. He had no reason to think his adversary was making progress while he had stalled, and yet knowing they'd met gave Mark the uncanny sensation that the killer was toying with him.

He had no evidence that the killer even knew who Mark was, or that he'd been any more aware than Mark of who he was talking to at the bookstore. But it was better to assume the killer knew who Mark was and engineered the meeting for his amusement than to assume otherwise.

Mark believed it was always wiser to assume intelligence over stupidity, planning over coincidence, because it forced him not to underestimate his adversaries. His feeling was you could never go wrong giving your adversary more credit than he might deserve; it only made you better prepared for the inevitable confrontation.

They *would* meet again, Mark was certain of that. And when they did, he wanted to be sure the encounter ended with the killer in handcuffs.

In his mind he went over their short conversation at the bookstore several times. Was there was anything Mark saw, or that the man said, that should have tipped him off? There was nothing. It had been small talk. A typical, meaningless conversation between two strangers.

Then again, that in itself was somewhat revealing.

The killer hadn't taken the opportunity to drop some kind of hint, to toy with him in such a way that later, upon reflection, Mark might realize how thoroughly he'd been duped. The killer didn't try to play with him, at least not as far as Mark could tell.

So this wasn't a mind game for the killer. This was about something else.

This was business.

Mark thought about what he knew, or rather what he could surmise, about the killer based on his actions. The man was no ordinary, professional killer. Most of them would kill anyone that someone was willing to pay to have murdered. However, this hit man was apparently selective about who he killed, choosing only fugitives from justice. And if Standiford was to be believed, he spared innocent bystanders.

What kind of man did that make this killer?

He wasn't a sociopath, or one life would be as meaningless to him as the next. And he wasn't a cold-blooded assassin, either. Most professional killers didn't think twice about murdering anyone who might present a threat to their freedom or livelihood. No one was an innocent in their world.

But this killer didn't see it that way. He only killed people who'd committed crimes. This killer seemed to be following some kind of ethical code, which suggested a greater purpose than the pleasure of killing.

Was he a vigilante?

Not in the usual sense, anyway. A vigilante killed for revenge or a personal sense of justice; he didn't do it for a living. Mark doubted the killer had any personal stake in the kidnapping and death of Connie Standiford.

So what drove him to kill? Was he some self-styled bounty hunter? Or was he simply a market-conscious killer who'd carved out his own commercial niche?

The killer had obviously staked out a corner of the murder-for-hire marketplace for himself, but Mark didn't think the hit man was doing it just for the money. The killer had extraordinary patience, the willingness to track his targets for months or years. Patience like that came from strength, from conviction. Money wasn't enough to sustain that kind of implacable will. The profit wasn't just financial for this man; he was rewarded on some deeper level.

The key to understanding this killer, and to beating him, would be to discover where his ethical code came from, what sustained his will, and what drove him to kill.

The answer to all those questions was going to be the same thing. Mark just had to find it.

For now, all Mark had to go on was a grainy picture and the memory of a fleeting encounter. He hoped for more. It was the only hope he had left of solving this case.

Mark figured it would take Feldman a few hours to get up to Keystone, a few hours to get back, and then the book had to be dusted and the prints run through AFIS. So it would be a day or two at best before he'd know if the book would yield any clues.

Mark would have to be patient.

Meanwhile, Steve, Amanda, and Jesse were beginning to compile the information on wealthy families who'd suffered the violent loss of a loved one. It was laborious and time-consuming work with no guarantee of a payoff.

Mark would have to be patient about that, too.

Patience. It was something the hit man was quite good at, a quality Mark wasn't sure he could match.

After a time, it grew chilly and a wind rose up off the sea. Mark finished his lemonade and went into the house.

The recipe cards and Dr. Plume's brochure were still on the coffee table from the night before. He gathered up the cards and glanced through Dr. Plume's brochure again. It amazed him how some people wore their bodies like clothes, changing them to match the fashion trends of the moment. Somehow, it seemed wrong to call the practioners of this kind of surgery doctors, or what they did medicine.

He closed the brochure and looked at the picture of the buxom woman on the back above Dr. Plume's address and phone number. Her breasts were clearly enhanced, but he wondered if the look was achieved from surgery or an airbrush. It was hardly a secret anymore that the pictures of models on the covers of magazines were heavily retouched to create a look neither nature nor medicine could match. Yet that didn't stop women from striving to achieve it, men from expecting it, or doctors from promising it, even if they couldn't actually deliver.

Mark put the cards on his desk and was about to set down the brochure, too, when the picture of the woman drew his attention again.

Did he know her? No. Was he attracted to her? No. So what was so interesting about the picture?

He put down the brochure, started to walk away, then turned back and picked it up again. There was something nagging at him, the mental equivalent of an itch demanding to be scratched. Mark had felt this sensation many times over the years, and had learned to respect it.

His subconscious mind was working. Some fact, some tidbit of information, was rising to the surface of his consciousness, fighting through the clutter to be noticed.

What was it?

He scanned the back of the brochure from top to bottom. And that's when he saw it, at the very bottom of the page. It was the name and address of the company that printed the glossy brochure.

Roswell Imaging in Albuquerque, New Mexico.

Mark had seen that name before. He picked up one of the recipe cards from the Royal Hawaiian. There it was, at the bottom of the card. The cards and the brochure were produced by the same company.

Dr. Morris Plume in Beverly Hills and Stuart Appleby in Kauai had both used a graphics and printing company in New Mexico. Why go to someone so far from home?

Mark picked up the phone and dialed the number for Roswell Imaging on the card. After a few rings, a woman answered.

"Roswell Imaging, how can I help you today?" She said energetically.

"I picked up one of your recipe cards at a restaurant in Hawaii and I'm very impressed with the quality of the work," Mark said.

"Thank you," she replied. "That's always nice to hear."

"I was wondering what kind of services you provide."

"I'd be happy to tell you all about them, but I'd rather show you," she said. "Our work itself best illustrates our versatility and attention to detail for any graphics job. I can mail you some materials or you can visit our Web site."

She gave him the Web site address. Mark thanked her and hung up. He sat down at his desk, logged on to the Internet, and went to the Roswell Imaging site. It was very slick and professional, full of colorful, animated graphics and crisp photos. Mark learned that the company specialized in printing graphics and digital imaging of all kinds: photographs, books, video presentations, magazines, brochures, and Web sites, among other things. Mark browsed through some examples of their work. Their clients included major corporations around the country, so it wasn't inconceivable that both Dr. Plume and Stuart Appleby could have stumbled on them independently.

But Mark didn't believe it was a coincidence.

Roswell Imaging was definitely a real, reputable company, not some kind of code, like Appleby's note about an "ideal oven."

Or was it?

Mark wrote down the company name on a piece of scratch paper.

Roswell Imaging.

Underneath it, he wrote the names of the two fugitives who remained at large.

Jason Brennan.

William Gregson.

He'd barely finished writing down Gregson's name when it fell into place for him. The letters, that is.

Two Gs. Two Ls. One W. One M.

Roswell Imaging might be a genuine company. But it was also an anagram for William Gregson.

"It didn't make sense to me that Stuart Appleby would only keep contact information on one of his fellow kidnappers," Mark said to Steve, who sat, nursing a beer, across from him at the kitchen table later that night. Between them was the recipe card and the sheet of photos that Kealoha sent. "Now I know why. He didn't. And neither did Diane Love. The location of the four fugitives was on that single recipe card all along."

"So where's Jason Brennan?" Steve asked.

"I haven't cracked that yet," Mark said with a weary sigh. "But I know it has to be hidden on that recipe card somewhere."

Steve picked up the recipe card off the table and examined it. "All that's left is the address of the restaurant, which we know is real, and the recipe for the lemongrass-seared island opah, whatever that is. You don't think he meant Oprah do you?"

"I don't think so," Mark said.

"Then you've just shot down the only contribution I have to make toward solving this puzzle," Steve said, dropping the card.

"If the recipe is an anagram, like everything else has been, I haven't figured it out yet," Mark said. "And I've stared at the picture of the entree until I've gone cross-eyed."

"So what's your next move?"

"I believe William Gregson is Jerry Bodie, owner of Roswell Imaging, which was founded five years ago in Albuquerque," Mark said. "So that's where I'm flying first thing tomorrow morning."

"Have you contacted the FBI?"

"Nope," Mark said.

Steve's expression hardened. "Dad, you can't do this alone. William Gregson is a murderer, and if you confront him he might kill you. And if he doesn't—" He picked up the sheet of paper with the pictures of the hit man on it. "Maybe this guy will."

"I have no intention of confronting Gregson alone," Mark said. "But I'd rather not involve the FBI just yet. I'd like to keep this 'in the family.'"

Steve grinned. "Terry is going to be sorry he ever said that to you."

"You wouldn't happen to have any friends in the Albuquerque Police Department who owe you a favor?"

"As a matter of fact, I do," Steve said. "Detective Norman Begay."

"How do you know him?"

"A couple years ago I helped him track down a runaway who witnessed a murder in Albuquerque. We found her hiding in Van Nuys. He took her back to New Mexico, and her testimony ended up putting the killer away."

"What kind of man is Begay?"

"Quiet," Steve said. "But determined."

"Perfect," Mark said.

Chapter Twenty-three

Albuquerque was a city that seemed to exist in three different eras at once, and Mark Sloan drove through all of them on his way from the airport to the police station where Norman Begay worked.

There was the Albuquerque that was forever stuck in the nineteenth century, when it was a dusty adobe settlement on the Old Chihuahua Trail along the Rio Grande river. There was the Albuquerque that was a colorful stop on Route 66, an endless street of hamburger stands and motels, all screaming for attention with their neon signs and jet-age architecture. And then there was the Albuquerque striving for tomorrow, with its gleaming high-rises, weapons labs, and software companies.

Norman Begay's police station seemed to straddle an invisible nexus where all three cities, in all three dimensions, quietly collided. The single-story, modern adobe-style police station was on busy boulevard, across from the outer edge of Old Town. On one side of the police station was a motel that looked the same as it did the day it opened in 1955. And on the other side was a striking three-story office building that mixed a variety of materials and architectural styles so that it simultaneously complemented and clashed with all the buildings around it.

Mark parked his rented Crown Victoria in the lot, where it blended right in with the city-owned Crown Victoria squad cars and Crown Victoria unmarked vehicles already there. He stepped out into the dry heat and walked quickly into the cool, air-conditioned station.

He announced himself to the uniformed officer at the counter, and after a few moments, Det. Begay came out to meet him.

Begay was a stocky and craggy-faced. He was what a rocky red mesa would look like if it came to life as a human being and bought itself a suit at a garage sale. The Navajo cop extended his huge hand to Mark. They shook hands.

"Norman Begay," the cop said.

"Mark Sloan," he said. "I appreciate you taking the time to help me out. Did my son fill you in on the details?"

Begay nodded affirmatively and motioned toward the door. "Let's walk."

They crossed the street to the Old Town, a maze of authentic and recreated adobe and frontier-style buildings grouped around a tree-shaded plaza and the 290-year-old Church of San Felipe De Neri. They walked around the plaza in silence for a while, the heat pressing on them, before Mark grew impatient.

"What's your take on things?" Mark asked.

"What things?" Begay said.

"On Jerry Bodie being William Gregson," Mark said.

"He could be," Begay said. "Then again, maybe he's not."

"Stuart Appleby hid the contact information for his fellow kidnappers in anagrams on a recipe card. Roswell Imaging is an anagram for William Gregson," Mark said. "The company was formed five years ago, right after the Standiford kidnapping, and they printed Appleby's recipe cards and the brochures for the plastic surgeon who gave the fugitives their new faces. I'm convinced Bodie is Gregson."

"You ever tried to use an anagram to convince a jury of something?"

"Nope," Mark said.

"You want to?"

"I'm hoping I don't have to."

"I don't blame you," Begay said. "But it would be pretty amusing to watch you try."

All along the plaza, Navajo street venders sat on the sidewalk under the shade of store awnings, their backs against the cool adobe walls, and displayed their handcrafted wares on blankets spread out in front of them. Tourists crouched over the blankets and examined silver and turquoise jewelry, belt buckles, and assorted pottery.

"Do you know anything about Jerry Bodie?" Mark asked.

"I know where he lives," Begay said.

"Is he still alive?" Mark asked.

"As far as I know."

Mark was relieved to hear that. It appeared, at least for the moment, that he was finally one step ahead of his adversary.

"I'd like to see him," Mark said.

"What makes you think he'll see you?" Begay said. "It may not be time for his annual physical."

"That's where you come in," Mark said.

Begay grunted in acknowledgment, or he was just clearing his throat—Mark wasn't entirely sure.

"What do you intend to do when you meet him?" Begay asked.

"I'm going to confront him, make him think I have more evidence than I actually do, and watch him crumble."

"Uh-huh," Begay said.

"But if he doesn't, I'll tell him about his dead friends and that he's next on the killer's list, and he'll be so terrified he'll confess to his crimes just to get your protection."

"So you think he's going to crumble and confess?"

"It's been known to happen," Mark said.

"For you?" Begay asked skeptically.

Mark nodded, projecting more optimism than he actually felt.

"I'd like to see that," Begay said.

"Me, too." Usually, when suspects cracked it was after Mark had confronted them with a lot more than some anagrams and the strength of his own convictions.

"What's your alternative?" Begay asked.

"Hope he survives long enough for me to build a case against him," Mark said. "With your help, I'll try to find cracks in his fake identity and his fictional past."

They walked in silence for a few minutes.

Mark glanced at the leather belts, rabbit skins, and dream catchers offered by an impossibly old Navajo woman, who was intently reading a Jackie Collins novel. He could feel his shirt sticking to his sweat-dampened back, but Begay, in his navy blue suit, didn't seem to be perspiring at all.

"You're a doctor," Begay said.

"Yes," Mark said.

"And you solve murders."

"I'm also a pretty good dancer," Mark said with a friendly smile.

Begay stopped, turned, and pointed to a small growth on his cheek, up toward his temple. "See this?"

"Yes," Mark said.

"Will I live?"

"I haven't met anyone who's died from a mole yet," Mark said. "But I suppose you could be the first."

Begay's lips curled into what Mark assumed was his approximation of a grin.

"Bodie lives in Corrales. I've got a patrol car watching the place," Begay said. "You can follow me out there."

Mark followed Begay north out of the city through an upscale neighborhood of homes that mixed Pueblo, ranch, and Mediterranean-inspired architecture with equally mixed results. There were no sidewalks. People on horseback rode on trails that paralleled the road, ran along the Rio Grande river, and disappeared into the thick wooded area known as the Bosque. The stores and restaurants they passed had hitching posts.

Jerry Bodie's house was an unassuming two-story contemporary adobe with a well-kept lawn, a small horse-riding ring, a detached garage, and a stable. The house, like all the others on the street, backed up against a dry irrigation levee and, beyond it, a forest of big cottonwoods.

Begay and Mark pulled up behind the patrol car, which was parked across the street from Bodie's house. Begay got out of his car. The officer rolled down his window. Begay leaned inside, said a few words to the officer, and the patrol car drove off. Mark joined him and together they approached the low front gate, which was more for show than protection. Begay hit the buzzer.

"Yes?" A woman's voice answered. It sounded familiar, even behind the crackle of static.

"Norman Begay, Albuquerque Police. I'd like to talk with Jerry Bodie."

"Come on up," she said, and Mark placed the voice. She was the woman who'd answered when he called Roswell Imaging.

The gate opened and they walked up the crushed gravel driveway to the house, where the woman was waiting for them, holding the front door open. She wore very short shorts, a loose-fitting shirt, and a big smile. Mark guessed she was in her early twenties.

"Can I see your badge?" she asked with almost childlike excitement.

Begay flashed his badge. She leaned forward and studied it, biting her lower lip.

"Cool," she said, then glanced at Mark. "What about yours?"

"I'm not a cop," Mark said.

"What are you?" she asked.

"I'm a doctor. My name is Mark Sloan. What's yours?"

She smiled. "Cloris O'Dell."

"What's your relationship to Mr. Bodie, if I may ask?" Mark said.

"I'm his squeeze," she said brightly. "And he's my stud."

"Do you live with Mr. Bodie?" Begay asked.

"Sometimes," she said, trying hard to be cute and largely succeeding. "Is that illegal now?"

"Depends," Begay said. "Are you underage?"

"That's the nicest thing anyone has said to me in a long time," She gave him a big smile. "You're a flirt, Detective."

Mark couldn't be certain, but he didn't think Begay was joking.

"We'd like to speak with Mr. Bodie," Mark said. "Do you know where we could find him?"

"Sure," Cloris stepped aside and let them in. "He's in the den, playing with his trains."

The house was lushly furnished with stone floors, leather furniture, and Native American paintings and artifacts on the walls. She led them to the den, where Jerry Bodie stood in the center of an elaborate, chest-high model of a small town and the surrounding countryside. A railroad system ran through the miniature town, over elaborately detailed bridges, and through tunnels, past ranches, cattle, cars, and people.

Bodie was dressed in a T-shirt and denim overalls and wore a conductor's hat. He was on the pudgy side and hairy everywhere except on his head, which was probably why he was wearing the hat, beyond the allure of getting into character.

The sound of the railroad train chugging along the track, its smokestack puffing and its whistle blowing, was loud enough to block Jerry from hearing the doorbell or Mark and Begay's arrival. Jerry didn't notice they were there until his girlfriend yelled his name.

Jerry looked up, startled at the sight of the two strangers in his den, and shut down his railroad.

"These guys came to see you," Cloris said.

"What are they selling?" Jerry said pleasantly to her, as if they weren't there.

"They're cops," Cloris said, then corrected herself. "Well, he is," she tilted her head toward Begay. "The other one is a doctor."

"I'm Det. Norman Begay, Albuquerque Police." Begay flashed his badge. "And this is Dr. Mark Sloan."

Jerry Bodie looked blankly at them both. "What can I do for you?"

Mark took a piece of paper out of his pocket and held it out for Jerry to see. The paper contained the photos Kealoha sent Mark of the suspected hit man.

"Have you ever seen this man?" Mark asked.

Jerry glanced at the pictures. "No, I don't think so."

"That's a relief," Mark said. "Because he wants to kill you."

"Me?" Jerry said, shocked. "Why?"

"It's a little complicated to explain, so please be patient with me," Mark said. "Do you remember the Standiford kidnapping? It happened in Las Vegas, about five years ago."

Jerry shook his head. "No, I don't recall that."

"It was around the time you moved out here and started up your business," Mark said. "You were probably too busy with all of that to be paying much attention to the news. Roger Standiford owns a bunch of casinos. A gang of kidnappers took his daughter and demanded a $4.5 million ransom. He paid it."

"I remember that," Cloris said. "The girl who was buried in a pit, right? She died, didn't she?"

"Yes, she did," Mark said. "And the four kidnappers disappeared with the ransom. We think Roger Standiford hired a hit man to track down the fugitives and kill them."

"What does any of that have to do with me?" Jerry asked.

"One of the kidnappers changed his identity, moved to Hawaii, and opened a restaurant," Mark said. "His name was Stuart Appleby, but he called himself Danny Royal."

"We know him!" Cloris shrieked, raising a hand to her mouth and looking wide-eyed at Jerry. "Oh, my God, we know him!"

"Why don't you go make us some iced tea," Jerry said. "I'll take care of this."

"Iced tea?" She said. "Since when do we drink iced tea? I want to hear this."

"Cloris, please." Jerry said firmly.

She glared at Jerry and stomped off. As soon as she was gone, Jerry turned to Mark.

"We don't know him, per se. He's a client of ours," Jerry

said. "We made some postcards for his restaurant. Souvenirs with pictures and recipes on them. That's where our relationship with him begins and ends."

"It's definitely ended," Mark said. "He's dead."

"Dead?" Jerry said, glancing at Begay, who's stone face revealed nothing.

"Murdered, actually," Mark said. "The killer fed him to sharks."

"Sharks?" Jerry took a deep breath and let it out slowly, the color draining from his face. "That's horrible."

"Worse than you can imagine," Mark said. "I saw what was left of him. He looked like a half-eaten sandwich."

"I still don't see what this has to do with me," Jerry said. "I hardly knew the guy. We just made some postcards for him, that's all."

"I wish it was," Mark said glumly. "One of the other kidnappers, Diane Lovc, was just murdered. And you know what she had in her kitchen?"

Mark took out a Royal Hawaiian recipe card from his pocket and held it up.

"One of these," he said.

"She must have visited the restaurant," Jerry said. "And took home one of the recipe cards as a souvenir or a way to keep his phone number handy."

"That would certainly explain it," Mark said. "But unfortunately, the name of your company is at the bottom of the card."

"Of course it is," Jerry said. "Because we made it. Whenever our clients let us, we put our name and address on our work so it doubles as advertising for us."

"That makes good business sense," Mark said. "Except the killer isn't going to see it that way."

"Why not?" Jerry said.

"Because you also did the brochure for Dr. Morris Plume's plastic surgery clinic," Mark said. "And your company name and address are on that brochure, too."

"So?" Jerry said.

"Dr. Plume gave the four kidnappers their new faces,"

Mark said. "And a couple days ago, someone broke into his office and stole all his files."

"I'm completely lost here," Jerry said. "We make a lot of brochures for a lot of doctors. Maybe this Danny Royal got the idea to hire us from our work on the brochure."

"I'm sure that's probably what happened," Mark said. "But I'm afraid the killer isn't going to believe the connection is so benign."

"Why not?" Jerry said. "It's the logical explanation."

"Because the name of your company is an anagram," Mark said.

"What's that?" Jerry said.

"A word or phrase made by transposing the letters of another word or phrase," Begay said.

Mark smiled at Begay. "Exactly."

"I still don't see the problem," Begay said.

"Roswell Imaging is an anagram for William Gregson," Mark said. "One of the kidnappers."

"Murderers," Begay corrected.

"Right," Mark said. "Kidnapper and murderer. Now do you see the situation?"

"No," Jerry said, swallowing hard.

"The hit man is going to think you're William Gregson," Mark said. "And he's going to kill you."

"It's a coincidence," Jerry protested. "That's all."

"It appears you're a victim of your own advertising." Mark said. "Of course, there's also the other coincidence."

"What other coincidence?" Jerry said, his voice becoming a bit shrill.

"You moved to New Mexico and started your company a short time after the Standiford kidnapping," Mark said. "That isn't going to look so good to the hit man. Fact is, you add it all up, I could even be convinced you're William Gregson."

"Me, too," Begay said.

"This is a terrible mistake." Jerry sat down slowly on a stool and took off his cap. He looked longingly at the small town in front of him, as if he wished he could shrink and disappear into it.

"At least you're still alive," Mark said. "We'd like to keep you that way."

Jerry looked up. "What do you have in mind?"

"Protective custody," Mark said. "We can put you under round-the-clock protection right here, or in one of the city's nicest hotels, until we can catch this guy."

Jerry sat for a long moment, thinking. Finally, he cleared his throat and said, "I don't believe I need protection."

"You would if you'd seen the parts of Danny Royal that the shark spit out," Mark said.

"Thankfully, there are no sharks in Corrales," Jerry said, standing up again, regaining some of his composure. "I appreciate your concern, but I don't think I'm in any danger. No offense, but I doubt anyone would see these events the way you have. It's a mishmash of coincidence and conjecture that's predicated on a huge contrivance and a complete disregard of common sense."

Begay glanced at Mark. "Aren't you glad he preceded all that with 'no offense' first?"

"The hit man is going to scrutinize your finances, pick apart your past, and look into every aspect of your life," Mark said.

"Then I'm even more confident that I'm safe, because then he will certainly discover his mistake," Jerry said, putting on his cap again. "Now, if you'll excuse me, I don't get much time to play with my trains."

Jerry turned his back to the two men and started up his train again, filling the room with the whistles and chug-chug-chugging of the locomotive on its tiny tracks.

Mark and Begay saw themselves out.

Chapter Twenty-Four

"He didn't confess," Begay said as they walked to their cars.

"Not overtly," Mark said.

"Not at all," Begay replied.

"All we have to do now is wait for him to run."

"We?"

"I can't watch him alone," Mark said. "His house opens up on a forest. It's going to take half a dozen men to do this right."

"I can't help you on that," Begay said, stopping at his car.

"I thought you owed my son a favor," Mark said.

"I did," Begay said. "And I've just repaid it. I can't justify the manpower or the hours necessary to watch this man."

"You don't believe he's William Gregson?"

Begay shrugged. "Whoever he is, I think he's right about your evidence. There isn't enough there, certainly not enough to convince my captain it's worth paying the overtime to watch this guy."

"You know he's lying," Mark said.

Begay nodded. "I'll check him out, work the phones a bit, maybe come up with something more convincing than an anagram."

Mark sighed. "Someone has to try to watch him. I'll park myself here as long as I can."

"Think what you'll save on hotels," Begay said, glancing

at his watch. "I'll ask for a patrol car to cruise by every hour or two. There's a shopping center up the street. I'll stay here while you get whatever you think you're gonna need."

"Thanks," Mark said and went back to his car.

Mark parked his car around the corner from Jerry's house and angled his rearview and side-view mirrors so he could recline comfortably in his seat and keep a constant watch on any comings or goings.

There weren't any.

He wasn't trained in surveillance nor did he have much experience doing it, so he didn't have any clever tricks for getting past the crushing boredom. Worse than that was the heat. He didn't dare keep the motor running so he could use the air conditioner, for fear of drawing attention to himself. So instead he rolled down the windows and toughed it out, his back sticking to the hot leather seat.

Mark kept himself hydrated with bottled water and munched on fresh fruit, raisins, and unsalted nuts. True to his word, Begay did send by a patrol car, the officers acknowledging Mark with a nod as they passed each hour. Between Mark and the patrol cars, it didn't amount to much surveillance or protection, but at least Jerry Bodie/William Gregson couldn't just hop in his car and speed off without being noticed. Still, Mark was keenly aware of the inadequacy of the effort, and the opportunities and dangers posed by the irrigation ditch and the forest behind the house.

He used the time in the car to study the recipe card, trying to figure out where in it Jason Brennan was hiding. The key to finding the fugitive was there somewhere, just as it had been for Stuart Appleby, Diane Love, and William Gregson. But as hard as Mark tried, he just didn't see it.

Shortly after nightfall, when the temperature finally dropped below three figures and Mark was reasonably comfortable for the first time, his cell phone trilled.

"Mark Sloan," he answered.

"Bart Feldman here," said the tired voice on the other end of the line. "I went up to Keystone, got the book, and ran the prints. It must not be a very popular title."

"Why do you say that?"

"Not that many unique prints on it," Feldman said.

"Were you able to match any of them?"

"We got yours, we got the bookseller's, and the guy you were talking to," Feldman said. "I got his picture here, and he's definitely the same guy in the Hawaii shots you sent me."

Mark felt his pulse quicken. "Who is he?"

"Raymond Wyatt," Feldman said. "Did some time in the military, mostly overseas doing covert wetwork for Special Forces. When he got out, he joined the Baltimore PD and rose up to the Major Crimes Unit, Special Investigations Division."

"He's a cop?" Mark asked incredulously.

"Used to be," Feldman said. "He quit about eight years ago, right after a big case he'd put together against some pedophile fell apart. The bad guy walked, and so did Wyatt."

"Where is Wyatt now?"

"Nobody knows," Feldman said. "Wyatt disappeared. Here's an interesting tidbit, though. The pedophile got himself killed a few months later. Fell asleep in his recliner, smoking a cigarette. His whole house burned down."

Feldman had more to say: that Wyatt was a decorated soldier but had been disciplined at the Baltimore PD for violating the civil rights of suspects and for using excessive force, though no formal charges were ever filed against him. He described Wyatt as an expert in hand-to-hand combat, firearms, electronic surveillance, interrogation, and undercover work.

There were more details, which Mark eventually wanted to hear, but he already knew what was important. He was beginning to get a sense of the man and, perhaps, the ethical code that drove him.

* * *

It was a great life, and Jerry Bodie hated to leave it behind, but it was better than having his ass fed to sharks.

Maybe in his next life he'd try being an actor, because he'd given an Oscar-caliber performance for the doctor and the Indian cop. When the doctor said Stuart and Diane were dead, it was all he could do not to start shaking. But he'd done it. He'd taken command of himself and overcome, as he would now.

He was lying naked in bed beside Cloris, listening to her breathing, waiting to be absolutely sure the sleeping pills he'd ground into her dinner had taken hold. The last thing he wanted was for her to wake up in middle of his escape. He'd miss her and her limber young body, though not as much as he'd miss his horses and his miniature trains.

Jerry got up and quickly got dressed. He didn't bother packing anything; the only essentials he needed were the overseas bank account numbers in his head, the false passports in his pockets, and the $50,000 in the money belt around his waist.

He'd sneak into the stable, hitch up one of the horses, and ride out the back into the Bosque, following it into the city unnoticed. In an hour or two, he'd leave his horse grazing in somebody's field, walk to a street, and phone a cab from a convenience store. Then he'd take a bus over the border, and then figure out where to go from there while enjoying a margarita and a nice rib eye steak.

By the time the cops or Standiford's hired gun showed up, he'd be long gone, starting his third life somewhere really different. France maybe. Or Australia.

In a way, it was kind of exciting. A year from now, he'd be living somewhere else with a new life, a new name, and new face. It was like a gift. How many people ever got the opportunity to start over, as if they'd never existed, and to do it without going broke first?

He was getting too fat and comfortable as Jerry Bodie, anyway. It was time to move on. He chose to look at this as a much-needed and welcome wake-up call. He'd let his guard down and nearly paid the ultimate price for it.

Jerry peered out the back door. It was pitch black outside, darker even than the night Roger Standiford went into the desert with his bags full of money. He took a deep breath and smiled. The air felt charged with excitement and possibility, just as it had five years ago.

He crept to the stable and slipped inside. The two horses, Enterprise and Voyager, stirred gently in their stalls. Jerry took a step toward Enterprise and was suddenly pulled backward, a muscular arm tight across his throat, a big hand clamped on his jaw, someone's warm breath in his ear.

"Roger Standiford sends his regards," a voice whispered.

Jerry whimpered pleadingly. "It was an accident."

"This isn't," Wyatt said and neatly broke Jerry's neck. He released his hold and let the body drop to the hay-strewn floor.

Wyatt stood for a moment, collecting his thoughts, formulating his plan.

He knew Mark Sloan was just a few yards away, sitting in his rental car. It would be so easy to kill him, if Wyatt was that sort of man. But he wasn't, and killing the doctor wouldn't do much good now, anyway. The damage was done.

Wyatt had been high up in the trees, watching the house and Mark with infrared binoculars, when he intercepted the cell phone call from Agent Feldman. Wyatt was astonished to learn how sloppy he'd been in Hawaii, and how stupid and careless in Colorado, and how quickly it had cost him his anonymity. Now he'd have to go to ground the way his prey did, maybe even resort to plastic surgery himself.

He'd always known his life as Raymond Wyatt was over, but he'd never reconciled himself to the possibility that he'd become as hunted as the men he pursued. He certainly never thought he'd be unmasked by an amateur like Dr. Mark Sloan.

Wyatt realized now that he'd let his huge advantage over

the doctor lull him into dangerous complacency. His ego had emerged and he'd indulged it. It was ego that compelled him to talk with the doctor in Keystone, to step out of the safety of the shadows. He never should have given in to that temptation. It had cost him dearly.

Now that he'd identified his own critical weakness, his inflated ego, he'd examine it and adjust his future behavior accordingly. He wouldn't make the same mistake again. If anything, the revelation of his own incompetence would become a psychological asset. He would remind himself of his failures every day. That should keep his ego in check.

But there was no time for regrets, only action, now. He had to erase any possible clues he'd left behind, and let Jason Brennan know, wherever he was, that his days of freedom, of simply breathing, would soon be over.

The first thing Mark noticed were the horses trotting out of the stable into the ring. He sat up in his seat and saw tongues of fire licking out of the stable doors.

Mark immediately started the ignition, shifted the car into reverse and, looking over his shoulder, floored the gas pedal. The car shot backward across the street, peeling rubber, and smashed through the white picket fence that surrounded Jerry Bodie's property. He shifted the car into drive and sped right up to the stable, which was already engulfed in flames.

He jumped out of the car. The back door of the stable was open and he could see a body on the floor, in the calm center of the firestorm. It was Jerry Bodie.

Mark took a deep breath, bent over, and dashed into the stable, which had become a swirling tunnel of fire. The air was heavy with the intense heat. It was like running through superheated Jell-O. He grabbed Jerry under the arms and dragged him out, but it was obvious to Mark that he was rescuing a corpse. Jerry's neck hung too loosely from his shoulders, his eyes open and unseeing, his face a death mask forever capturing his last seconds of terror.

He dragged Bodie's body to the car, a safe distance from the inferno, then grabbed his cell phone and dialed 911.

Mark reported the fire and the murder to the operator, then realized, as he saw the flames lapping against the house, he hadn't seen Cloris leave. She was still inside. He tossed the cell phone into the car and ran into the house.

"Cloris!" he yelled as soon as he entered, but there was no response. Already smoke was beginning to fill the house and he could see the fire against the windows.

He hurried up the stairs to the master bedroom. Cloris was naked, sleeping deeply, in the large bed. Mark nudged her hard, shouting her name, but she barely stirred. So he yanked off her sheets, sat her upright, and shook her.

"Wake up," he shouted.

Her eyes fluttered open, and then widened in surprise when she saw Mark staring her in the face.

Mark yanked her to her feet. "The house is on fire—you have to get out of here."

She looked back to the bed for Jerry.

"He's gone," Mark wrapped a bathrobe loosely around her and steered the dazed woman out of the room.

Once she was in the smoke-filled hallway and saw the fire lashing against the windows, her head instantly cleared. Cloris charged past Mark and ran screaming out of the house ahead of him. She flung open the front door and bolted into the night, her untied bathrobe flaring out behind her like wings.

Mark emerged from the house a few moments later, coughing hard, just as the fire trucks, paramedics, and police cars came screaming up the street, sirens wailing.

The blazing stable collapsed into an enormous campfire, smoke and embers spiraling up into the night sky in a thick plume. The next instant fire spit out of the top-floor windows of the house. By morning, William Gregson's existence on the earth would be cleansed by fire.

Mark glanced at Cloris, hunched sobbing over the body of her dead lover, then he shifted his gaze beyond the fire to the darkness of the Bosque. The dense forest was cold and implacable, like the man it hid.

Wyatt was in there somewhere, watching. Mark could feel it.

Chapter Twenty-five

Mark didn't wait for Terry Riordan to arrive from Las Vegas and execute his wrath. He gave a detailed statement to Norman Begay, filled out reams of insurance papers at the rental-car agency, and flew out of Albuquerque as fast as he could.

It looked like the cowardly act of a defeated man, running away in shame, unwilling to face the consequences of his failure.

That's exactly the way Mark wanted it to look.

Terry Riordan would believe it and so would Wyatt. They would believe it because it was pretty close to the truth.

He *had* been defeated. And he didn't want to face the fury of the FBI just yet. But he wasn't ashamed and he certainly wasn't giving up.

Mark was far too angry to quit now. He'd been bested too many times by Wyatt. It was as if the hit man knew Mark better than he knew himself. He seemed to know what Mark was thinking before Mark was thinking it. And as a result, Diane Love and William Gregson were dead.

Of course, Wyatt had several advantages he didn't. Wyatt had five years to study and track the kidnappers. And unlike Mark, he knew all about his pursuer. If Wyatt wasn't aware of him in Hawaii, he was after Mark's meeting with Roger Standiford. Learning all about Mark would have been simple. There was plenty of information about him, going back decades, in the public record. There were countless newspaper articles and trial transcripts that detailed the cases he'd solved and the methods he'd used to do it. Wyatt would have studied those, as Mark would have studied Wyatt's past had he known who the hit man was earlier.

Intellectually, Mark knew and accepted all of that. And yet emotionally, it didn't matter. He was furious with himself for not being smarter and faster than his opponent. It was as if Wyatt was feeding off Mark's progress, rising to the challenge of an adversary.

Mark knew the feeling and understood its power, because it was driving him, too. It had been driving him ever since he'd discovered the shark attack was a murder and he'd felt presence of the killer lurking in the shadows.

No, that was a lie.

It didn't begin for Mark Sloan then. It began a long, long time ago. Deep down, Mark knew he didn't solve murders to see the guilty get punished for their crimes or for the intellectual challenge of solving a complex puzzle. What always compelled him, what kept him going without sleep for days on end, was the thrill of the hunt, the pure adrenaline rush of the chase. It was a drug, and he was an addict.

In that way, Mark probably wasn't so different from Wyatt. From what little Mark knew about Wyatt, he was sure the man also believed he was motivated by a desire to see justice done. It would explain Wyatt's ethical code, his unwillingness to kill innocent bystanders and potential witnesses.

But that's where the similarities between the two men ended. Mark worked within the law, Wyatt outside it. Mark apprehended criminals, Wyatt killed them.

It was those differences that Mark Sloan couldn't abide and why he would continue to pursue Wyatt no matter what happened to Jason Brennan.

Or was it more personal than that? Was it anger at being consistently outsmarted?

Perhaps Wyatt didn't really know Mark at all. Perhaps

he'd tracked Diane Love and William Gregson based on information he'd found at Stuart Appleby's home in Kauai. Maybe Wyatt hadn't outsmarted Mark; it just *appeared* that way. Maybe all this time Mark was simply catching up to Wyatt, only not quite fast enough.

Regardless of which explanation was true, Wyatt was definitely feeling the pressure, too. It showed in his work. The hit man was killing quickly and brutally now, without the detailed planning and careful execution he'd displayed in Stuart Appleby's murder. He hadn't bothered to make William Gregson's death look accidental. Wyatt knew there was no point anymore, that his time to act was running out.

And Mark was the reason why. Knowing that, and accepting it, suddenly made Mark feel better.

This was the endgame now, and Mark was determined to win. He was convinced that the key to second-guessing his adversary was right in front of him, like the anagram that hid Jason Brennan's identity, he just couldn't see it yet.

He had to clear his head and relax. Let his unconscious mind sort through the thousands of bits of information he'd accumulated in his investigation. Mark closed his eyes, reclined his economy-class seat, and mentally returned to Hawaii, to the beginning, and walked through it all again, following the path that had led him to Las Vegas, Keystone, and Albuquerque.

The flight was thirty minutes outside Los Angeles when Mark opened his eyes again. He wasn't sure if he'd actually been thinking or dozing, but it didn't matter. He understood more now than he did before. The recipe card was his Rosetta stone, and he knew how to use it.

Mark removed the in-flight phone from the seat back in front of him, swiped his Visa through the credit card reader in the handset, and made a call.

Steve rushed back home, summoned by an urgent phone call from his father. He'd already heard about the debacle in Albuquerque from Terry Riordan, who, without Mark Sloan to yell at, had taken his fury out on Steve instead. He'd also heard from Norman Begay, who said he felt responsible for what had happened because he wasn't able to provide the surveillance Mark had asked for. As far as Begay was concerned, he still owed a debt to Steve, and now Mark, as well.

When Steve got home, he found his father at the kitchen table, the Royal Hawaiian recipe cards spread out in front of him, the floor littered with balled-up pieces of yellow legal paper covered in handwritten scrawl.

His father looked terrible, wearing the same wrinkled clothes he'd left in the day before, his white hair askew and dark circles underscoring his bloodshot eyes.

"Maybe you should have called the paramedics instead of me," Steve said. "You look like hell. When was the last time you slept?"

"I've had a few minutes here and there," Mark said. "But that's not important."

"It is to me," Steve said. "I don't want you killing yourself to save a couple of murderers."

"They're still human beings," Mark said.

"That's debatable," Steve said.

"Tell that to Diane Love's husband and kids," Mark said. "I know how to find Jason Brennan."

Steve raised his eyebrows in surprise. "The way you look, I'm surprised you're even able to speak."

"Maybe I had to be a bit deranged to see the solution to the puzzle," Mark said, holding up the recipe card he'd made to replicate the one they'd found in Appleby's safe-deposit box. "Stuart Appleby saved this recipe card because it told him where to find the others who helped him kidnap Connie Standiford. He hid the information in anagrams."

"We knew that already," Steve said. "We just couldn't figure out how it pointed to Jason Brennan."

"This recipe card points to a lot more than that," Mark said. "It's a Rosetta stone, not only to the location of Jason Brennan, but the accounts where the ransom money is hidden. The recipe on this card is actually the key that unlocks the true meaning of the recipes on the other cards."

"How does it work?"

"It's too complicated to explain now and we don't have the time," Mark said. "It's easier for me just to show you."

He handed Steve a legal pad, the pages thick with Mark's hurried, and very sloppy, handwritten notations. Steve quickly scanned it, his eyes widening in shock.

"My God, it's so obvious," Steve said. "Why didn't I see it before?"

"The same reason I didn't," Mark said. "It was so obvious, it was invisible."

Steve stared at the pages for a long time before speaking. "Are you sure about this?"

Mark nodded. "Jason Brennan is Ian Ludlow, the mystery writer. He came out of nowhere five years ago with his first best-seller."

"The timing is certainly right," Steve said.

"He's notoriously press shy," Mark said, "No one knows anything about him."

"Hopefully," Steve said, "that includes Standiford's hired gun."

"Do you think we can move fast enough?"

"Do we have a choice?" Steve asked.

While Steve Sloan tried frantically to reach Ian Ludlow's publishers and agents on a Saturday in New York, Raymond Wyatt lurked in the back alleys and secret passages of the Internet, where passwords and databases were bartered like flesh.

First, he scoured the public record for information about the reclusive author. There were no photographs of Ludlow, who was reportedly single and lived in Los Angeles. The hard-boiled author never attended book-signing events; instead he had his publisher or the bookstore drop ship books to his home for him to inscribe and return. It was widely believed that Ludlow was a pseudonym, perhaps for some already famous writer who wanted to dabble in a different genre.

Wyatt searched the Department of Motor Vehicles, the major credit reporting agencies, and Southern California utility company accounts and couldn't find any record of Ian Ludlow in the Los Angeles area. It seemed that Ian Ludlow was a pseudonym on top of a fake identity. So Wyatt hacked into the computers at Ludlow's publisher, found out which package shipping service they used, then tracked down the address where Ludlow's books were sent for him to autograph. There were two addresses, one in Santa Monica and another in Palm Springs. Both homes were owned by Ian Ludlow's loan-out corporation, so Wyatt wasn't able to determine the author's so-called real name. But he was able to dig up a phone number for each residence and then snoop in the Pacific Bell database to find out which number was the most active over the last forty-eight hours. Nothing was happening on the Santa Monica line, but the Palm Springs number was used as recently as ten minutes ago to call a Chinese restaurant.

Jason Brennan was in Palm Springs.

Wyatt checked out Mark Sloan's location using his laptop, which was tracking feedback from all the electronic surveillance devices. The doctor was at home and surfing the Internet for information on Ludlow while his son worked the phones. From what Wyatt could determine from the digitized records from the wiretaps, Steve Sloan still hadn't been able to reach Ludlow's editor or agent.

The hit man packed up, left the hotel, and headed for Palm Springs. In three to four hours, Jason Brennan would be dead, the Standiford assignment would be over, and Raymond Wyatt would disappear for good.

And in a few months time, a new man with a new face would emerge to carry on Wyatt's legacy of retribution and absolute justice.

* * *

Palm Springs, California, was the last place on earth where Cadillacs and Lincolns were still considered the classiest cars money could buy. Of course, most of the drivers of those cars were old enough to remember a time when *everybody* thought that was true.

This once glamorous resort was, like most of its inhabitants, a mere shadow of its former self, withering away and waiting to die.

There were some people who weren't yet collecting social security who saw a certain retro charm to the place, buying up homes built in the 1950s and '60s and restoring them to their original mediocrity.

One of those people, it seemed, was best-selling author Ian Ludlow, better known to law enforcement and hired hit men as wanted fugitive Jason Brennan. Ludlow lived on an unfenced plot of desert just outside town in a modernistic, flat-topped house that was all glass and stone and light.

It was the light, in fact, that Wyatt saw first that night, gleaming against the impenetrable darkness of the shale mountainside behind the house. It was an isolated retreat, the nearest neighbor more than a hundred yards away, separated by a bleak expanse of dry gravel, gnarled cactus, and lifeless clumps of scrub grass.

Wyatt turned off his headlights, pulled off the road and into the dry desert. He checked his laptop. Mark Sloan was still at home and, according to the captured screen shots from the doctor's computer and the digitized recordings of his phone calls, he had only just discovered Ian Ludlow's addresses. It would be at least an hour or two before anybody would show up here looking for Brennan, and by then it would be too late. All they would find was a corpse.

He took his gun out of the glove box and screwed on a silencer. This kill would be fast and efficient. He removed the bulbs from the interior light of his rental car, opened the door, and got out.

Wyatt was dressed in black and blended seamlessly into the night as he made his way to the house. The property was landscaped with cactus and boulders around a kidney-shaped swimming pool, it's light radiating an unearthly blue glow that reflected off windows and walls of the house. He skirted the circle of light, staying in the shadows until the last possible moment.

The front door was unlocked. He eased the door open, slipped inside the house and into the 1970s: loud patterned wallpaper, thick shag carpet, brightly colored vinyl furniture, and globe-shaped lamps and hanging light fixtures. With the bright light and unshaded windows, Wyatt felt uncomfortably exposed. There were no shadows to hide in. It was as if he was naked. He wanted to end this and get out as fast as possible.

Wyatt heard the soft clickety-clack of fingers on a computer keyboard and followed the sound to a back bedroom that had been converted into an office. The drapes were closed. It made Wyatt feel a bit more comfortable.

A youthful looking man in his thirties, wearing a ratty sweatshirt and faded jeans, sat at his desk with his back to the doorway, all his concentration on the last words he'd ever write for a novel he'd never finish.

The hit man crept silently into the center of the room, his footsteps muffled by the deep shag carpet. He raised his gun and pointed it at the back of Brennan's head.

"Are you sure you want to do that, Ray?"

Wyatt was startled, but his aim didn't waver. The only part of him that moved were his eyes, shifting their cold gaze briefly in the direction of the voice.

Dr. Mark Sloan stood in the adjacent bathroom, leaning casually against the door frame, his arms crossed loosely under his chest.

"Because that isn't Ian Ludlow," Mark said. "Or Jason Brennan."

Wyatt glanced back to the desk, where the man at the keyboard slowly raised his hands and swiveled around to face him, a sheepish grin on his face.

"Hey, you must be Wyatt," Dr. Jesse Travis said. "I've heard a lot about you. Cool gun."

The hit man took a few steps back, angling himself slightly so he could keep Mark, Jesse, and the doorway behind him in view at the same time. But he kept his gun aimed at the young doctor's head.

"How did you know you were wired?" Wyatt asked Mark.

"I didn't," Mark said. "Either you were eavesdropping on me electronically or you were way ahead of me to start with and I was always two steps behind you. This was the only way I could think of to find out which explanation was correct."

"The notepad you showed your son didn't explain how you solved the anagram," Wyatt said. "You warned him that the house, phones, and computers were bugged and you outlined your plan."

Mark nodded. "Ian Ludlow is actually the literary pseudonym of an LAPD detective I know. I'm his medical consultant on the books. I called him from the plane on the flight back from Albuquerque. He was only too glad to help out."

"Because he's got writer's block," Jesse explained. "I think we're all gonna end up in his next book."

"You haven't cracked the code," Wyatt said to Mark, ignoring Jesse's comment. "You still have no idea where Jason Brennan is."

"I wish I did," Mark said.

Wyatt said nothing. He thought he could hear the sound of a helicopter in the distance and the crunch of footsteps on gravel outside. He took two steps back, positioning himself out of view of the open doorway and the line of sight of any marksman.

"By now, the house is surrounded by the SWAT team that was hiding on the hillside," Mark said, as if reading his thoughts. "And that's a police chopper you hear closing in.

You're trapped in a house in middle of the open desert. You might as well drop your weapon and surrender."

Wyatt knew instinctively where each officer was, the weapons they were carrying, even the expressions on their faces. He'd been one of them once. The tactics and training were ingrained in him. He was outnumbered and cornered but not without options.

"You're forgetting that I have hostages," Wyatt said.

"I'm afraid you don't," Mark replied, almost sympathetically. "Jesse and I are leaving in just a minute."

"Take one step and I'll shoot you both."

Mark shook his head. "I don't think you will, Raymond. You've never killed an innocent bystander."

"You aren't innocent," Wyatt said.

"I haven't committed a crime," Mark said. "I haven't evaded prosecution. That's why you became the man you are, isn't it? To get the criminals the law couldn't reach?"

"Right now it's about saving myself," Wyatt said.

"Killing us would make you the same as your prey," Mark said. "What part of yourself do you think you'd be saving?"

The helicopter was over them now, the walls shaking from the rumbling of its blades, the harsh glare of its spotlight illuminating the desert around the house.

It was obvious to Wyatt now that he'd gravely underestimated the doctor from the start. Mark Sloan was far more calculating and perceptive than he'd ever imagined.

Unfortunately for Wyatt, Mark Sloan wasn't guilty of the same devastating miscalculation. Mark had estimated his character, his strengths and weaknesses, with uncanny precision and amazing speed.

The hit man glanced at Jesse. "You can go."

Jesse rose slowly from his seat, his hands still raised. "Not without Mark."

Wyatt looked at Mark and studied him for a moment. "You won't stop until you find Jason Brennan." It was a statement, not a question.

"I'll find him," Mark said. "It's just a question of when."

"That's good to know," Wyatt said. "I wouldn't want one of them to get away with it." He motioned to the door with his gun. "You can go now, too."

The two doctors walked out of the room, Mark pausing in the doorway to look back at Wyatt, who now held the gun down at his side.

"Are you sure this is how you want it to end?" Mark said.

Wyatt allowed himself a tight smile. "It's not what I want, Dr. Sloan. It's just the way it has to be."

Mark knew there was no point arguing with the man. He turned his back on Wyatt and walked away.

The moment Wyatt was alone, he calmly put the gun to his head and squeezed the trigger.

Mark didn't even hear the shot.

CHAPTER TWENTY-SIX

"Wyatt is dead," Mark said.

He sat in one of the uncomfortable seats in Roger Standiford's grandiose office. It was two days after the incident in Palm Springs.

Standiford remained seated behind his massive desk, making no effort to be cordial, regarding Mark with cool detachment.

"Who is Wyatt and why should I care?" Standiford said.

"He was the man you hired to kill the kidnappers who murdered your daughter."

There was a moment of silence. Mark had been scanned for listening devices in the elevator, and he knew the office was secure, so Standiford wasn't silent out of fear of incriminating himself. The casino magnate was considering something else.

"I never knew his name," Standiford finally said. "But I will mourn him. He was a good man."

"Wyatt was a murderer," Mark said. "The only difference between him and the people who killed your daughter is that he enjoyed it."

"He was justice," Standiford said.

"With a Swiss bank account," Mark said. "Or was it in the Cayman Islands?"

"Even justice has a price, Dr. Sloan," Standiford said.

"Not that we'll ever be able to trace how you paid it," Mark said. "Which makes you a very lucky man."

"I've lost my daughter and, for all intents and purposes, my wife," Standiford said. "There isn't an hour that goes by that I don't imagine the terror and agony my daughter endured. They chopped off her finger and they buried her alive. For hours she sat curled up in a corner of that dark, hot pit, slowly suffocating to death, and all because of me and my money. I'm responsible for what happened to her, and I carry that guilt every day. Oh yeah, I'm a very lucky man."

"You could be imagining all those things in a jail cell," Mark said. "But that isn't going to happen, because the one person who could have linked you to three murders is dead."

Standiford met Mark's gaze. *"Three?"*

"Wyatt didn't finish the job," Mark said. "There's one fugitive still out there somewhere. But you're not going to hire somebody else to kill him."

"Why not?" Standiford said.

"Because the FBI and the Justice Department will be watching you," Mark said, "And so will I."

Standiford smirked. "Do you think you frighten me?"

Mark shook his head and stood up. "I didn't frighten Wyatt, either."

And with that, Mark Sloan walked away from Roger Standiford—and from any effort to prove the casino owner hired Raymond Wyatt to murder Stuart Appleby, Diane Love, and William Gregson.

Mark didn't walk away because he sympathized with Standiford or believed the three fugitives deserved their grisly fates. He walked away because Standiford was already enduring a life sentence of unimaginable suffering no amount of wealth could ever alleviate.

He was walking away from Roger Standiford, but not the pursuit of the one surviving kidnapper who could still be held accountable for the heinous murder of Connie Standiford.

As Mark emerged from the T-Rex casino and stood in the

long line of tourists waiting for a taxi, he thought about what his next move might be.

Since he was in Las Vegas, Mark considered going back to see if he could learn more about Jason Brennan from Patsy Durkin, his showgirl ex-girlfriend. But then he recalled her most vivid memory of her old boyfriend was that he urinated frequently and never put the toilet seat down. It wasn't exactly vital information that would give him blazing new insights into Jason Brennan's character.

He would have to return, yet again, to the deceptively simple, and yet aggravatingly complex, little recipe card.

All of Stuart Appleby's coconspirators were on it somewhere. Why couldn't he see where Jason was?

Over the past two days, Mark had done virtually nothing except study the recipes, trying to twist them into anagrams that might reveal who Jason Brennan was and where he could be found.

But it was fruitless.

A taxi pulled up to the curb with a placard across the trunk advertising the Girls of Glitter Gulch strip club. It got him thinking about Patty Durkin again and the other things she'd said about Jason.

"He was thirsty all the time, always had a Big Gulp in his car. Liked to put catsup on rice, which is pretty disgusting if you ask me. And he wore lots of tank tops and sleeveless shirts."

"Which leads me to my next question," Mark said. "How would you describe him physically?"

"Great," she said.

"Could you be more specific?"

"Buff, tight, in good shape," she said. "How much more specific do you want me to get?"

"Any defining characteristics?"

"Oh yeah," she said, grinning.

"I meant tattoos, scars, birthmarks."

"He had a little scar on his forehead from a construction accident. A few two-by-fours fell on his head . . ."

Mark smiled to himself.

A few days ago at the beach house, when he'd been acting for the benefit of Wyatt's listening devices, he'd told Steve he'd unlocked the secrets of the recipe card, that the answer to Jason Brennan's identity was so obvious, it was invisible.

The irony was that Mark had actually been telling the truth, he just didn't know it at the time.

But he knew it now.

Chester Greene was sitting on a couch at the Inxpot the next morning, sipping a large mug of coffee, looking contemplatively into the roaring fire in the fireplace, when Mark Sloan came in and took a seat across from him.

"Dr. Sloan," Chester said in surprise. "What are you doing here?"

"Your coworkers at the real estate office told me I could find you here. There's been some progress in the investigation," Mark said. "And I thought it would be was best if I told you about it face-to-face. But before I do, how are you and the kids holding up?"

Chester shrugged. "They're too young to really understand—they just know that Mommy is never coming back. I don't know how I'll ever tell them the rest. I'm still trying to get a grip on it myself. I just try to take life day by day. I've been going into the office, but I can't really get myself worked up about real estate, you know?"

Mark nodded. "I'm sure your coworkers understand. Is your family helping you take care of the kids until things settle down?"

Chester took a sip of his coffee. "Our friends are helping out. I haven't kept in close touch with my family. You know how it is sometimes."

Mark nodded again.

"So what did you come here to tell me?" Chester asked.

"We caught the man who killed your wife," Mark said. "You don't have to worry anymore—you're safe now."

Chester leaned back on the couch, took a deep breath, and let it out slowly. "Thank God. Where is he now?"

"The morgue," Mark said. "He took his own life rather than face prosecution."

"So, then, it's all over," Chester said.

"Not quite," Mark replied.

Chester sat up again, setting his mug on the coffee table between them. "You're going to go after the guy who hired him."

Mark shook his head. "No."

"Why not?" Chester said, color rising in his cheeks. "He's responsible for my wife's death."

"We can't prove it, not with the hit man dead," Mark said. "Besides, don't you think he's suffered enough?"

"I wouldn't know," Chester said.

"Sure you would," Mark replied. "You're partly responsible for it."

"I loved Stella," Chester said. "I never knew the woman you say committed those crimes. The caring, nurturing woman I was married to could never have been a kidnapper."

"And a murderer," Mark said. "Just like you."

Chester's face turned rigid. "This conversation is over, Dr. Sloan."

He got up and turned toward the door. That's when he saw Agent Barton Feldman in his FBI parka, sitting at the counter. Two other agents were outside the door.

"Sit down, Chester." Feldman said.

He sat down, his face still hard and flushed with anger.

"When I told you we'd caught your wife's killer, and that you were safe now, you didn't say anything," Mark said.

"Is that what this is about?" Chester said. "Okay, thank you. I really appreciate everything you've done."

Mark smiled. "That wasn't what I was looking for. I was expecting you to ask what made me think you were ever in any danger. After all, the hit man was chasing your wife for a crime she committed. Why would he want to hurt you?"

"When someone murders your wife for revenge, it's only natural to assume you and your family might be in danger, too."

"Especially if you committed the crime with her," Mark said. "But the hit man didn't know that. I didn't realize it myself until yesterday."

"I didn't even know Stella five years ago," Chester said.

"I suppose that's technically true, since back then she was Diane Love and you were Jason Brennan," Mark said. "You were living with a showgirl named Patsy Durkin and working for Standiford Construction. You know what Patsy said about you? That you were thirsty all the time, went to the bathroom constantly, and always left the toilet seat up."

"That's the crime this Brennan guy committed? Leaving the seat up?" Chester glanced over his shoulder at the FBI agents. "When did that become a federal offense?"

"Patsy also said you were hit on the head in an accident at work," Mark said. "None of that clicked for me, not even when I saw the desmopressin acetate inhaler in your medicine cabinet."

"You went through my medicine cabinet?" Chester said, his flush getting even darker.

Mark shrugged. "I can't help myself. That's why I don't get invited to many dinner parties. Desmopressin acetate is prescribed for people with pituitary insufficiency, which is characterized by excessive thirst and frequent urination."

"What does that have to do with him getting bonked on the head?" Feldman asked, taking a seat next to Chester on the couch.

"The condition can be caused by head trauma," Mark explained to Feldman. "But the real ah-ha for me was the Royal Hawaiian recipe card."

Mark addressed himself to Chester again. "Stuart Appleby hid contact information about all three of you in anagrams on a recipe card that he kept in a safe-deposit box. I was able to find anagrams for everybody but you. It was driving me crazy. And then I realized I'd already found it.

Stuart didn't do an anagram for you because you and Diane were in the same place."

"Sounds pretty airtight to me," Feldman said, turning to Chester. "I bet if we got a court order compelling you to undergo a facial X ray, we'd discover you've got an entirely new face."

Feldman snapped his fingers, as if something had just occurred to him, then reached into his coat pocket and pulled out a neatly folded piece of paper.

"Well, what do you know?" Feldman said, placing the paper in Chester's lap. "I've got a court order right here."

Chester's whole body seemed to sag, sinking deeper into the couch, as if he alone were feeling the effects of gravity.

"We never meant to hurt her," Chester said, his voice barely above a whisper.

"You didn't think amputating her finger with a meat cleaver would hurt?" Feldman asked incredulously.

"She was giving us attitude," Chester said. "Laughing at us, not taking any of it seriously. She was a spoiled rich kid calling us a bunch of miserable losers. Stuart just snapped. If she didn't believe we were serious, what was her father going to think? We had to do something to show them who was in charge. So we cut off her pinkie. She fainted after that, which made her a lot easier to handle."

"You just threw her in a pit and buried her alive." Mark said.

"That's not what we did," Chester said. "We hid her underground—it's a totally different thing. We made sure she had air and plenty of water. She only had to be down there a few hours."

"It was too hot and there wasn't enough air," Mark said. "She couldn't have survived more than two hours, let alone six or eight. Nobody could have."

"We didn't know that," Chester whined, tears welling in his eyes. "It was an accident."

"Tripping over your shoelace is an accident," Feldman said. "Getting kidnapped, maimed, and buried alive isn't."

"How do you think we felt? We were sick with remorse," Chester said, tears rolling down his cheeks. "We've had to live with the unbearable guilt ever since."

"Not to mention a couple million bucks," Feldman said. "Boo-hoo."

"We aren't monsters. The guilt ate away at us," Chester said, wiping away his tears with the back of his hand. "Diane was tormented by nightmares and panic attacks every night. It was horrible. We thought it would end when the kids were born, but it only got worse."

"Because now you could imagine the horror of your children suffering the torture you put Connie Standiford through," Mark said. "And you saw yourselves the way we see you."

Chester nodded, spilling more tears, then looked pleadingly at Mark.

"How am I going to tell my kids what we've done?" Chester asked softly, beginning to sob. *"How?"*

Two days after Jason Brennan's full confession, a team of FBI agents, led by Special Agent Barton Feldman, arrested Dr. Morris Plume, who'd not only given the fugitives their new faces, but also supplied all their phony identification. It turned out that Dr. Plume had offered the same one-stop shopping for new identities to scores of other wanted felons, including several on the FBI's most wanted list.

Dr. Plume agreed to tell everything he knew and testify in court as often as necessary in return for a new identity of his own and inclusion in the Witness Protection Program.

The arrests earned Barton Feldman an immediate transfer to Chicago and a key post on the Bureau's high-profile special unit on wanted fugitives, where he could mine the mother lode of data gleaned from Dr. Plume's files.

Special Agents Terry Riordan, Sandra Flannery, and Tim Witten were quietly reassigned to clerical posts at FBI field offices in Spokane, Wichita, and Sacramento, respectively.

Nearly a month after Jason Brennan and Dr. Plume's arrests, Mark Sloan received a nice letter from the FBI thanking him for his assistance in their investigation.

But his most rewarding memento of his experience on the case arrived a few days after the letter. It took four men close to two hours to get it into Mark's house. He tipped them generously and was still appreciating the many intriguing facets of his keepsake when Steve came home.

An enormous overstuffed recliner dominated the living room. The chair's wood-grain trim and leather upholstery reminded Steve of the interior of a cheap car with luxury pretensions. It was the ugliest piece of furniture he'd ever seen.

He stared at the chair, warily approaching it from the back as if he was nearing a potentially dangerous animal.

"Dad?" Steve shouted.

"BRING ME TORTILLA CHIPS!" Mark's voice boomed thunderously out of the recliner.

Steve staggered back, startled, and was instinctively reaching for his gun when suddenly the chair spun around to reveal Mark sitting on it, a big, boyish grin on his face, his legs resting on the footrest.

"ISN'T THIS WONDERFUL?" Mark boomed, forgetting that his voice was still amplified by the recliner's built-in loudspeaker. He gave Steve an apologetic shrug and switched it off. "Isn't this wonderful?"

"I heard you the first time," said Steve, self-consciously taking his hand from his holster and trying to look casual about it. "What the hell is it?"

"The Captain's Chair, the recliner for the new millennium. I forgot I even bought it. Would you like a refreshing, ice-cold soft drink?" Mark lifted up the armrest to reveal a six-pack of root beer in a mini-icebox.

Steve peered into the icebox. Along with the drinks, Mark had stowed some cheese, salami, grapes, and a Godiva chocolate bar.

"You've got to be kidding," Steve said.

"You keep telling me I need to relax. Now look at me.

I'm in total command of my relaxation." Mark hit a switch, the recliner hummed, and his body began to jiggle as he enjoyed a vigorous massage. "This is comfort-tech engineering."

"Let me try it," Steve said.

"No," Mark replied, hitting another switch. Classical music began to play on the recliner's hidden surround-sound speakers and subwoofer.

"I just want to see what it feels like," Steve said. "I'll get right out."

"I don't think so," Mark said. "What happened to those tortilla chips?"

"C'mon, Dad, I'll only sit in it for a—"

Mark pressed a button and interrupted Steve with a voice that could have parted the Red Sea.

"GET ME CHIPS!"

Steve jerked back, startled again. "Okay, okay. I'll get your chips. Geez."

As his son trudged sullenly to the kitchen, Mark gleefully operated the tiny joystick, spinning the recliner around and steering it out onto the deck, where he parked facing the surf.

The sun was shining. He had cold drinks on ice, great music playing on the speakers, a skilled masseuse kneading his tired muscles, and a spectacular view of the Pacific.

Mark Sloan smiled to himself and closed his eyes.

Who needs a vacation?

Turn the page for a preview of Dr. Sloan's next adventure

THE SHOOTING SCRIPT

Coming from Signet in August 2004 . . .

Over the years, dozens of hospital administrators have tried to force Dr. Mark Sloan, Community General's eccentric Chief of Internal Medicine, to follow some simple rules of conduct.

All they asked was that he maintain a professional demeanor, attend regular administrative meetings, operate his department within a strict budget, and not indulge his inexplicable interest in homicide investigation on hospital time.

By and large they were an impressive bunch of administrators. Smart, capable, often fearsome, but Dr. Sloan had conquered them all.

That wasn't going to happen with Noah Dent. Community General's new chief administrator was fresh from the Hollyworld International corporate office in Ft. Lauderdale, where the 31-year-old had been a rising star in the acquisitions department. Although primarily known for its amusement parks, Hollyworld had diversified into cruise lines, fast-food franchises, office buildings, and hospital ownership.

Dent's aggressive, hard-line approach to the hostile takeover and absorption of businesses into the Hollyworld corporate family impressed his superiors, who felt he was just the right person to wring a wider margin of profitability from Community General.

Before Dent was transferred to his new post in Los

Angeles, he put together a detailed file on Mark Sloan and the administrators the doctor had defeated. Now, in advance of Dent's first meeting with Dr. Sloan, the administrator once again studied the case histories of his immediate predecessors to see what lessons he could learn from their embarrassing failures.

Kate Hamilton came to Community General after steering two miss-managed hospitals from the brink of bankruptcy to profitability. But within a year, Dr. Sloan defanged her, convincing her to quit her job, sell her home, and use the proceeds to establish a non-profit food bank in the inner city.

Norman Briggs, her successor, showed great promise as a hard-line bottom-liner, having spearheaded the hostile take-over of the hospital by Mediverse Corporation. But somehow Dr. Sloan managed to compromise Briggs completely. Not only did Briggs let Dr. Sloan use hospital resources and staff as he pleased in his murder investigations, but the administrator became his eager flunky.

When Community General was sold to Healthcorp International, they brought in General Harold Lomax, who'd spent ten years running battlefield medical operations for the United States Marine Corps before being lured into the private sector. Healthcorp was certain that Lomax could bring Dr. Sloan, and the Community General budget, under control. But eight months later, Lomax resigned with an extreme case of irritable bowel syndrome and left behind a hospital literally in ruins, decimated by a serial bomber stalking Dr. Sloan.

From what Dent could tell, it wasn't that Dr. Sloan possessed any Machiavellian political skills. In fact, it was quite the opposite. He wore his administrative adversaries down with his utter affability, gentle humor, and relentless good will.

Those days were about to end.

Noah Dent was immune to humor and good will, especially where business was concerned. Mark Sloan would find himself powerless against him.

Mark showed up promptly at the appointed hour, which was at end of a long shift on a weekday afternoon. Dent had chosen that time purposely to catch Mark at his lowest ebb, when he was tired and off his game. Even so, Mark entered flashing a warm smile and extending his hand.

"Welcome to Community General," Mark said. "I'm Dr. Mark Sloan, but I hope you'll call me Mark."

Dent offered the tightest of polite smiles in return as he shook Mark's hand. "It's a pleasure to finally meet you, Dr. Sloan. Please, take a seat."

He motioned Mark into his spartan office and tried to hide his disappointment. In the flesh, Mark Sloan just didn't live up to Dent's expectations.

Although Dent knew Mark's weapons were his charm and good-natured humor, he still expected the doctor to be an overpowering force of nature, to fill a room with his indomitable personality. But compared to the corporate executives Dent had symbolically beheaded in the past, men who commanded a room and exuded hurricane strength and charisma, Dr. Sloan seemed decidedly weak. He was just a white-haired old doctor in a wrinkled lab coat.

Mark took the seat that was offered to him and smiled as warmly as he could, considering the chilly temperature of both the room and the man who inhabited it.

"I'm sorry we haven't had a chance to get together until today," Mark said. "My life has been kind of chaotic lately and is only just settling down again."

"Indeed," Dent settled into his chair behind his desk and opened the file in front of him. "You've been traveling a lot over the past few weeks. Hawaii, Colorado, New Mexico, Palm Springs. Quite an itinerary."

"I wish I could say it was for pleasure, but I was helping the authorities pursue a killer," Mark said, well aware that Dent already knew that. The details had been widely reported by the media, mostly because the case involved the kidnapping and murder of a Las Vegas casino owner's teenage daughter.

...sure the FBI and the LAPD appreciated having an ...ist on the case," Dent said. "I just wish you put as ...ch effort into your duties at this hospital as you do playing amateur sleuth."

Mark was prepared to defend himself to Dent, as it was something of a ritual for each new administrator to try and exert some control over him. But he didn't expect such a direct attack.

"I've been on the staff of this hospital longer than any other doctor here," Mark said. "I've treated generations of families and trained countless physicians over the last forty years."

"I don't doubt your qualifications, Dr. Sloan, or your skills as a physician. You're a respected member of your profession," Dent said. "What I question is your commitment to this hospital and your blatant abuse of the privileges you've been granted here."

"I haven't been *granted* anything, Mr. Dent. Whatever I have, I've earned." Mark was surprised how quickly Dent had managed to get under his skin.

Dent sighed wearily. "An inflated, and misplaced, sense of entitlement. That's usually the excuse employees use to justify to themselves stealing office supplies, padding the expense account, and making long distance calls on office phones."

"I admit I sometimes forget to take my pen out of my pocket before I go home," Mark said. "If you like, you can deduct the cost from my paycheck."

Dent referred to the file in front of him. "Your son, Steve, is a homicide detective with the Los Angeles Police Department. Frequently over the years you've assisted in his investigations."

"I'm a consultant to the police," Mark said.

"Really?" Dent said. "Do they pay you?"

"No, I volunteer my time."

"That's not all you volunteer," Dent said. "You also freely offer the resources of this hospital and the services of its employees. Who do you think pays for the overtime when Dr. Bentley pulls an all-nighter dissecting a corpse for you?"

"Amanda is the Adjunct County Medical Examiner," Mark said. "The city compensates her for her work."

"Yes, they do, for the work they order, not the work *you* ask her to do," Dent said. "Let's be honest, Dr. Sloan. The Medical Examiner's satellite office is here for your amusement and convenience, a personal playground cleverly paid for by our stockholders and Los Angeles taxpayers."

"The Medical Examiner's office is here because they desperately needed additional manpower and more morgue space," Mark said. "We're providing a service to the community."

"But it was you who suggested they open their morgue here at Community General and staff it with one of our pathologists."

"Because it was a fast, simple, and inexpensive way to solve a serious problem facing the county and help shore up the hospital's finances at the same time."

"And it brought you a constant supply of fresh corpses to play with," Dent said, shaking his head with disgust. "I don't know how you managed to pull it off, Dr. Sloan."

"As I recall, the board voted unanimously for the project," Mark said stiffly, trying to keep his rising anger in check.

"The same board that drove Healthcorp International into bankruptcy," Dent said. "Which is why they no longer own this hospital and we do."

"I can't tell you how thrilled we all are about that too," Mark said. "I've always wanted to work for a division of an amusement park company."

"Hollyworld International has diversified into many areas," Dent said. "But we treat each of them as if they were our core business."

"Which is to make as much money as possible," Mark said.

"Of course," Dent said. "You say that as if it's a bad thing. Making money is the whole point of operating a business, Dr. Sloan."

"I don't look at medicine as a business."

"That is abundantly clear," Dent said. "You look at it as a way to subsidize your detective work."

"It's unfortunate that you see things that way," Mark glanced at his watch and rose from his seat. "As much as I've enjoyed our chat, I'm coming to the end of a long shift. I should be getting home."

"Well, there's one thing we agree on, Dr. Sloan," Dent said. "In more ways than one."

Cleve Kershaw was irresistible and he knew it. He had the complete package: money, charm, and power. Looks had nothing to do with it, though by his estimation he was no slouch in that department, either.

Part of his undeniable allure, he knew, was his casual self-confidence, which came from having an accurate sense of who he was and where he stood in the Hollywood universe. He was a player. Certified, bonafide, and blow-dried. Somebody who made things happen. Somebody that nobodies aspired to be. A producer, with a capital "P."

"God, it's beautiful," Amy Butler said, standing on the wide deck of Cleve's Malibu beach house, the gentle breeze rippling the thin fabric of her sheer, untucked blouse as she admired the view. "Just awesome."

Cleve was also admiring an awesome view, at least what he could see of it when the wind hit her shirt just right.

Amy was irresistible and probably knew it, too. She had it all: beauty, youth, and innocence, though the fact she was with him now put that last quality in doubt. Not that he cared. Amy's ability to project innocence she didn't have revealed a natural talent for acting, which was more valuable than innocence anyway.

Amy was in a great shape, but not in the surgically-enhanced sense, also a plus. She was a one-hundred percent natural beauty with the lean, strong, supple body of someone in complete control of their physicality. There wasn't a molecule of body fat on her. She exuded so much youthful vitality, she made Cleve feel elderly at forty, but not so elderly that he doubted for one second that he'd have her in bed before the afternoon was over.

They were two irresistible people who wouldn't be resisting each other much longer.

"Do you live here?" she asked.

Cleve shook his head. "This is just where I go to get away from it all."

"Get away from what?"

He shrugged. "The hustle and bustle."

"I thought you liked to hustle and bustle," she said with a sly grin.

"It depends with whom," said Cleve, so smooth his words could be poured. He saw himself as Dean Martin in his prime, only without the singing voice.

"So where do you live?" she asked.

"I got a place in Mandeville Canyon."

It was a loaded and carefully premeditated reply. By calling his house a *place*, he made it seem unremarkable, which made him come across as relaxed, easy-going and self-deprecating—the very definition of charm.

By slipping in that his *place* was in secluded Mandeville Canyon, he was actually saying he lived in a mind-blowing estate and that he could afford the ridiculous extravagance of owning two magnificent homes, each worth the high seven figures, that were barely twenty miles apart.

If all the subtext in that deceptively simple remark didn't make her swoon, she wasn't a woman.

"The movie business has been very good to you," Amy said.

It was a good thing she was holding on to the rail, Cleve thought, or she might swoon right into the surf.

"It's going to be very good for you, too."

"Starting when?" Amy said, her eyes sparkling with mischief and possibility.

"Starting now," he said.

The formal seduction had begun at lunch at Granita. The informal seduction began six months ago when he saw her picture in a *LA Times* ad for Macy's fall clearance sale. What most people saw, if they noticed her at all, was a fresh faced girl modeling a discounted sports bra. What Cleve saw was a potential action superstar. He tracked her down, talked her into dumping her agent, and immediately began remaking her.

Of course, she knew Cleve was married, and who he was married to. Everybody did. That was half the attraction for her. Maybe two-thirds. She knew exactly what he was bringing to the party. But so far, she'd been doing all the partying. There hadn't been any festivities for Cleve yet.

That was about to change.

After lunch, Cleve invited her to see his "little beach place" just down the road. Amy said sure, left her Volkswagen Bug in the lot, and let him drive.

She'd ceded control of the afternoon to him the moment she'd slid into the hand-stitched, leather interior of his SL. Of course, she'd ceded control of so much more six months ago.

And now here they were at his beach house on an exclusive stretch of sand on a bright, sunny, perfect California afternoon. What was going to happen next was as inevitable as the setting of the sun, the dawn of a new day, and the thousand-dollar minimum he spent every time he took his Mercedes in for service.

Cleve went inside and uncorked a bottle of champagne.

"I hope you like Dom Perignon," he said, filling their glasses.

"What are we celebrating?" she asked as she joined him.

"The future," Cleve said.

They clinked their glasses together, unaware that they were sharing a toast to their last two hours alive.

The first in the series based on
the hit TV show

Diagnosis Murder:
The Silent Partner

by

LEE GOLDBERG

Dr. Mark Sloan is assigned to LAPD's "unsolved homicide" files. As he reopens one case on the murder of a woman whose killer currently sits on Death Row, Sloan learns that the wrong man was charged. And the real killer is still at large...

"A whodunit thrill-ride that captures all the charm, mystery and fun of the TV series...and then some."
—Janet Evanovich

0-451-20959-1